Praise for Sydney Somers's
Trust Me

"*Trust Me* is like a high speed chase, it gets the adrenaline pumping from page one and doesn't let up until you cross the finish line."

~ *Joyfully Reviewed*

"If you are ready for an edge of your seat suspense with a boatload of super-hot romance then Sydney Somers' *Trust Me* is just what you are looking for. From the introduction I was hooked and I quickly turned page after page eager to discover how everything would pan out... I can't wait to see what Ms. Somers has in store for her next installment within this series."

~ *Fallen Angel Reviews*

"Romantic suspense fans, don't miss this one! If you enjoy a story about a woman on the run, a man who wants only the truth and stops at nothing to get it, sizzling sexual tension, then trust me, this book is for you."

~ *Long and Short Reviews*

Look for these titles by
Sydney Somers

Now Available:

Pendragon Gargoyles
Primal Hunger
Primal Attraction
Primal Pleasure

Shadow Destroyers
Unbreakable
Stripped Away
Storm Warning
Dark Obsession

Spellbound
Say You're Mine
Don't Let Go
Whatever It Takes

Enslaved
Waitin' on a Hero
Call Me Cupid
Talons: Caged Desire

Print Collection
Primal Seduction

Trust Me

Sydney Somers

SAMHAIN
PUBLISHING

Samhain Publishing, Ltd.
11821 Mason Montgomery Road, 4B
Cincinnati, OH 45249
www.samhainpublishing.com

Trust Me
Copyright © 2011 by Sydney Somers
Print ISBN: 978-1-60928-293-6
Digital ISBN: 978-1-60928-249-3

Editing by Lindsey Faber
Cover by Kanaxa

First Samhain Publishing, Ltd. electronic publication: November 2010
First Samhain Publishing, Ltd. print publication: October 2011

Dedication

To my parents, who have always encouraged me to follow my dream. Your unwavering support has meant the world to me.

Chapter One

Babysitting a gift shop wasn't the smartest way for an alleged murderer to keep a low profile. But then what were friends for, right?

At least that was how Maxine Walker interpreted the look on her friend's face a moment after Sherri insisted she watch the place while she took her daughter to the hospital.

Max winced at the blood running down Ellie's leg from where she'd split her knee open after falling off her bike.

"You'll be fine."

For a second she wondered if Sherri was talking to her or nine-year-old Ellie.

"Sherri—"

Her friend finished wrapping a hand towel around Ellie's knee. "You can handle it, Max."

"That doesn't make it a good idea." In fact, it was a very bad idea. Bad like the first time Sherri had talked her into going to a keg party. Only this time she could end up with more than a crescent-shaped scar on her chin and fuzzy memories of people chanting *Chug. Chug. Chug.*

Like twenty-five to life in prison.

"Since when has that stopped you?" Scooping her daughter up, Sherri carried Ellie out to her car. "*You* will be fine, but my shop won't be if I have to close early with only a week left to go before tourist season is over."

She stuck to Sherri's heels, hoping her brother's high school girlfriend would come to her senses and remember Max excelled at shooting range targets and busting drug-pushing criminals, not selling stuffed humpback whales and chocolate-covered peanuts some marketing whack-job had repackaged as Reindeer Poop.

"There could be a customer inside right now." Sherri finished getting Ellie settled in the back seat.

"Maybe they can run the shop."

Sherri rolled her eyes, her determined expression eerily mirroring the morning after said keg party when she had insisted a breakfast of stale beer, marshmallows and three-day-old pizza would cure Max's hangover—and Max had believed her.

"You know how to use the cash register and debit card machine. If anyone thinks you're slow or awkward, just tell them you're still in training."

This is what she got for hanging around the shop helping Sherri with stock. If she hadn't wanted to pay her friend back for giving her a place to stay for a while, she could have insisted she didn't have a clue how either machine worked.

"I could take Ellie," Max hurriedly offered, knowing she'd be way more comfortable with blood and stitches than gift wrapping and customer service small talk.

Ellie made a sound of distress, a few more tears tracking down her cheeks, and Max winced in sympathy, wishing she could make her feel better.

Sherri slid behind the wheel. "Call me on my cell if you run into any problems."

"Like someone recognizing me?" If anyone in Riverbend, New Brunswick even followed news from New York City, which was unlikely given the local Canadian coverage of American stations, they would doubtfully link her to a four-month-old story of a detective wanted for murder, at least that's what she tried telling herself.

On the other hand, over half the tourists who waltzed through the gift shop doors were American and many from the upper east coast.

"I was talking about problems with the store. Your own mother would pass you on the street without recognizing you, let alone anyone else."

Unless someone was looking specifically for her. She knew better than to believe cutting her blond hair to shoulder-length and dying it black would be enough to keep her safe.

"Just relax and try not to pick an argument with Dave if he gets bored and stops by later, okay."

Max shuddered at the thought of the sporting goods store owner from across the street stopping by at *any* time.

Seeing the look of exaggerated horror on Max's face, Sherri laughed. "He's not that bad."

"That man has his head up his ass more often than all the dogs in the local shelter combined."

Ellie sniffed and used the back of her hand to smear her runny nose across her cheek. "Mr. Stiles sticks his head up his ass?"

Ignoring Sherri's scowl, Max grinned down at Ellie, relieved she'd stopped crying. "Yes, he does. Your mom just can't say it out loud since Mr. Stiles owns her building."

Owned half the buildings on the street and took the opportunity to remind Max of that every time their paths crossed. Listening to the man yammer about his real estate prowess was as nauseating as him sharing intimate details of every woman he'd dated but turned out to be not good enough for him.

Sherri started the car. "I'll check in with you in a little while. You've got this," she added, probably to encourage Max to release her white-knuckled grip on the driver-side window.

"Okay." She stepped back from the car, preferring not to lose a toe. Sherri had a great head for business, but behind the wheel of a car, she was a maniac.

Max waved as the car pulled away, finally dragging her butt inside when she swore she glimpsed Dave in the window across the street, watching her.

She hadn't planned on staying with Sherri and Ellie for more than a night or two after she'd crossed the border into Canada. Two days had turned into three weeks when she found herself relaxing for the first time in months, lulled by the laid back pace of the community.

But she still wasn't any closer to figuring out her next move, and after spending the afternoon watching the shop, assessing every person who stepped foot inside, she knew she couldn't hide out here forever.

Thankfully the last two hours had passed without incident—knock on wood—and in another five minutes she could flip the sign in the window to *Closed* and lock up.

Max glanced at the guy looking over a selection of homemade preserves, placing him in his early thirties, a couple years older than her maybe.

Dressed in expensive running shoes, beige cargo pants and a black T-shirt that showed off his muscular arms, he was likely an outdoor enthusiast with a bike or kayak strapped to an SUV parked out on the street. Maybe he was part of the group staying up at the lodge that had come for some fishing or to check out the sea caves. Sooner or later most of them wandered in for a look around.

He was the type Sherri had suggested Max should hook up with for a night to relieve some tension. Tall, good looking and preloaded with the kind of stamina it would take to really wear her out, according to her Sherri.

Max could think of numerous things she needed more than a fling with an outdoorsman—like her name cleared and her job back. Even if she gave serious thought to Sherri's suggestion, she would go with someone less...intense.

She'd dealt with enough scrutiny before her suspension to be remotely interested in the kind of thorough study Mr.

Weekend Warrior seemed to excel at. Everything he stopped to look at seemed to capture his complete attention before he moved on, his expression serious despite the occasional crooked grin that curved his lips.

Startled by the sound of her prepaid cell phone, Max dragged her gaze away from him and answered.

"How are things going?"

Max smiled at the sound of Sherri's voice. "I didn't burn the place down."

"Not ignoring customers?"

She glanced at the tourist she hadn't so much as waved at. "Nope. How's Ellie?"

"She needed ten stitches, but she's been a trooper. Especially once I promised her ice cream on the way home."

Max laughed, but the mention of ice cream suddenly made her stomach rumble. A hot fudge sundae when she got out of here would take care of that.

"I'm going to take her home and I'll close out today's sales first thing in the morning. Did you lock up yet?"

"Just waiting on a last-minute customer." She watched said customer bend down to look at something on a lower shelf. The guy did have a really great ass.

"Is he hot?"

"I never said it was a guy." She angled away from him and lowered her voice, though he probably couldn't hear her from across the room with the radio playing from overhead speakers.

"You wouldn't have sounded as impatient if it was a woman. Guys make you twitchy."

"No they don't." She just tended to be a touch more suspicious of unfamiliar men, and with a drug and arms dealer gunning for her, who could blame her?

Maybe the right guy wouldn't make her twitchy at all, but she wasn't about to find him while on the run. Even before she'd become a fugitive, decent guys who weren't intimidated by

11

the fact she was a cop were hard to come by.

"What color are his eyes?"

She chanced a quick glance, but he was still too far away to tell. "Blue," she guessed.

"Liar. You hesitated, Max. You don't have a clue, which means you haven't even approached him to see if he needs any help." A fact Sherri clearly expected her to correct ASAP judging by her the-customer-always-comes-first tone.

"I'll take care of it."

"Him, not it. And ask him to meet you for a beer afterward while you're at it."

Rolling her eyes, Max stared at the display of ships in bottles behind the counter. "I never said he was good looking."

"With you it's all about what you don't say. When was the last time—"

"If you're about to ask me how long it's been since I got laid, I'm locking the guy in the store and leaving him here for you to deal with."

Sensing movement behind her, Max whipped around to find the guy in question had soundlessly crossed the room and stood on the opposite side of the counter.

A little rattled by the slick approach, she forced a smile. "Gotta go, boss. See you later."

"Be nice," Sherri warned before Max hung up.

If there had been any question in her mind about him standing there long enough to overhear the last bit of their conversation, the knowing smile on his lips said it all.

Awesome.

Ignoring both the warmth she felt creeping up her neck and the tingling that started low in her belly at the undeniably sexy grin, she set her phone on the counter. "Was there something I could help you with?"

"I'm not holding you up, am I? I know it's probably almost closing time. I can always stop by tomorrow if it's a problem."

"No problem at all." She owed Sherri more than a couple hours of her time for giving her a place to stay without asking too many questions and promising not to tell her family where she was.

She knew Samuel Blackwater wouldn't hesitate to hurt any of them if he thought they knew something. She'd made sure of that when she'd screwed up his last deal and left him with a token to remember her by.

"Are you sure? Because if you've got plans or someone waiting at home for you..." His tone was nothing more than polite, but his eyes, a deep penetrating green, were almost...hopeful?

She smiled easily. "It's fine. But if you happen to be around tomorrow, feel free to pop in and remind my boss that I didn't ignore you."

"The same boss who thinks you should meet me for a beer later?" He looked down, his expression bordering on remorseful. "Sorry, I've got really good ears."

"What was it that I could help you with?"

"Should I assume the quick change in subject means you wouldn't be interested in grabbing a beer?"

Laughing, she crossed her arms. "You can assume whatever you'd like." He wasn't the first guy to hit on her while she was hanging around the shop, but he was the first to tempt her to follow Sherri's advice.

Maybe if it had been another time or place, or if she'd been living her life instead of running from it.

"Can I see the small blue dream catcher?"

Lucas McAllister let his attention slide all the way down her body, his interest genuine enough to mask his surprise at finding Maxine Walker less than two feet away.

If he wasn't caught in some surreal place between attraction and utter disbelief that he'd stumbled across the woman he'd been hunting for months, he might think he'd absorbed some of Eli's inherent good luck through osmosis or something.

Whether it was women, contraband or intel, it always landed right in Eli's lap like a gift from the heavens. Today though, Lucas's luck was definitely on the upswing. That might have been enough to lift his mood if finding Detective Walker didn't slam the past right to the forefront of his brain, bringing with it emotional baggage he really didn't have time to deal with.

"Here you go."

Lucas took the offered dream catcher, noting the dark purple polish on the detective's nails. Part of her disguise? It certainly fit the slightly goth image she had going for her with the dark hair and heavy liner around her eyes. The only thing throwing it off was the pink sweater that was probably borrowed since it looked a couple of sizes too big.

He'd spent weeks learning everything he could about the woman linked to Cara Beckett's death, hoping for a clue that would lead him right to her. Every member of the Lassiter Group, a private paramilitary unit outsourced by the U.S. government for covert operations and intelligence gathering, had done their homework, but none of them had been able to get a line on Walker when she'd disappeared.

Since no leads had panned out and there hadn't been a price tag put on Walker's head, either Blackwater was looking for her quietly or she was dead. A dirty cop wouldn't be useful to him once exposed. Either way, it had left them with jack shit.

The rest of the team had slowly given up, assuming drug and arms dealer Samuel Blackwater had taken her out.

Before Cara's death, the Lassiter Group had been tasked to gather intel on Blackwater after word got out that he was stepping up his game and entering the biological weapons market. They'd been working on identifying all the players involved in an upcoming deal when things had fallen apart and they'd lost Cara.

Unfortunately, Lucas's boss had ordered him to let it go as of three weeks ago. He would have been reassigned along with the rest of the team if he hadn't insisted on some vacation time. The vacation time Joe had been pushing him to take for weeks.

If Joe had learned Tess passed along the tip that led Lucas to Riverbend, he would've had his ass in a sling before he'd stepped so much as a toe into Canada.

Lucas glanced around the shop. Was she alone, or was there someone else here with her, like the owner, Sherri, or another employee?

"Was there anything else?"

He held up the dream catcher, but his eyes remained locked on the detective. "Does it work?"

A small grin curved her lips. "You'll have to let me know."

"What, no nightmares you want to escape?"

An unreadable emotion blinked across her face, then she offered him that polite smile that looked as genuine as the chocolate-covered peanuts with the Reindeer on the package. "I think everyone has bad dreams they wish they could wake up from."

"Some more than others," he said, holding her gaze. "Actually it's not for me. I screwed up and took my nephew to a scary movie and my brother is holding me accountable for his bad dreams."

"Well, for your sake I hope it works."

"You and me both. I don't suppose you've got a gift box?" Or anything else that would drag this out a little longer. He needed to know whether or not anyone else would be interrupting what came next. Like someone out back.

"Sure." She bent down to check under the counter. "Looks like we're out."

"Too bad. My nephew likes opening the package as much as finding out what's inside."

"I can check out back." It came out almost grudgingly.

He nearly smiled in triumph. "That would be great. I wanted to check out the snow globes anyway. My brother's wife is a sucker for them."

"Okay then." She moved around the counter, and although she betrayed no suspicion he had an ulterior motive for being there, she was careful to keep him in her peripheral vision, never turning her back on him entirely.

Smart girl.

She turned a corner, and instead of bolting down the narrow hall toward the back door, she disappeared into a room on the left. He let out the breath he'd been holding, half-anticipating that she would run.

A chime over the door tinkled.

So much for being alone with her. He glanced at the front of the store and went perfectly still. *Fuck.*

Picking up a red and blue windmill from the closest display, he ran through his options, eliminating every one that involved walking Maxine Walker past the two men who just stepped through the door.

The first one inside—tall and dressed in a green Aloha shirt—had a tattoo that wrapped around his throat and supposedly ran down the length of his body. James "Snake" Martin was Blackwater's muscle and had been working for the dealer for over twenty years. He usually stuck close to Blackwater though, unless he was with...

His gaze darted to the second guy through the door.

Fantastic. Blackwater's son.

Christ, he needed to talk to Tess. Whoever her source was, they'd apparently shared their information with Blackwater, and god knew who else. It would be really helpful to know who else might end up breathing down his neck before he got Max the hell out of here.

He was hardly a fan of hers, considering more than one

person had implicated her in Cara's death, but he could guarantee what he had in mind didn't involve roughing her up for the hell of it. He'd bet his next bonus that neither man wandering around the front of the store could claim the same.

Sensing movement, he spotted his target in the doorway, a box in her hand. He started forward, planning an interception that began with getting her down the hallway and ended with them slipping out the back door, without attracting the attention of Blackwater's men.

It would have worked out fine if she'd kept her eyes on him and didn't glance at the two men who'd joined them. He had to give her props, though, since the only indication she'd recognized them was the squaring of her shoulders as she strode to the counter, closer to the men.

He knew from his homework that Maxine Walker was a risk taker, reckless according to some, and had earned the nickname Mad Max. If he had doubted what he'd read, every determined step forward would be proving him wrong.

Either she was confident neither man would recognize her, or there was some tactical advantage in heading back to the cash register. Moving to catch up with her since she'd dodged around another display to get ahead of him, he undid the snap on the side pocket of his pants where he had stashed his Sig Sauer.

Seeing as he was supposed to be fishing in Florida, using the pistol was at the bottom of his to-do list.

Ahead of him, Max set the box on the counter, hollered out about the shop being closed in a deeper-sounding voice than earlier, and bent down to grab something. He saw her dig a gun from a bag beneath the counter and tuck it in the back of her waistband as he approached from her left.

She stood, sparing him only a glance before slipping the dream catcher in the box.

"Just had a couple questions." Snake strolled closer. "For the owner, actually."

Max's hands momentarily stilled, then she continued to slip the box into a paper bag with the shop's logo on the front. "She's away on vacation," she lied. "Won't be back for a couple of weeks."

"That's too bad. Maybe you can help us. We're looking for someone."

"Sure. Just give me a minute."

She motioned to Lucas. "The dream catcher comes to nineteen seventy-five." She kept her face angled away from the two men the whole time, but Lucas didn't doubt she was keeping track of them.

Still, there was no way she'd be able to have a conversation without one of them seeing right through her new look.

Lucas turned toward them, cutting them off before they got any closer to the counter. "I'm friends with Sherri, the owner. Maybe I can help."

Blackwater's son shrugged and dug a picture out of his pocket. "We're tracking down a missing person." He offered the photo to Lucas.

It was the same one he had in his own file on Maxine Walker. "She's pretty, though I don't usually go for blondes myself. And she's missing? Do you guys think anything bad happened to her?"

"Not yet. We hope," Blackwater tacked on, forcing a smile that was probably supposed to pass for concern.

"I haven't seen her around town. Is she local?"

"No. It's an old case, actually."

"You know, you should probably talk to Constable Herring. He's the RCMP officer running the BBQ on the wharf today, the big guy massacring the burgers. He's pretty vigilant about what goes on in Riverbend. He might have come across your missing woman." All of which Lucas had learned in the two minutes he'd spent scoping the area out earlier.

Turning his back, he kept his body between them and Max.

He offered her the picture. "Have you seen her?"

Her eyes snapped to his, suspicion glittering in the steel-blue depths. "I don't think so. No."

Before Blackwater Junior got any closer, Lucas pivoted around, handing back the picture. "If one of you guys has a business card or contact number, I'm sure Sherri would have no problem getting in touch with you guys when she gets back into town."

Blackwater's son tucked the photo back into his suit. "We'll be in touch with her later." He nodded to Snake, who lingered another moment, then headed for the door.

"You need to go," Max hissed under her breath, all but shoving the bagged and boxed dream catcher down his throat. "Now."

He lowered his voice to match hers. "I can't do that."

She stepped around the end of the counter, putting herself a few feet closer to the back door. "Who are you?"

The chimes sounded and Lucas waited to hear the door close. And waited...

Max froze. The cool resignation in her eyes said it all—Snake had recognized her.

How in the hell had Blackwater's men found her? And of all the lowlifes he could have sent after her, why did one of them have to be Snake?

Three months ago she had figured out how he'd earned the nickname, had witnessed the sick bastard drape his albino python around a snitch, grinning as it wrapped itself around the guy and squeezed the life out of him.

But it was the presence of Blackwater's son that really unnerved her. Samuel Blackwater wouldn't have sent his oldest son, his right-hand, if he wasn't dead set on getting her back to New York. She knew she'd crossed the line in that rundown warehouse three months ago, had made it impossible for him to forget her.

The same way he'd made it impossible to forget what had gone down that night. The nightmarish images hovered at the back of her mind, and she quickly shut them down. She couldn't afford the distraction. Not when she was determined to avoid being stuffed in a trunk with Snake's python and taken back to Blackwater.

The stranger opposite her snapped his head around, his gaze locking onto Snake. Whatever he'd come looking for, it didn't have anything to do with a souvenir for his nephew. He knew who she was, which left him with the advantage. He also knew who Sherri was, and the local law officials. How long had he been hanging around town?

Across the room, Snake went for his weapon.

"Down!" Max threw herself against Mr. Unknown, and they crashed to the floor.

She ignored his surprised grunt and rolled to a crouch, yanking her gun out as the first set of silenced shots tore into the display case behind her. Shattered glass rained down on her head.

Damn it. Sherri was going to kill her. Thank god she'd said she planned to wait until morning to come back in.

Angling around a shelf filled with some locally crafted pottery, Max slid to her feet, catching sight of Snake. Her first shot missed, but the second nailed him in the side. Since she hadn't pegged Mr. Unknown—who'd crawled off somewhere—as anything but a tourist, it was good to know her aim wasn't as far off-base as her instincts.

Heart drumming against her ribs, she edged behind the counter. She dug another magazine of ammo out of her bag and tucked it into her pocket for the time being before looping her bag over her head and across her body.

Another of Blackwater's guys could be waiting out back for her, but she'd have to take the chance seeing as she wouldn't be leaving through the front.

Counting on the men's view of her being obstructed by more overflowing shelves—and to think she hadn't appreciated Sherri's determination to use every square inch of space before now—she maneuvered behind a stack of wooden crates.

Breath held, she waited. The only sound in the shop was the occasional sharp breath—more of a wheeze really—from Snake. With her eyes on the shelf in front of her, she inched backward around the last corner between her and the back hall.

At the sound of a magazine sliding home, she spun around.

A gun pressed against her side, and she lifted her head to find Mr. Unknown inches away.

Who was this guy?

A ghost of a smile touched his mouth, and then vanished as she nudged the tip of her Glock against the inside of his thigh. One dark brow arched, but she couldn't tell if he looked impressed or annoyed.

"I'm on your side."

Uh huh. And tonight Santa Claus would bring her a cherry-red Chevy Silverado pickup truck and an all-expenses paid vacation to Maui.

"Who do you work for?" Her eyes never left his face as she heard the other two men move in their direction. She was running out of time.

Gunfire ripped apart the model ship display next to them.

"No one needs to get hurt, Detective. Just come along and your *friend* gets to walk out instead of being carried in a body bag." The strained voice came from the right.

Her *friend* rolled his eyes, then tipped his head to indicate the hall behind him. "You go, I'll cover you." He started to stand.

Max yanked him back down. "So you can shoot me in the back?" she hissed.

Splinters of wood skimmed above their heads.

"Fine." He sprang up, fired off a few rounds and then crouched beside her. "You cover me and I'll go."

With no way to believe him and Snake and Edward Blackwater closing in, he was the lesser of two evils. She hoped.

"Better get going." Before she could argue, he moved around the crate in the opposite direction of the back door.

There wasn't enough time to speculate on who he was, or more importantly, who he worked for. A succession of shots plowed into the far wall, and she ran low, sprinting down the back hall. She only hesitated for a heartbeat, unsure if anyone waited for her outside.

Short on options, she shoved the door open and pressed back against the inside wall. Outside, the private parking lot was deserted.

At least something was going for her.

She sprinted across the empty lot, digging her keys from her pocket. With nothing worth stealing in the ancient, battered pickup, she hadn't bothered to lock the door earlier.

Breathing hard, she slid behind the wheel, jammed the key into the slot and turned it over. The engine sputtered and died.

"Son of a bitch." She cranked the key in the ignition again. The engine coughed, almost caught and quit.

Fuck. Fuck. Fuck.

On her third try the engine jerked, shook like a bulldozer overdosing on nitro and died.

Darting a look at the shop's back door, she realized she hadn't closed it. Anyone who pursued her would have a clean shot.

Slamming the heel of her hand on the wheel, she glared at the console. "Start or I'm going to shoot holes in your fucking transmission myself."

As if it understood her perfectly, the truck revved to life on her next try.

Her foot remained on the brake. *So go already.*

She glanced once more over her shoulder wondering what the hell she was doing. The guy was armed and knew who she was. Clearly he wasn't in the area to check out the hiking and fishing opportunities, and if he was a cop or belonged to some agency with an interest in Blackwater he would have said so.

Screw it.

Max wrenched the gearshift into drive and punched the gas. The tires spun in the gravel before tearing across the lot.

Something thumped in the back of the truck, and she twisted around, not surprised to see the back of a black T-shirt pressed against the window.

Chapter Two

Who the hell was this guy?

Anxious to get some space between her and the biggest threat—Snake and Edward—she floored the pedal and zipped onto the main road. The sound of sirens made her turn down a side street and then another as she zigzagged her way out of the small town.

So much for keeping a low profile. And now she'd dragged Sherri into it. People were going to want to know what the hell had just happened in her shop, people like Constable Herring. She'd told Sherri as few details as possible, wanting to keep her out of it and now this.

God, if Sherri and the munchkin had been in the shop... Her stomach churned. Coming here had been such a mistake. If she'd thought for one minute they would have tracked her across the border, she would never have taken Sherri's invitation to stay.

There hadn't even been time to grab her phone off the counter so she could give Sherri a heads up. And once her friend caught a glimpse of the damage done to her shop and no Max, she'd really start to worry.

Knowing that only made Max's stomach hurt worse.

Fifteen minutes later, the town miles behind her, her unwanted passenger knocked on the glass. Max ignored him. She was content to leave him there until she could figure out what he was after.

The moment he'd handed her the photo of herself, it was clear he recognized her. She just didn't know what he wanted or why he'd bothered to go through the motions of buying something and making up the whole story about his nephew. If he'd been hired to take her out, why hadn't he put a bullet in her head when they'd been alone in the shop?

She'd expected Blackwater to put a price on her head, had spent the better part of three months looking over her shoulder for any jerk-off out to make a few bucks or a name for himself.

"Hey!" He banged on the glass. "Pull over or I'm coming through the window." The wind didn't quite rob his words of the menacing tone, but it didn't faze her. He was hardly in a position to make demands.

With one hand on the wheel, she tugged the inside windowpane open a crack to talk to him. That still left the screen for him to claw through if he wanted in, which, given his build and the size of the small window, would be interesting to watch. His gun wasn't visible, but she didn't doubt for a second he had it within reach.

"Who are you working for?" The rearview mirror kept her from having to look over her shoulder to see him.

"No one." All traces of his earlier sexiness had faded. She'd seen a lot of street-hardened faces and cold eyes throughout her law enforcement career, but his were almost enough to give her chills. Almost.

"That's the best answer you can come up with? I suppose you're just some Good Samaritan passing through town and just happened to carry a gun and extra clips tucked in your pants? In case of emergency, right?"

"It doesn't matter if you believe me or not. Pull over."

Max shut the window, drowning him out. Maybe if she left him back there a while longer he'd come around.

The sun was only a thin strip of orange on the horizon now. The late October day that began unseasonably warm was quickly cooling off, and Max flicked the heat on. She blamed the need for warmth on her earlier adrenaline rush.

In the mirror she saw her passenger huddled against the back window. She slid the window open, not even a little bit tempted to pull over and let him into the cab.

"Why were you in the shop?"

No answer.

Max craned her neck to get a better look. His eyes were closed.

"Hey." She knocked on the glass, dividing her attention between the road and the rearview mirror. "Wake up."

Still no movement, but with a second glance over her shoulder she noticed the blood running down his bare arm. A lot of it.

Swearing under her breath, Max guided the truck to the shoulder of the road. She really didn't need this right now. It was only a matter of time before the RCMP, Royal Canadian Mounted Police, started keeping an eye out for her truck.

Still cursing, she rummaged through the glove box and pulled out a travel size first-aid kit. There was little sunlight left as she got out and climbed into the back of the truck, cautious in her approach toward the slumped form.

She set the kit aside, keeping one hand tight on her gun while she looked him over. The source of the bleeding was either his upper chest or shoulder.

"Hey, can you hear me?" Max waited, then kicked his foot. "Hey." It wasn't a good sign if he'd lost consciousness.

Keeping her weapon trained on him, she struggled to get his shirt out of the way to check the wound before finally deciding to set her gun aside. Being a person of interest was bad enough, but getting pulled over with a dead man in the back of her truck would really screw her over.

She tugged at his shirt, the drenched material sticking to

his skin, and he moaned. His eyelids fluttered then stilled once more. Not dead apparently, but she wasn't counting that as any kind of a bonus.

Finding only sculpted abs and some blood beneath his shirt, she frowned and turned her attention to his shoulder. Tearing up through the bloodied fabric, she found only a flesh wound in need of a few stitches.

Had she missed something? Had he caught a bullet in his back, one with no exit wound? She leaned in, and froze. Her gaze snapped to his face.

As she expected, his eyes were open, assessing. Her attention drifted down to the gun clutched in his hand.

Her gun.

Shit.

Rocking back on her heels, Max met his lethal stare with one of her own.

"Climb out and move very slowly. Keep your hands where I can see them."

Max slowly lowered herself to the pavement, backing out of the way when he jumped effortlessly to the ground. Sneaky bastard.

"Walk around to the passenger side and get in," he ordered.

Since he had her own weapon pointed at her, she complied and bit back the *Or what?* perched on her edge of her tongue. Barely.

Something on her face must have betrayed her thoughts because he motioned impatiently for her to slide behind the wheel.

"You're driving and don't get cute with me either." He climbed in after her.

"That's a shame, I do cute pretty well."

He ignored her comment and waited for her to turn the

ignition. The truck started up sweeter than a kitten's purr. Naturally.

Once she'd maneuvered the beast of a vehicle back onto the quiet highway, she watched him from the corner of her eye. The fleeting grimace of pain as he shifted on the seat next to her didn't escape her notice. Nor the fact his being injured was a definite advantage. Maybe her only one.

"So how much is he paying you?" she asked.

He stared straight ahead, giving her the impression he wasn't interested in talking. Not that she cared. If talking provoked him, it just meant their confrontation would come around sooner rather than later.

"Whoever *he* is, it's obviously not enough."

"Right." Max packed as much skepticism into that one word as she could manage.

"I only wanted to talk to you."

"Really? Because where I'm from people usually strike up conversation with, 'Hi, how are you?' Pointing a gun in my face is sort of counterproductive if you want to exchange astrological signs and scary ex stories over beers."

"I said talk to you, not hit on you. And spare me the sarcasm, Max. Do us both a favor and keep quiet so I can think."

"What? Things not go as planned? Bummer." Given how smoothly he'd taken the picture from Edward and acted as if he really knew Sherri, it was probably too much to hope that he was new to the professional killer gig.

Testing to see how jumpy he was, she deliberately stretched and adjusted the rearview mirror. "So what's your name?"

Instead of answering her, he set the gun on the dashboard, freeing up both hands to inspect his shoulder. "Even if you try,

I'll still get to it before you," he stated without looking at her.

Although not inclined to believe he was *that* good, it still wasn't worth the risk. He had managed to lift her gun from beneath her nose. New or not, the guy was very slick.

Lips compressed, he examined the wound, then murmured something she didn't catch.

"Lucas," he repeated, awkwardly wrapping a ripped piece of his shirt around his arm.

"Well, *Lucas*—" Was she actually supposed to believe that was his real name? "—I assume you already know who I am." She reached for the radio, testing him as much as to check if they'd made the local news yet.

His hand closed over hers, stopping her.

She yanked her hand back, surprised at the warmth she felt beneath his touch. Professional killers should not have warm hands.

Lucas went back to adjusting his makeshift bandage, giving her an opportunity to study him further.

His dark brown hair tapered neatly to his collar, a few damp strands curling across his forehead. Beneath them, two dark brows were pulled together in concentration. Already she knew he had dark green eyes that betrayed little of what he was thinking. If eyes truly were mirrors to the soul, Lucas might not have one. Considering his profession, it wasn't surprising.

Relaxing back into the seat as much as she could, she temporarily gave up on trying to read him. Until Lucas made his intentions clear, nothing could be gained by trying to guess what he had planned, except maybe a migraine. Considering the pressure thumping between her temples, one wasn't far off.

Determined to keep a cool head, she stared straight ahead and made no further attempts at conversation. Sooner or later he'd say or do something that would give her an opening, and she didn't plan on missing it.

Cursing under his breath, Lucas shoved his cell phone back in his pocket. He hadn't been able to get a decent signal for the last fifteen minutes and he needed to talk to Tess. Needed to know what other players might be in the area looking for the woman next to him.

As pissed as Joe Lassiter was going to be with him for going solo on this, he and the rest of the team needed to know he had the only person tied to Cara's death. Keeping ahold of her until secure travel arrangements back to headquarters in Boston could be made would be the tricky part.

Resourceful. Max's commanding officers had used that word a lot in his file on her. Even without him there to cover her—and getting shot in the process—she likely would have ditched Blackwater's men. She'd been one step ahead of them for the last three months. One step ahead of everyone.

He eyed the dark hair and painted nails. Resourceful, determined and creative. The goth girl image might have made it harder to fully blend into the small tourist community, but on the surface it was a better disguise than many. If he'd passed her on the street, he might have missed recognizing her.

He had meant what he said about wanting to talk. He just didn't mention that he'd planned for that conversation to take place in his rental car. The one still parked a few blocks down from the shop. Once the tourists cleared out for the night and his car remained on the street, it was bound to draw attention.

Just one more reason he needed to get ahold of Tess. Nothing in the car could be linked to him or the Lassiter Group, even the passport in his bag was under an alias in case Joe had decided to follow up on his whereabouts, but it didn't hurt to see if Tess could make the rental information disappear.

He planned on being long gone before the local law officials, in this case the Royal Canadian Mounted Police, went looking for the owner. The fact that he'd rented the car in Maine before he'd crossed the border would slow them down. Still, he'd feel better knowing they'd have little to go on when they got to that point.

Not that any of that was going to happen unless he started getting some cell phone reception.

"Turn here." He motioned with his injured arm, and clenched his jaw at the flair of pain that burned through his shoulder.

If he'd arrived five minutes earlier, not only might he have gotten the shop door locked before Snake and Edward Blackwater arrived and avoided being shot, he might have had an easier time of getting Max to talk to him.

After the way she'd nearly left him in her dust back in Riverbend, he wasn't holding his breath that she'd spill her guts about what went down the night Cara died. And no matter what story he came up with, the odds of her trusting him on even a superficial level fell somewhere between not in this lifetime and when hell freezes over.

Running short on some of that earlier good luck he'd been enjoying, he indulged in a small victory when she made the turn without objection.

He didn't intimidate her at all unless he had a gun pointed at her, and even then he could see her mind working behind those stormy blue eyes. Eyes he knew from the hours he'd spent going over her file, wanting to get a handle on her. Eyes that turned out to be far more striking in person.

That wasn't the part that worried him, though. He'd come across plenty of attractive women on assignment, some when he'd still been in the military and running an op, and although he'd entertained a thought or two about a handful of them, it took more than pretty eyes to pull his head out of the game.

It was that jolt of awareness that slid through him when she'd turned around at the counter and he got his first up close look at her that made him wary. That and the subtle kiss-my-ass attitude of hers that had trouble written all over it. Especially when the attitude belonged to a woman wanted for his partner's murder.

Makeover aside, he doubted anyone in her department would have pegged her as a murderer, but some people were damn good at masking their nastier sides. He wasn't convinced she had killed Cara or he wouldn't have been so nice about it up until this point, but he wasn't about to hand over her gun and give her the opportunity to prove him wrong.

Once he got ahold of Tess, he could plan his next move. He wasn't looking forward to pointing a gun at Max indefinitely, though, and that was probably the only way to ensure her reluctant cooperation.

Across the seat, she gave a good show of focusing on the road. Strong, slim fingers clenched the steering wheel, the only indication she was tense, and under his scrutiny, they too relaxed as though she suspected he was sizing her up.

"How did you find me?" Her velvet-edged voice still carried the unmistakable tone of someone used to getting what she wanted.

Lucas considered ignoring her then changed his mind, figuring he might as well push a button or two himself. "You made it rather easy."

She arched a brow. "If it was so easy, how come it took so long to catch up with me?"

"I found you when I needed to," he lied. "You should have

done a better job of covering your tracks." Lucas retrieved the gun and settled against the seat's faded and worn upholstery.

Max shook her head, her knuckles turning a little white. "I covered my tracks—"

"Whatever you say."

Her shoulders stiffened, but she let it go. "Where are we going?"

"Don't worry about it. Just drive."

"Is it much farther?"

He didn't know if it was Max, his shoulder, or that he still couldn't reach Tess—or any one else for that matter—that was testing his patience. "I'll let you know."

"I think—"

"You don't need to think. You only need to drive."

Right near the top of his to-do list was ditching the truck and finding something a little less conspicuous. The lemon-colored rust bucket stuck out like an original Volkswagen Bug parked between two brand new BMWs.

Finding something else might have to wait until morning, though. The secondary highway they were travelling on wasn't exactly overflowing with potential vehicles. It wasn't overflowing with much of anything except trees. At least the truck was getting them where they needed to go for the time being, which was far away from Riverbend.

As soon as the thought took root in his mind, the truck shuddered and rolled to a dead stop.

"Out of gas?" Lucas echoed a minute later, certain he couldn't have understood Max's faint murmur.

The barest hint of a smile tugged at the corner of her mouth.

"What do you mean by out of gas?" He crossed his arms,

33

waiting. What kind of murder suspect on the run didn't keep their vehicle filled up at all times?

"Well," she began. "You see methods of transportation such as my truck here are powered by a fuel that some of us like to call *gasoline*. And when this—" she tapped on the fuel gauge, "—little arrow gets down on E, which coincidently stands for *empty*, you need to stop at a place that sells *gasoline* and fill up the tank."

Lucas could only stare at her. "Are you finished?"

She shrugged. "That depends."

He managed to stop himself from asking, *On what?* knowing the question would encourage her to keep talking. Seeing how quickly his good luck had gone to shit, he could do without inviting that kiss-my-ass attitude he heard in her voice.

Ignoring the drumming ache in his shoulder, he checked his phone—surprise, no signal—then stared out into the night.

No headlights cut through the darkness in either direction. Probably a good thing since flagging down a ride was a last resort. He was betting Max's unpredictable streak ran at least a mile wide. Who knew what she'd pull if they managed to catch a ride.

"Trying to figure out your next move, huh?" She glanced over at him.

He wasn't buying the innocent expression on her face for a second. If he was in her shoes, he'd be focused on using the unexpected development to his benefit. Which left him coming up with a plan *and* anticipating how she'd try to work it to her advantage.

Too bad his car was stuck back in Riverbend, though he doubted Max would have found being locked in a trunk with a very big gag over her mouth a more promising situation, even though according to some, she deserved a lot worse.

A crushing numbness squeezed his chest and grief over Cara's death overwhelmed him. God, he missed her. When he caught up with the bastard who killed her...

Half his team was convinced Max did it, but the deeper he dug, the less sense things made. Of course sharing that opinion had pissed off a number of people, including Cara's brother Caleb.

But Cara had been convinced her friend Max had a better handle on Blackwater and wanted to team up with her to bring the bastard down. That had been the last thing she'd said to him. A few hours later she was dead.

From the corner of his eye, he watched Max pick at the driver's seat. If she was concerned at all over her present situation, she kept it under wraps. If she wasn't worried about him, she should damn well be concerned that Blackwater's men had tracked her here.

They needed to get the truck going or leave it.

"Why didn't you say anything about needing gas?"

Max nibbled on her thumbnail. "I just did as I was told and drove. Besides, the gauge is broken."

Lucas leaned over and confirmed the arrow still indicated the tank was full.

"Out," he ordered.

She cocked her head to the side. "What?"

"Get out of the truck, Max." He pointed the gun at her chest. "Now."

Her answering sigh was quintessential drama queen, but she obeyed and hopped out.

"Hands on your head."

"I suppose you want to frisk me too," she quipped.

Lucas ignored her, clamping down on the frustration lodged in his chest. She wasn't the first person to shoot her mouth off at him, and in his six years in Special Forces and three as part of the Lassiter group, most of those people had been more dangerous than Max. Heads of drug cartels, terrorists, arms dealers, even a who's who on Interpol's most wanted list.

But few who purposely goaded him had a fraction of the success she was having. Which meant he needed to get back in control and focus.

"Get the gas can out of the back of the truck."

"What gas can?" she drawled.

"The one I saw back there a while ago."

"It's empty."

"Get the can," he growled.

"Whatever you say. You're the one with the gun." She flung a leg over the side and hauled herself up.

Lucas ignored the way her jeans molded snuggly to her ass. He might have helped her out with a soft push if she were anyone else.

Max picked up the can. "I told you, it's empty." She carried the orange jug to the edge and straddled the side of the truck, glaring at him. "Is that scratch on your arm leaving you a little slow on the uptake or are you always so thick headed?"

He checked the urge to drag her out of the truck. Barely. "Get. Down."

Her eyes narrowed. "You could say please, you know."

"Don't push it."

"Or what?" Max lifted her other leg over the side and jumped down. "No, wait, don't tell me. It might be so terrifying I'll pee my pants."

"Listen, smart ass—" Lucas stopped at the widening of her eyes as she glanced past his shoulder.

"They found us," she whispered.

Lucas followed her gaze but saw only darkness.

Too late, he realized the amateurish mistake. Pain ricocheted through his head. Stunned by the unexpected blow, Lucas staggered a few steps, tripping over the very full gas can she'd blindsided him with.

He fell against the truck, his injured arm taking the brunt of the impact. Pain sliced across his shoulder.

Fuck.

He was seriously going to enjoy restraining her.

It took him a few seconds to see past the blinking colored lights popping behind his eyes, and he raised his head. He caught a glimpse of Max's pink sweater disappearing into the woods. *Shit.*

Lucas stumbled after her, ignoring the way the world still dipped and wobbled. Judging by the pressure pounding at the back of his skull, like someone had slammed his head in a door a few times, he had a concussion to go along with his *scratch.*

Stepping into the woods, he paused to listen. Crickets, an owl hooting, something scampering over branches in a nearby tree.

Silently he slid between the trees, his eyes slower to adjust to the dark than he liked. Probably had something to do with getting nailed by a gas can.

Resourceful was turning out to be pretty damn accurate.

Every few steps he stopped and listened before continuing. She couldn't have gone far and she wasn't tearing through the underbrush, meaning she had to be close, hiding somewhere in the surrounding shadows. Sooner or later she'd give herself away. She'd want to be on the move.

Another branch snapped, heightening his senses. Grateful for the clear night and full moon, he scanned the darkness, breath held as he waited...waited...

A muted crunch came from his left, then another. Watching his steps, he moved toward the sounds inch by inch. Dull scraping, like someone rubbing two sticks together to get a spark, echoed through the trees.

What the hell was she doing? Either she thought he was still clinging to the truck, trying to stop the stars from circling his head, or she wanted to draw him closer.

Having been blindsided once this evening, he sure as hell wasn't going to make it easy for her to surprise him. Even unarmed and with the gas can abandoned by the truck, she was still dangerous. He wasn't about to make underestimating her his second mistake of the evening. Third if he counted not getting that shop door locked the second he recognized her.

Circling a massive pine tree, he approached from the opposite direction. Each time the scraping sound stopped, he did too, edging forward only when the noise masked his approach.

A few minutes later, he reached a small clearing less than twenty feet across. A small blur zipped along the ground. A fat raccoon paused, eyes glittering like torches in the dark before the animal growled and darted under a bush.

Great, he'd been stalking a raccoon. Definitely a detail he'd be leaving out in his update if he ever got his cell phone to work.

The hair on the back of his neck rose to attention.

Something changed, a shift in the air, and he glanced up to see a blur of pink bearing down on him.

Chapter Three

Max ignored her cramping legs, her grip on the tree branch so tight she was half convinced she'd never be able to peel her fingers off the bark.

Ten feet down, maybe less, Lucas stepped from the cover of trees. He closed in on the same raccoon that had growled at her moments ago from the opposite end of the branch she presently occupied.

Too bad the furry little bugger didn't take his friend with him. The second raccoon was smaller, but that didn't make his claws or teeth any less sharp. And when faced with going head-to-head with the nocturnal creature stalking toward her or the guy circling below, she'd take Lucas.

She didn't know what exactly he was after or how much she could possibly be worth that he'd covered her back at Sherri's shop, but either way he was going home empty-handed.

The raccoon snarled and lunged forward, and God help her, she jumped.

Either the raccoon had impeccable timing or fate was on her side, because she hit Lucas dead-on.

He grunted in surprise and his knees buckled, pitching him forward and taking her with him. She landed on her side, the impact knocking the breath from her lungs. Recovering quickly, she rolled to her feet and kicked the gun Lucas had dropped out of his reach.

He glared up at her, already to his knees. She pivoted on

instinct, snapping her leg around to deliver a kick to the jaw. Lucas blocked her with his forearms, then caught her ankle and shoved her backward.

Off-balance, she stumbled and hit the ground, but drove the heel of her boot into his stomach before he could pin her. Doubled over, he still managed to snatch a handful of her sweater and jerked her toward him.

Son of a bitch.

"You keep this up and one of us is going to get hurt."

"Worried?" Snapping her elbow back, she caught his bad shoulder, but damn it he was fast and managed to wrench her arm behind her back.

"Not really."

"Wait," she breathed, the white-hot pain running from wrist to shoulder turning the last syllable into a wince.

"Are you done playing games, Max?"

"Absolutely." She didn't give him a chance to wonder if she meant it. She smashed her head back into his, then twisted free.

Grabbing his shirt, she spun and shoved him at the tree only a couple feet away. He couldn't get a hand up in time to prevent a full-on collision and skidded across the bark before hitting the ground.

It should have been enough of a head start. Maybe if she'd managed to keep out of range of the kick that caught her across the thigh as he dropped. She stayed on her feet, but he rolled and tripped her before she got another foot of space between them.

Her back had barely touched the ground and he was on her, using every inch of his solid frame to trap her beneath him.

Breathing hard, she glared at up at him, cursing the fucking raccoon that had forced her to jump when she'd been prepared to stay up there all night if she had to. Or until Lucas gave up and moved on, whichever came first.

"Okay. Now I'm done."

His body didn't give an inch. "Somehow I doubt that."

She cracked a smile that probably fell miles short of sincere. "Maybe I'm ready to cooperate."

Surprisingly, he didn't call her on the lie, and since he had blood dripping into his eye from the scrape on his forehead and running down his arm from his flesh wound, she knew there wasn't a hope in hell he believed her.

Between breaths, he shoved her onto her stomach, planting his knee in the center of her back.

"Take it easy, damn it." She sank her teeth into her bottom lip when he yanked both arms back and cold metal encircled her wrists with a deafening click.

Wasn't he a regular Boy Scout coming all prepared? Handcuffs would certainly slow her down.

The pain in her arms had subsided by the time he flipped her back over. Lifting her head off the ground, she watched him move around the clearing. Probably looking for her gun. Maybe she'd get lucky and he wouldn't find it, though he probably still had his own on him somewhere.

The audible click of a magazine being checked and reinserted squashed that hope. Hell, something had to start going her way soon.

Cursing the tender muscles she already knew wouldn't be very cooperative come morning, she rolled to a sitting position just as Lucas stalked toward her.

"What the hell were you thinking?"

The narrowed eyes and thin line that barely passed for a mouth indicated he wasn't actually looking for a response, but that seldom stopped her. She could have retired at the age of eighteen if she'd earned a dollar for every time her father or three older brothers had given her the same look.

Strangely enough, reminding herself of that helped to slow the adrenaline that was still pumping through her veins.

"Which time?"

He gave her a blank look.

"Are you referring to me hitting you over the head? Nice goose egg by the way. Or jumping you?"

His whole body tensed, but Max didn't think for a second she'd gone too far. He wouldn't be that easy to crack, but she had a feeling that when Lucas lost his cool—he *really* lost it.

All she had to do was hope she wasn't wearing the cuffs when it happened.

"You're a real piece of work." Lucas jerked her to her feet.

Max bit the inside of her cheek against the rough grip. He obviously didn't care he'd nearly pulled her arms out of their sockets getting the cuffs on.

Standing so close, she had to raise her chin to meet his gaze. "Now don't go getting all sweet on me, Lucas. We won't be together *that* long."

The lethal glitter in his eyes did wonders to improve her mood. She was definitely getting to him and that knowledge made the lingering ache in her arms more tolerable as he shoved her in the direction of the truck and fell into step behind her.

She supposed she should be thankful he hadn't killed her yet, but not knowing what he had planned left a bitter taste in her mouth. If he wasn't working for Blackwater—and if he was, why had Snake and Edward shown up too?—then why bother to track her to Canada?

Even Blackwater knew she couldn't risk returning to New York and have any hope of beating the murder charge. He'd made damn sure of that, him and the supposed eye-witnesses he'd paid off.

Max started to turn around.

"Not one word or I'll shoot you."

She snorted, but kept walking. "You're not going to kill me."

"Who said anything about killing you?" Though his granite-edged voice warned her he was thinking about it.

They reached the truck, the dark stretch of road just as deserted as before.

"Face down, Max." He urged her to her knees, then down onto her stomach, leaving her on the ground next to the truck while he filled the gas tank.

When he finished, he settled her in the truck's passenger side this time and slid behind the wheel.

He reached across her—

"What are you doing?"

—and snagged her seatbelt. "Safety first."

Safety first? Jesus, who was this guy? A driving instructor moonlighting as a hit man?

His brows drew together as he struggled to jam it into the slot, and his eyes met hers. Intensely aware of how close he was, she looked out the window, relieved when he finished buckling her up and slid back to his side of the truck.

More than a little disturbed by how hot she suddenly was—and who wouldn't be after what just went down in the woods, right?—she took a perverse amount of pleasure in watching him curse under his breath when it took three times to make the truck's engine turn over, a task she sensed drained Lucas of any lingering patience.

She opened her mouth, but a tiny voice warned her not to ask to see a valid driver's license, considering he was still the one with the gun. Instead, she kept quiet as he popped the gearshift into drive and pulled onto the road.

Her silence lasted a full five minutes before she tried again to get some information out of Lucas. He continued to ignore her, even when she'd insisted on needing to stop and use a bathroom somewhere, which wasn't exactly a lie. His only response involved a muttered warning to hold it or end up sitting in it.

Ten minutes later, Lucas surprised her by turning into a motel parking lot. Long past its prime, the motel's yellow paint was faded and peeled away in places and the blinking vacancy sign was like something out of a low budget horror film.

He parked the truck in front of a pair of vending machines, one of which was leaning to the right due to the large dent in its side where someone had probably backed their car into it.

Lucas shut off the truck, pocketed the keys and faced her. He'd barely opened his mouth to say something and already she knew she wasn't going to like it.

"Take off your shirt."

Really, *really* not like it. Max scoffed. "You first."

Holding her gaze, he reached behind his neck and tugged his shirt over his head, then down his arms, careful of his shoulder. "Now are you going to take it off, or will I?"

"As much as I'm sure you'd enjoy that—" she jiggled her wrists to remind him she was handcuffed, "—neither of us will be taking it off while I'm still wearing these."

When she didn't immediately lean forward to give him access to the cuffs—which had absolutely nothing to do with wondering if he bench-pressed Volkswagens to get such sculpted abs—he made a move to help her out.

"Paws off, bud. Exactly when did I give you the impression I got friendly with every perp who made a pass at me?"

"Trust me, if I was making a pass, you'd know."

It would have been so much easier to blow off the remark if his voice didn't have the same sexy edge he'd used before her evening had gone to hell.

Lucas blew out a breath. "I just need to borrow your shirt. I can't exactly go in and rent a room wearing this." He fingered his torn and bloody shirt.

"And how is that my problem?" She had no idea what dragging out the conversation would actually accomplish, but talking seemed to be about the only thing she had any control over at the moment.

"Max," he warned, coming remarkably close to the same bordering-on-exasperated tone her father and brothers used whenever she said something to piss them off. Nine times out of ten they deserved it, though.

"You know, I don't think pink is your color."

His eyes narrowed. "I'll make do." He reached for her once more. "If you try anything—"

"Yeah, yeah, you'll shoot me. I know." At least that's what he said earlier. Considering he'd taken the time to belt her in, he either had no intention of killing her, or he needed her alive.

Reminding herself that a night at a run-down motel was better than getting any closer to the border, she leaned forward so Lucas could unlock the cuffs and free one hand. Assuming that he wouldn't care if her wrists were sore, she didn't waste time rubbing them before yanking her sweater over her head in one fluid motion.

If she'd been banking on Lucas being distracted by the sight of a little skin, she would have been sorely disappointed. His eyes never left hers.

At least there was no question about him being a professional. Only the mission-focused type wouldn't sneak a peek, which made her feel less optimistic about her odds of ditching him in the very near future. She would have felt much better if he'd shown a little interest in her navy push-up bra.

Sherri had insisted she splurge on something when they'd gone shopping last week. New lingerie was something every woman needed, even murder suspects, apparently.

"Are you gay?"

Lucas frowned. "What?"

She cocked her head as though sizing him up. "Are you gay? Just wondering if that's why you really want my sweater."

"I'm not gay." He sounded both amused and a little confused.

45

She shrugged and handed him the sweater. "Whatever."

"I'm not gay," he insisted.

Max hid her smile by turning her face to the window. "If it makes you feel any better, I'm completely comfortable around gay men. My cousin is gay. He and his partner got married last year. Cute couple. He did have a hard time coming out of the closet though."

Without warning, Lucas jerked her toward him, his palms warming her skin as though he were branding her with his touch. Hot, green eyes burned into hers, daring her to pull away, daring her not to. Seconds ticked by until her lungs ached to drag in the breath trapped between her throat and her chest.

Thirty seconds ago this was the exact response she would have taken advantage of, but with his hands on her, his thumb sweeping across her skin, she couldn't stop thinking about how long it had been since any man had touched her, caressed her.

And the lazy brush of his thumb—god, she never had to work so hard to suppress a shiver in her life—was definitely a caress.

Except it was all wrong. The time, the place, the guy. That still didn't stop the heat that simmered in her stomach when Lucas's gaze dropped to her mouth and then lower, to her breasts. Like the half-starved traitors they were, her nipples hardened at the hunger that flashed across his face.

Slowly, he raised his head. "I *am not* gay." Deep and loaded with enough delicious intent to worry her, his voice managed to drag her attention from his lips to his eyes.

"Should I put together a press release?"

His expression darkened and her heart kicked against her ribs—in preparation of going head-to-head with him or kissing him?

So caught up in her growing awareness of Lucas and the

fact that she'd succeeded in rattling him, she failed to notice the handcuff until he'd shackled her to the steering wheel.

Sneaky son of a bitch.

With a sound of disgust, she tested the give of the cuffs, more than a little annoyed with herself, then inched over as much as she could.

Lips pressed in a pained line, Lucas tugged on her sweater. The fuzzy pink fabric stretched taut across his chest and fell just past his elbows.

"I was wrong," Max corrected. "Pink is *so* your color, girlfriend."

Lucas scowled at her, then grabbed a napkin from the console under the radio. Next he grabbed the half empty bottle of water on the floor by her feet and cleaned the dried blood off his face.

"I'll be right back, and seeing as how I'll be able to see every move you make through that window, I suggest you be a good girl."

Max resisted the urge to kick him in the ass when he climbed out. Better that than the thoughts she'd been entertaining when he'd put his hands on her. He checked the safety on her gun and tucked it into the side pocket of his cargo pants, leaving his own weapon at the small of his back.

After one last look over his shoulder, he walked toward the motel's office.

Max waited until he was halfway to the door then used her foot to feel around on the floor for her bag. Not there. Damn.

Under the seat maybe? Not wanting to bend down, she used to foot to tug it out, then pulled it into her lap. She glanced up, relieved to see Lucas still preoccupied with the desk clerk.

Digging through the bag with one hand slowed her down, and when she couldn't find anything to pick the cuff with, she settled on something else, forced to take her eyes off Lucas long enough to look in her bag. God, how did she end up with so much crap anyway? Like she had time to dig through old receipts, makeup and wet nap packages from drive thru's.

She jiggled the oversized bag farther up on her knees so she could use her cuffed hand to hold it open. Her fingertips just grazed the can of pepper spray when the door swung open.

What the hell was she up to now?

Lucas had just turned from the desk, key in hand, when he noticed Max duck her head.

Behind him, the desk clerk went back to watching the football game he'd been engrossed in when Lucas walked in, cursing under his breath when he noticed the score.

Wearing the pink sweater went against his preference for avoiding attention, but thankfully the clerk was so distracted by the Patriots' third down while getting Lucas registered, he'd barely glanced away from the television.

Considering just how ridiculous he must look in the sweater, not to mention the scrape on his face, it said a lot more about the clerk than it did about how many wrong turns the last hour had taken.

Outside the air had grown cooler and countless stars glittered in the black sky above. If not for the five-foot-six-inch package of trouble looking at something in her lap, he might have enjoyed the star-lit view.

There was a lot of scary shit that went down in the world and the only way to keep your head on straight when wading hip deep in it was to find an anchor. A lot of the guys he knew used family, friends or a favorite place they couldn't wait to get back to. For those who couldn't envision a life outside of the military, it was getting to the next assignment.

The stars were his anchor. He'd spent so much of the last

eleven years stationed around the globe, first with the military and then with the Lassiter Group, that the stars were one of the few things he could count on to stay the same.

Lucas wrenched the truck door open, snatching the bag off Max's lap. "Tsk, tsk."

He waited for her slide over, ignoring the bra and enticing cleavage that had screwed with his head just long enough to make him cross the line—and with a murder suspect for Christ's sake.

Poking through her belongings, he slanted her a suspicious look. "So what were you trying to get your pretty little hands on?"

"Gum," she answered easily.

"Right." Whistling, he withdrew the three-inch can. "This is nasty stuff, Max. I'm sure you understand that I need to confiscate it." He tucked the pepper spray into his pocket, and dropped the bag on the floor at her feet.

"Stop calling me Max like we're friends or something."

"Whatever you say, *Max*." He unlocked the cuff around the steering wheel, waiting until she sighed and offered up her other wrist.

Once both hands were secured in front of her, he drove the truck around to the rear of the motel. He didn't pull into the empty spot in front of their room, but parked behind the dumpster near the edge of the surrounding woods instead.

If Snake and Edward Blackwater somehow managed to pass by the place looking for them, they'd have to drive all the way to the end of the rear lot to spot the truck.

Grabbing his shirt, he climbed out and moved around the vehicle to open the door for Max. He reached for her when she didn't look interested in getting out on her own. The look on her face as she snapped up her bag and hopped down said she'd rather follow the devil to hell than go anywhere with him.

Good thing he hadn't been shot, nailed in the head, jumped on, kicked, punched and shoved into a tree or his feelings might be a little hurt.

Chapter Four

Max shivered next to him, but he didn't stop to return her sweater. He wanted her inside first, contained, and maybe buried under enough blankets that he didn't have to think about her breasts.

Nudging her up against the door, he dug the key from his pocket, then hustled her inside when he got the door open. After maneuvering her into the closest chair, he locked the door and slid the chain into place.

He didn't immediately turn a light on, leaving only the moonlight streaming through the open window to see by as he leaned against the door for a moment.

"Aw, rough day at the office, honey?"

Maybe he could find some duct tape in that bag of hers.

Pushing away from the door, he crossed to the bedside table and switched on the lamp. The sudden brightness overpowered the small room, and he turned to drag the drapes shut.

Just large enough to accommodate the double bed draped in a faded gold bedspread, the room's remaining furniture consisted of the chair Max occupied, a battered dresser and TV stand, all crowded within inches of each other. Beneath it all, the shabby tan colored shag carpet was a testament to the last time the room had been redone.

But it was clean and a much better place to plan his next

move than camping out in the woods waiting for Max to give herself away.

Inside the bathroom, he barely glanced at his reflection when he noticed Max cast a speculative look at the room's only exit. He snagged a towel from the shelf above the toilet and turned toward her.

"You won't get very far."

She didn't argue with him, but he knew her earlier failure to ditch him wouldn't stop her from trying again.

He leaned in the doorway. "For a woman who needed to use the bathroom so badly, you're certainly not begging to get in here."

"You won't see me begging you for anything."

"Not even for your life?"

Her chin rose a notch, defiance flashing in her eyes. "I wouldn't give you the satisfaction."

He didn't doubt the conviction in her voice for a second. Cara had called Max a scrapper and everything he'd seen so far backed that up. That still didn't mean Max hadn't killed her, though.

Moving back to the chair, he snatched her bag off the floor and dumped the contents out on the bed.

"I'm all out of pink nail polish if you're looking for some to match the sweater."

"So I guess giving each other pedicures tonight is out then." He dragged her sweater off and tossed it at her before getting back to snooping through her stuff. A large hair elastic caught his eye and he slid it up his arm to hold the small towel over the wound that had started bleeding again.

The extra magazine clips for her Glock looked to be the only interesting things in the pile, and once he tucked them in his other side pocket, he stretched out on the bed and closed his eyes.

For a full minute he felt Max's gaze drilling into him. When she cursed under her breath, he cracked open an eye and watched her snatch up her shirt and stalk into the bathroom, stubbing her foot on the corner of the TV stand as she sailed past.

"Don't lock it."

She poked her hand out of the bathroom long enough to flip him off.

Jesus, the woman had balls. Either he hadn't been intimidating enough, or she excelled at masking her fear with some serious attitude.

Or maybe it something to do with the minute he'd lost his mind back in the truck, when she taken her shirt off and asked if he was gay. People with worse reputations than hers had done a better job of baiting him in the past and he'd never once let it get to him.

He'd gone one-step further with her—proving she was wrong. There had been absolutely no tactical advantage in letting her know he was attracted to her. If anything, he'd sacrificed information she could try to use against him. Emphasis on *try*.

His judgment might have been temporarily clouded by a sexy, determined woman he might have admired if not for her questionable role in Blackwater's organization and Cara's death, but he'd be damned if it happened a second time.

Frustrated with failing to keep his mission objective— getting Max back to Lassiter Group headquarters—front and center, he grabbed the extra pillow off the bed, along with the bedspread and crossed to the bathroom.

When she didn't answer his knock, he shoved the door open.

She turned from the sink, a towel in her hands. "Do come in," she scoffed.

The less than spacious bathroom left only a few feet between them and his gaze dropped to the open buttons on her pants. Dropping the blanket and pillow, he closed the distance between them.

She backed up against the vanity, but didn't push his hands away when he stepped in to fix her pants for her.

"I'm handcuffed, not paralyzed. But if you're inclined to be so helpful, why not take the cuffs off?"

"Injured, not brain dead." He made quick work of fastening the buttons but didn't retreat until he realized how still she was, like she was holding her breath.

He glanced up, searching her face to be sure she wasn't about to try something. Their gazes met, held and then she broke eye contact.

"Fuck, no."

So she'd finally noticed the pillow and blanket.

Without waiting for a thank you, he made a strategic retreat, falling back to the doorway.

"Wait a minute."

Lucas shook his head. "You're sleeping in here. In the tub, on the floor, I don't particularly care."

Max stepped over the pile on the floor. "What about the bed?"

He blocked the doorway with his arm just in case she was serious, and God help him, she looked like it. "What about it?"

"It's big enough for the two of us."

"But I thought you didn't get friendly with every perp who made a pass at you?"

Her eyes shrank to murderous slits, and she slammed the door in his face.

"Bet you're wishing you'd stayed in the tree, huh?"

No matter how thick the door was, he very clearly heard, "Asshole."

Satisfied she'd stay out of trouble for a few minutes at least, he returned to the bed and picked up the phone to call Tess.

Hoping last night had only been a dream, Max opened her eyes.

No such luck.

Same cracked light fixture and drab bathroom—minus the potato bug that she'd seen scuttling across the floor last night. She didn't even want to think about where it might have crawled for the short time she'd actually spent sleeping. Between wondering about Lucas and who he worked for and running through countless scenarios to get herself out of this mess, sleep hadn't been high on her priority list.

Sleep hadn't been a priority for three months actually. Staying one step ahead of Blackwater, finding places to lay low, conserving what little money she had left and doing her best not to think about what the bastards had done to Cara made sleeping difficult at best and pretty much impossible when a nightmare took hold and wouldn't let her go.

Staying with Sherri had been the closest she'd come to any kind of peace, and thanks to Lucas and Snake she was back to square one. Damn them.

Recognizing the first stirring of anxiety press down on her lungs, she stood and scrubbed her face with cool water, rubbing until she felt the cold seep into her pores, waking her up all the way.

A flash of color caught her eye and she spotted her bag on the floor by the door. She must have slept deeper than she thought since she hadn't heard Lucas come in.

Listening at the door, she didn't hear any signs of movement. Either he was still asleep himself or he was sitting there waiting for her to get moving. Actually, the latter seemed unlikely. Barging in and telling her to get her ass in gear seemed more probable after how things had gone down last night.

Either way, she had a little time to get cleaned up and pull a few random twigs from her hair while she tried wrapping her mind around the only option she had left.

She'd lie.

Lie and use his attraction to her for all it was worth. She hadn't imagined the way he'd responded to her in the truck. She couldn't see the point in him playing her and then pulling away. If he'd felt that brief—*extremely* brief—moment of mutual awareness and planned to do something about it, he wouldn't have left her in the bathroom all night.

She'd done worse things than make promises she couldn't keep. Getting two people killed weighed far more on her heart than leading Lucas on ever would.

She couldn't guarantee another physical confrontation would go her way any more than the last one had. He was strong, fast and seemed to know a hell of a lot more about her than she knew about him. He had every advantage and if she didn't do something to level the playing field, she was going to regret hiding out in New Brunswick more than she already did.

The slim tube of tinted lip gloss in her bag caught her attention, and she pulled it out, rolling it back and forth in her palm. It had belonged to Cara. She'd been carrying it around for weeks as though she could use it to hold onto her friend a little longer.

She'd found Cara's purse when she'd been fleeing the warehouse but the contents—lip gloss, Blackwater's business card, a hotel keycard—hadn't offered any clues about what information Cara had claimed to have for her.

Twisting off the cap, Max ran the gloss over her lips. She

stared as her reflection, trying to gear herself up for something she might not even be able to pull off. Three months of running had carved away pieces she wasn't sure would fit back together again. Some never would, the same way Cara would never take another breath, never smile, never laugh.

Don't.

She squeezed her eyes so tight they hurt, praying she wasn't about lose it. Giving in to the horrific memories stirred up after yesterday was the quickest way to ensure she ended up dead.

As much as part of her wanted to stop running, just wanted it to all be over, she desperately wanted to find a way back to her life. The one Blackwater had ripped away from her, first when he screwed with her family, then her career and then Cara.

More than anyone she wanted to call her partner, Glen. For three years he'd been the one backing her up, reinforcing her instincts or talking her out of one of her more radical ideas. But even if he'd heard or uncovered something that could help her, she couldn't risk calling him, no matter how much she could use his advice right now.

Blackwater was responsible for that too. Glen hadn't blamed her for their suspension or losing his fiancée, but she might as well have killed Jillian herself. If she hadn't pushed Glen so hard to help her find something to bring Blackwater down for good Jillian might still be alive. Glen was better off if she didn't involve him, leaving her on her own.

Max just wasn't sure if that was enough anymore.

"You're not looking too hot."

Her head snapped up and she caught Lucas's reflection in the mirror. She'd been so preoccupied with talking herself down from some kind of meltdown that she hadn't heard him come in.

She tucked the lip gloss into her pocket. "I could say the same about you. How's your shoulder this morning?" The question had way too much bite if she wanted to talk her way out of this mess, and she let out a breath. "Sorry. For all I know you got hit by a bullet meant for me." She picked up her bag and stepped back from the sink, taking a seat on the edge of the tub when he made no move to let her pass.

"You're not actually going to cooperate this morning, are you?"

Massaging the back of her neck, she offered a weak smile. "I'm not interested in starting the morning the same way we ended last night."

He rinsed his face and ran a damp hand through his hair. He wore a different shirt this morning, dark blue and long sleeved, along with a blue and white ball cap. Had he borrowed them from the desk clerk or perhaps stolen them from the occupants staying in the closest room?

She leaned against the wall, eyes closed, as she felt him studying her.

"I've got coffee," he said finally.

"Really?" She didn't have to exaggerate how appealing that sounded. She hadn't eaten since lunch yesterday and her system could benefit from a boost of caffeine.

He started out of the room then stopped when he noticed her sweater was still on the floor.

She shrugged. "I think the cuffs make a much bolder fashion statement without the sweater."

The corner of his mouth twitched, and he dug the key from his pocket. He hadn't hesitated to touch her last night, but this morning he seemed careful to keep any physical contact to a minimum.

He uncuffed one wrist and handed her the sweater. Dropping her bag, she pulled it over her head, aware of the moment his attention slid down her chest. She ducked her head, the nervous flutter in her belly having nothing to do with the game she was playing.

A full ten seconds passed before he cuffed her again, and she intentionally brushed up against him as she squeezed past. Without a lot of wiggle room, she had to turn her body into his to fit, drawing the slow slide out an extra second or two.

He only let her get a couple feet ahead of him into the main room before he circled around, giving her a wide berth.

Grateful to have more than ten square feet to move around in, she sat on the edge of the bed. Lucas handed her one of the two coffees from the bedside table. Ten bucks said Lucas had given the desk clerk a nice tip to deliver them right to the room.

She brought the Styrofoam cup to her lips, letting every bit of the uncertainty she felt play across her face. "You're not going to tell me where you're taking me, are you?"

Leaning back against the dresser opposite her, Lucas only shook his head.

"What if I told you I could pay you more than whatever Blackwater is?"

"Then I'd wonder where a cop comes by that kind of money."

When he skipped asking her who Blackwater was, any hope she might have been clinging to that he had nothing to do with the drug and arms dealer was shot all to hell.

"Does it really matter?"

He crossed his arms. "Depends on if you actually expect me to believe you or not."

His suspicion wasn't entirely unexpected. The hesitation to lie to him was, though. Why should it matter what he thought of her when Blackwater had made sure even her own friends and family questioned her involvement with his dealings?

It didn't, she reminded herself. She took a sip of her coffee, letting the hot liquid slide down her throat and buying herself a few more seconds.

"There was a shipment that came in a three months ago. The deal went south."

"Drugs?" He sounded only mildly curious, but he stood a little straighter, his sharp gaze locked on her every move.

"No. Something else." Something Cara had gotten caught up in somehow. "Blackwater was just the middle man on this and whatever it was, he was in over his head. The merchandise was seized during the exchange and everything went to hell."

"DEA?"

"I don't think so." She hadn't seen much of anything to know for sure. The second Blackwater had realized the location had been compromised he'd fled, dragging her along with him to take care of later.

Cutting off that train of thought right there, she glanced at Lucas. He stared at her, waiting.

"The bust never made the news and not a single agency claimed anything went down that night."

"I'm still waiting for the part where you explain how I can benefit from a deal that already blew up in someone else's face?"

She took another sip of her coffee. "Blackwater's buyer was killed that night." At least she couldn't imagine how he'd survived being shot in the head. "But the money was never recovered."

"And you know where the money went?"

"I saw where the Russian hid it."

"Russian, huh?" He searched her face, probably trying to figure out if she was lying. "And how do you know it wasn't already found?"

"You wouldn't be here if it had," she lied. Even if Blackwater had found the money, he hated how she'd constantly put her nose in his business. And it was apparently her fault that some dangerous players on the world stage were not too happy with him for losing both their money and the merchandise.

Lucas grabbed the chair by the door and turned it around backward before sliding into it. "You don't really expect me to believe you're driving that clunker and hiding out here when you've had some terrorist's blood money at your disposal."

Terrorist? Did Lucas know something about what had gone down that night?

"If I had a prayer of getting to that money on my own, would we be having this conversation?"

He gave her a tight smile. "Maybe. Maybe not. But then we also wouldn't be having this conversation if you'd managed to ditch me in the woods."

She set the coffee aside. "I promise I can make it worth your while." Just a little desperate to gain some small measure of control over her fate, she gripped his hand. "Please."

His gaze dropped to where her fingers were curled around his, and plan or not, she didn't let go, wanting to hold on to something, someone for just a second.

One second turned into five, then ten, and Lucas's jaw grew tighter with every one of them.

Somewhere along the way she'd either overestimated his attraction to her, or her ability not to panic when he looked at her like he could see all the way into her soul.

Suddenly feeling way too vulnerable, she let go of him, wishing she'd gone with another plan altogether. Any other plan.

Lucas leaned in, catching a loose strand of hair and wrapping it around his finger, his eyes dark and intense. "What all are you promising me, Max?"

Half afraid he wouldn't believe a word if she answered him,

Max angled her face a little closer to his hand. To test him or herself?

His thumb brushed her jaw, the caress incredibly intimate coming from a stranger.

"I've been afraid and alone for a long time." Slowly, she raised her head, letting him see the truth in her eyes. She meant every word. She just didn't have any intention of using sex to get out of this mess. At least she was determined that it not come to that.

And she would have found it so much easier to believe that if Lucas wasn't too damn good looking for her peace of mind. Keeping him squarely in the bad guy column was turning out to be a little trickier when she was playing the attraction card.

Lucas cupped her face, his fingertips sliding around her nape. "How long?"

Hoping this wouldn't be the last game she ever played, she let her gaze drop to the mouth just inches from hers. "Too long."

Her heart pounded to keep up with her lungs and every breath she sucked between her lips. She forced herself to hold his gaze, though the sizzling intensity in the green depths burned along her nerve endings.

Lucas edged closer, running his other hand along the outside of her thigh. His warmth seeped through the denim, and she pulled in another shallow breath, realizing too late she *had* overestimated herself.

Lucas was dangerous, a threat to her survival. But as he leaned in, his unshaven jaw rasping against her skin, she didn't feel threatened. She felt—

His lips grazed her jaw and she almost leaped out of her skin.

God, she needed to pull back or shove him away. Something. Except when he dropped his head and gently dragged his teeth across to her neck, following the teasing scrape with a hot sweep of his tongue, a soft sigh fell from her parted lips.

The reasonable part of her brain ordered her to get a grip and not be sucked in by the role she'd stupidly chosen to play. Only the part that enjoyed his touch, that bone-deep craving for more, was all but impossible to drown out. And the longer he stared at her like she was his for the taking, the harder it was to pay attention to anything reasonable.

"Lucas," she pleaded, but for what exactly she wasn't sure. She wasn't even sure if Lucas was his real name, but she couldn't make herself care. Her body hungered for a moment where she didn't have to think about running or hiding or clearing her name.

Just one moment...

"Max?"

The sound of her name on his lips, all deep and rough, had her eyes sliding shut. "Yeah?"

"Exactly when did I give you the impression that I got friendly with every woman who promised me money to let her go?"

Max's eyes snapped open, shock at the abrupt response giving way to anger she directed first at herself for thinking he wouldn't see right through her, and then at him.

More specifically at the mocking smile on his face.

He didn't give her a chance to work up an appropriate response before hauling her to her feet and steering her toward the door.

"Walk or be carried." His sharp voice carried a warning that had Max rethinking any kind of sarcastic response.

In the short time she'd spent with him she'd heard charm, annoyance, frustration, but not anger. The unmistakable razor edge made her a little wary, but strangely reassured her that she was getting to him.

At this point, though, she was no longer sure if that was a good thing.

Outside, the sun had barely topped the treeline. Dragging her feet, Max stared at the truck with as much enthusiasm as she would a prison cell.

Lucas ignored her sluggish pace and continued to propel her forward. Her booted heels bit into the pavement. She couldn't get back in the truck with him. She didn't care that the odds of getting away with her hands still cuffed weren't great. She refused to get back in the truck. Period.

The cold barrel of a gun dug into her side. "You're not getting any crazy ideas, are you, Max?"

Lucas opened the door and despite the fact that he held a gun, she contemplated burying her knee in his groin. It was the least he deserved for pretending to go along with her, for making her forget who he was for even a heartbeat.

A beige Winnebago rolled to a stop in front of them, snaring both their attention. A sixtyish woman with long silver hair pulled back under a blue bandana rolled down the passenger side window. Smoothly, Lucas turned so that his body shielded the gun he pointed at Max's chest.

"Hey, there. Could either of you give us directions to Fundy National Park?"

Lucas smiled, his expression sliding from don't-fuck-with-me to happy-to-oblige between one beat and the next. "Wish we could help. I've always wanted to see the Hopewell Rocks myself."

Max rolled her eyes.

"I'm sure the motel clerk inside would know," Lucas added.

"Thanks." The woman waved and the Winnebago pulled away, leaving them alone once more.

After helping her into the passenger side and belting her in, Lucas locked and shut the door before climbing behind the wheel. It took three tries before the reluctant pickup roared to life, but this morning Lucas appeared unruffled by the temperamental vehicle.

Too bad.

Stone-faced, Lucas stared straight ahead, guiding the truck out of the lot and putting them back on the road. Was he taking her to Blackwater? Or was he waiting on orders and planned to kill her the second he got the go ahead?

Ten minutes later, his gaze drifted in her direction. He opened his mouth to say something at the same time a blur cut across her peripheral vision.

Max braced herself a heartbeat before Lucas slammed on the brakes.

Chapter Five

The coopery taste of blood rolled across Lucas's tongue, and he winced at the pain that branched from the center of his forehead, to his temples and down his neck. He dragged in a deep breath, bringing his hand to his chest, which ached like someone had nailed him with a sledgehammer.

What the hell happened?

He frowned, but even concentrating seemed to intensify his colossal headache. They had been driving and...

The colored spots exploding across his vision started to clear at the same moment he sensed movement beside him.

Something cold and sharp dug into his neck, and he hissed out a breath. His gaze slid left absorbing the dark bruise on Max's cheek and the trickle of blood at the corner of her mouth.

Hard eyes stared back at him.

Well, he'd obviously been out long enough for her to find the key to her cuffs in his pocket, but how long had that been exactly? And where was his gun? He didn't need to look down to known it wasn't on him.

Had she already removed it? Or had it been dislodged on impact?

"Who are you?"

He might have laughed at the unexpected one-eighty his life had just taken—both figuratively and literally—if not for the cold metal sinking a little deeper into his neck for every second he didn't answer.

He'd like to think Max wouldn't sever his jugular, but he wasn't stupid enough to bank on it. Although he'd been apparently stupid enough to think ill-timed and idiotic thoughts about how close her mouth had been to his earlier, and how ridiculously long it had been since he'd kissed a woman.

Her mouth was the last thing on his mind now, though, unless he counted the determined press of her lips until they were all but leached of color. If Max really had killed Cara, she wouldn't think twice about killing him.

His gut told him she wasn't a murderer or a dirty cop, but his instincts had failed him before. Like the night he'd let himself be separated from his partner and ended up losing her.

He swallowed carefully, not particularly caring if he answered her question or not. "What happened?"

"We hit a moose."

Lucas glanced through the shattered windshield, taking in the pickup's smashed front end butted up against a tree. "That's an awfully solid moose."

"We only clipped him. Can't say the same about the tree."

"You're bleeding." He motioned to her side, where something had ripped her sweater, but she kept her eyes fastened on his.

The corner of her mouth lifted as though she saw right through the attempt to distract her. She shoved the makeshift knife under his chin and the sharp tip sliced him.

He clenched his jaw, wanting to rip the blade out of her hand and knowing any move he made to take it from her might cost him.

"I want to know who you really are and what Blackwater's orders are. Now."

He knew he had to say something, but the truth wouldn't go over well. If he admitted he worked for an organization outsourced by the government and that he was taking her in for interrogation she'd either take off, kill him or both.

Neither of those possibilities was particularly appealing.

Lucas released a pained breath. "You won't believe me."

"Probably not, but humor me anyway." When he didn't immediately answer, she tapped the blade with her index finger. "Time's a wasting."

"I'm Cara's brother."

Silence filled the truck's cab.

Lucas searched her eyes, but the crisp blue depths remained guarded.

"You're lying," she said finally.

Lucas started to shake his head, but she jabbed the knife deeper. "I'm telling the truth," he insisted, hoping like hell Caleb and Max had never crossed paths.

Caleb had been stationed overseas when Cara had been in the police academy, where she'd met Max, so the odds were slim the two had met. Even if she had seen a picture of Caleb years ago, there was a good chance Max wouldn't remember what he looked like, but did she still know enough to see right through his lie?

Clearly skeptical—and that was putting it lightly—she arched one dark brow. "So why didn't you say something before?"

"I didn't really get the chance before your friends showed up—"

"They are *not* my friends."

"After that you were so determined to get away from me, I knew you wouldn't even listen to me, let alone believe me."

A brittle smile cracked her lips. "I still don't."

"It's the truth."

"And did Blackwater provide you with Cara's background information in case you needed it? Or did you take the initiative and do some digging on your own?"

"Ask me something only someone close to Cara would

know." He'd worked side-by-side with her for the last three years and had known her through Caleb for a few more before that. There wasn't much about his partner that he didn't know.

She snorted, still not buying it.

"I know Cara was at Samuel Blackwater's party before she met with you the night she died."

The knife eased off. A little. "And how do you know that?"

"I called in some favors." He nodded, hoping he was getting somewhere with her. Otherwise, one or both of them was going to wind up hurt when he disarmed her.

"And what was Cara doing at Blackwater's party?"

"Working on something classified, but that's all I know." Joe was going to have his balls on a platter for not only lying about his fishing plans, but following a lead alone and worse, losing control of the situation. Telling her anything about the Lassiter Group at this point would earn him a one-way ticket to the unemployment office, and he happened to like his job.

Most days.

Today wasn't looking to be one of them, though.

"Classified," she repeated, sounding unimpressed. "That wasn't Cara's answer." She reached for the door handle with her free hand.

"You're the only one who can help me, Max."

"Help you what?"

"Nail the real killer." At least that part wasn't a complete lie. If Max didn't kill Cara then she was his only connection to finding the bastard who did.

She tipped her head, her expression betraying nothing. "And what makes you so certain that I didn't kill her?"

"You two were tight once." He knew they'd gone through police academy together and Cara had shared more than a few stories when they had time to kill while on assignment.

"People turn on each other all the time."

"Maybe I just don't think you've got it in you." Christ, he

69

almost sounded like he believed it.

Her eyes narrowed dangerously. "You don't have a clue what I'm capable of." The deceptively soft tone only managed to emphasize the warning. A warning he'd be stupid to ignore since she'd nearly knocked him out, used him to break her fall and attempted to seduce him.

Now he knew why Joe had been relieved when he said he was taking a little time off. Clearly only a man bordering on burn-out would let a minor attraction cloud his judgment. Right now that kind of complication would be about as helpful as Max cutting him another airway.

Lucas frowned. "Are you trying to convince me that you killed her?"

Pain blinked across her face. "I might as well have."

He could say the same. Hell, he *had* said the same thing, but not nearly as often as he'd thought it. Things had gone wrong on missions in the past, both with the Lassiter Group and when he'd been Special Forces, but what happened with Cara was different.

He'd let himself get too close to her, to all of the team, making it that much harder to accept his role in her death. He should have had her back that night.

"Look, I know more about you than you think, Max. You're a first-rate detective with a knack for following your gut, which usually turns out to be right. You've had more arrests than most senior officers in your precinct and your quick thinking and loyalty to the department has not only earned you respect and admiration, but three commendations."

Max laughed, the sound cold and sharp. "And here I thought I was going stump you on the pop quiz."

"You're also well known for your...quick wit." Calling her a smartass when she had a piece of jagged metal jammed against his throat wouldn't be all that bright.

"Are you always so...diplomatic?" she mocked.

"When the occasion calls for it."

Her narrowed gaze suggested she doubted that very much. "And how exactly do you think I can help you?"

"By going back—"

"I'm not going back to New York." The patient amusement vanished from her expression and her spine straightened.

"That's the only place we can even hope to figure this out." Especially by making a stop at Lassiter Group headquarters on the way.

She arched a brow. "We? There *is* no we. And there's nothing in New York but a warrant for my arrest."

"I can help you."

Max withdrew the knife from his neck and slid back across the seat. "No, you can't. No one can."

Her hair shielded her face, but the vulnerability echoing behind her words tugged at him. Probably because he wasn't sure anyone could fake the kind of blame he'd heard in her voice when she'd mentioned Cara.

Lucas probed his neck, studying the few drops of blood on his fingertips. "Max," he began, but any words that might convince her escaped him.

"I don't care if you're Cara's brother or the next Dalai Lama. I'm not going back to New York." She pushed open the door and jumped out.

Lucas squeezed his eyes shut. How did this situation continue to slip further and further out of his control? Without either gun, he didn't hold any leverage to gain her cooperation and even if he did, they'd lost their only method of transportation.

Gearing himself up for another fight, Lucas undid his seatbelt and climbed down out of the truck. A sliver of pain under his ribs made him pause. He glanced toward the smashed front end. Christ, they were damn lucky to walk away from this with only minor injuries.

Before he followed Max, he reached in and grabbed the

handcuffs she'd left on the floor. He couldn't see the key anywhere, but pocketed the cuffs just in case.

Ahead of him, Max glanced up and down the road, indecision drawing her brows together.

"Wait up." There had to be something he could say to convince her to go along with him. Peacefully.

Her pace didn't slow.

Lucas jogged to catch up to her, shaking off the fading dizziness. His ribs felt bruised, but he ignored the discomfort. What were a few more injuries anyway? Between the aching shoulder and the headache that hammered at the back of his skull, bruised ribs he could live with.

He reached out to catch her elbow. She whipped around, her gun in her hand and aimed at his chest.

He backed off, holding his empty hands up. "Whoa. I'm not the bad guy here."

Her lips parted in feigned surprise. "Really? I guess I should give you your gun back then." She swiveled back to the road, dismissing him as a threat.

"You're scared," Lucas called after her.

"You give yourself too much credit," she tossed over her shoulder.

"Not of me, of going back to New York."

Max stopped, but didn't turn around. He noticed her knuckles tighten around the gun's grip. "You don't know what you're talking about."

"You're a good cop, Max. Cara must have trusted you enough to bring you into her investigation even after you were suspended. I know you didn't kill her, just like I know that without your help the person who did will get away with it." The more he said it, the more convinced he sounded.

She turned around and Lucas studied her so intently everything else faded from awareness.

Max's ice-blue eyes wavered, then hardened. "Forget it,"

she snapped and started walking just as the same beige Winnebago rumbled up and pulled to the side of the road.

The same older woman who'd asked for directions earlier rolled down her window. "You two all right?"

No, Max thought, they weren't all right. The jerk wouldn't take the hint and get lost. He couldn't seem to absorb the fact that she wasn't going anywhere with him.

"You two have an accident?"

Max nodded, resisting the urge to glare at Lucas when she felt him step up beside her. "We hit a moose, but we're fine. Our truck isn't going anywhere, though."

"You guys need a ride?" The woman offered.

"You're headed for Fundy National aren't you?" The opposite direction of the border. "You sure you wouldn't mind dropping me in the next town?"

The woman frowned. "What about your husband?"

"Oh, he's not—"

"Now, *darlin'*, let's not waste any more of these nice peoples' time."

Darlin', was it? Max glared at him. "I thought you were going to wait with the truck, *honey*." She spoke through her teeth, subtly motioning to the gun she'd slipped into her bag when the couple had driven up.

His lips parted in such a genuine, breath-stealing smile she almost believed the melting warmth behind it wasn't an act.

"You know I was just teasing you. I wouldn't let the love of my life hitchhike all alone, would I? What if something were to happen to you? I'd never forgive myself."

And the Oscar goes to... Max rolled her eyes. There was no way the older couple could possibly—

Sentimental smiles were glued to their faces and she knew the poor fools were soaking it up.

As Max contemplated her next move, Lucas reached past

her and opened the door. "After you."

She gave serious thought to driving her knee between his legs, but the woman appeared in the open doorway, ushering them inside. Holding her bag in front of her, Max started up the stairs.

"Up you go, *muffin*," Lucas said. He followed the sickening sweet tone with a stinging slap across her ass.

The man had a death wish.

The older woman beckoned them inside. "Why don't you two take a seat? I'm Charlotte and that's my husband Henry at the wheel."

When the door closed, Henry maneuvered the vehicle back onto the road and Max sighed in relief. Lucas wouldn't try anything as long as Charlotte and Henry were close by, especially with his gun tucked safely away in her bag. By sheer luck she'd managed to remove it from his pants before he came to in the truck.

Accepting the woman's invitation, Max took a seat at the table.

Instead of sitting opposite her, Lucas nudged her. "Scoot down a bit, *sweet cheeks.*"

Max tipped her face up. "*Baby,* I think you'd be much more comfortable in the chair." She clamped her teeth around the inside of her cheek to stop herself from doing something stupid. Like punching his wounded shoulder.

"You know I like to be close to you."

Feeling the weight of Charlotte's curious stare, Max had little choice but to scoot over and make room for him beside her.

He pressed up against her, draping an arm across her shoulder. She opened her mouth to tell him where his could shove his freaking arm.

"Would you two like something to drink?" Charlotte asked, cutting Max off. "You know," she continued. "I've got a first-aid kit in the bathroom. You two could use a little bandaging."

The moment Charlotte moved out of ear shot, Max jerked out of his embrace. His determination to play up this phony relationship unnerved her. But more alarming was the fact that her insides were drawn tighter than a bow. Every move he made warmed her from hip to shoulder.

Ignoring the confusing tightening in her stomach, she glared at him, lowering her voice to a whisper. "What the hell are you doing?"

"I'm not letting you walk away from this."

"And you think pretending to be my husband is going to stop me?"

"Better they think us lovers than two suspects from yesterday's shootout."

Max snorted. "Lovers? Honey, the only thing I'd love to do to you right now—"

"Found it," Charlotte sang out. The petite woman deposited the white tin in the center of the table. "I'm pretty sure there is a small bottle of rubbing alcohol in there to clean out those nasty little cuts."

To humor the woman kind enough to give her—*them*—a ride, Max used the materials inside to clean the scrape on her chin and dab at the blood she tasted on the corner of her mouth.

Of all the injuries Lucas had, he choose to pay particular attention to the small cut she'd inflicted on his neck. If he thought he could guilt her into cooperating, he'd need to get a number and wait in line. There were already people ahead of him who'd been hurt by her determination to nail Blackwater—Sherri, Glen, Cara.

"So are you two on vacation, maybe a honeymoon?" Charlotte asked, that same sappy grin falling into place.

Max shook her head. "No."

"Yes," Lucas said at the same time.

Charlotte frowned.

He covered Max's hand with his own. "What my wife means, is that, this isn't our first honeymoon."

The older woman beamed. "So you two renewed your vows? That's wonderful. It's so nice to see a couple still so in love. Nowadays married people just don't spend enough quality time together."

"Yes, well, it's the least he could do after cheating on me with his assistant," Max shot off, giving her a reason to shrug out of his grip. Not that it helped when her skin still felt warm from his touch.

Lucas didn't recover as quickly as she expected and gawked at her.

Instead of being appalled by Max's admission, Charlotte slid into the seat across from her and patted her hand. "Oh, dear."

Lucas flashed a tight smile. "I thought you promised that was behind us, sweetheart? Or did you want me to bring up your indiscretion with your yoga instructor?"

The truck swerved and Max realized Henry was being drawn into their childish game.

"We both know that if you'd admitted your problem," she glanced pointedly at his groin, "and started taking medication earlier, none of that would have happened."

Lucas's mouth fell open.

Max stole a peek at Charlotte who didn't seem the least bit thrown by the conversation.

The older woman turned her attention to Lucas. "And why do you think it took you so long to admit you had a problem?"

"I've never had a problem with...my performance," Lucas choked out.

Charlotte gave his hand a thoughtful squeeze. "It's all right, dear. This kind of thing is very normal." She leaned over the table. "Actually, Henry had some difficulty in that area too."

"Sure did," Henry chimed in. "And I got through it thanks to the support of my wife." His and Charlotte's eyes met in the rearview mirror.

For a moment Max envied their close relationship, one she'd become convinced wasn't in her future. Aside from few men lining up to get involved with a cop who always put her job first, forgetting that she was presently wanted for murder, she wasn't sure her heart was ready to trust anyone after her last boyfriend, Wade, had used her to advance his career.

Dating Wade had made sense in the beginning since they both understood the job, but as far as reasons to get married went, it fell short. It just shouldn't have taken Wade breaking things off when he was promoted to make her see that. Adding insult to injury, Wade had also been one of the first to believe she'd been taking bribe money from Blackwater.

She had foolishly believed everyone who knew her would instantly dismiss the possibility she was a dirty cop. Turns out it didn't matter how many lives she'd improved through her job or how many criminals she'd help put away. One seed of doubt planted by Blackwater was all it took to make conversations cease the second she walked into the room at work. "And now our sex life is better than ever," Henry added, drawing her back into the present.

This time it was Max and Lucas's eyes that met and held. Somewhere in the intense green depths she swore she glimpsed the same surreal humor she felt at the course their conversation had taken.

"We're only a couple of miles from the next town. Where about would you like to be dropped off?"

"A gas station would be fine," Lucas answered.

Charlotte stood up. "I certainly hope you two get back on track. It would be a real shame for such a lovely young couple to drift apart over something like this."

The amusement vanished from his eyes when he glanced at Max. "It would be a real shame, especially when I need you so much."

"We're done talking about it, Lucas." Ignoring him, Max focused on the scenery sliding past the window.

He leaned toward her, his gravelly voice deep and his breath warm on the back of her neck. "I'm not giving up."

"I'm going to enjoy shooting you then," she snapped under her breath, trying to tamp down the rising awareness of exactly how close he was.

Charlotte and Henry dropped them in front of a gas station situated right across from a *Tim Hortons*. Her mouth salivated at the thought of the steaming coffee she'd become addicted to since she'd been staying with Sherri.

Before she could thank the couple, Charlotte enveloped her in a motherly embrace and told her to be patient with Lucas. Erectile Dysfunction was a challenge she and Lucas needed to overcome together.

Oh, how she wanted to laugh out loud.

She didn't wait for Lucas, who was still shaking hands with Henry, but thanked the couple and strode across the street for coffee. As she walked, she dug into her bag for change. The first steaming sip would be exactly the jumpstart her brain needed to figure out her next move.

Lucas followed her from the counter to the table. She did her best to pretend he wasn't there as the hot liquid slid down her throat. She gulped down more than half of it before she acknowledged him.

"You still here?"

"You know I need—"

"My help," she finished. "I get it, but what you don't seem to understand is that I don't care."

"I thought you and Cara were friends."

"Cara's dead," she snapped. The second the words left her mouth, she wanted to take them back. A cold fist squeezed her heart and she looked down at the table.

"Come on, Max, you were there. You must have seen something."

Too much. Too fucking much. Nausea swirled in her stomach, and she jerked to her feet.

"Where are you going?"

"Ladies' room." Max brushed past him when he stood to block her path, her annoyance level spiking when he followed on her heels.

Outside the door, he leaned against the wall. "I'll be waiting right here for you."

A scathing reply perched on the tip of her tongue, but being on the verge of throwing up she only glared at him and rushed inside.

She didn't wait for the door to shut completely, but darted into one of the stalls. Her stomach heaved as she collapsed over the ceramic bowl. Chills raced across her skin and her hands trembled.

Images whirled through her mind of what some faceless bastard had done to Cara, his back to her as she'd been forced to watch it happen. *Christ.*

Max heard the door open, knew it was Lucas before he spoke. "You okay?"

Like he cared. "Yeah, fine. I'll be out in a minute." Max squeezed her eyes shut when the door closed, wishing she were anywhere but here.

It took a few minutes before she regained control and climbed to her feet. In front of the mirror, she took note of the dark circles under her eyes.

Cara.

Another twist of guilt made her insides wobble. If she hadn't agreed to help Cara with her investigation maybe she could have stopped it and—

Silencing the pointless train of thought, Max clenched her hands until they stopped shaking. Was Lucas on the level? Was he really Cara's brother?

For the last half hour she'd wracked her brain, trying to remember anything Cara had mentioned about her brother, but she continued to come up with nothing. She was sure Cara had mentioned him frequently, but the details were fuzzy with time, even his name.

Did he really just want to see his sister's killer brought to justice? Or did he have another motive? Either way it meant nothing to her. She was on her own—no one else could get hurt that way.

And then there was Sherri. Max still hadn't called her. Had she told the police Max's name, or shown them a picture? It would make it more difficult to move around if the RCMP was keeping an eye out for her.

The door burst open, a thousand pounds of teenage girls swallowing the small space with their high-pitched voices and ear piercing giggles.

It took Max only a few seconds to realize these girls were her ticket to get free and clear of Lucas.

"How's the fishing?"

Lucas froze at the sound of Joe Lassiter's voice on the other end of Tess's phone. "Not too bad."

"Any bites?"

Was he still talking about fishing, or had Tess changed her mind about keeping Joe out of the loop? "Here and there," he answered vaguely.

If Joe was still unaware of the situation, Lucas wasn't about to fill him in until he had Max cooperating. There was little point in getting Joe's hopes up if she somehow managed to ditch him.

"How are you doing, really?"

"Surprisingly, ready to get back to work." He eyed the bathroom door, wondering how Max was holding up. Either she'd been more shaken up by their accident than she let on, or the mention of Cara had upset her.

"I should have something for you and Eli in another few days," Joe said.

"Great."

"I'm glad you took some time, Luc." Joe lowered his voice. "I know I've said it before, but no one blames you. And even Caleb has been asking where you disappeared to."

Lucas leaned against the wall to let a group of girls pass him. "The same Caleb who rarely speaks to me at all and when he does only uses one or two syllables at a time?"

"When you actually stay in the room long enough for anyone to talk to you, you mean?" Joe sighed. "Caleb's coming around."

"Yeah, maybe I'll have him up to a full sentence or two by the end of the year."

"She'd be pissed at the two of you, you know."

He blew out a breath, imagining just how furious Cara would be. "I know."

"I'll see you back here in a day or two." Joe hung up, and Lucas slid his phone into his pocket.

He heard the door open and looked up just as a dozen hysterical females pounced on him.

Jesus.

He had just enough time to brace himself before the girls surrounded him.

"Can I have your autograph?"

"Me too."

A third girl yanked down her shirt. "You can sign me right here." She pointed to her cleavage.

He whipped around, swearing that one of them had just grabbed his ass. Had they all skipped breakfast this morning or something, or were they high?

"Hey!" he snapped at whoever at pinched his ass a second time. "I think you have me confused with someone else."

Two of the girls shook their heads. One of them, a short blonde with wide brown eyes and braces said, "We know who you are, the lady in the bathroom already told us."

"What lady...?" Max. Damn it.

Taking an opening, he slipped past the shortest two and checked the ladies room.

Empty.

She must have slipped right by him when the girls had surrounded him.

"Let me by," he insisted turning around to squeeze past his entourage. As a group, the girls pressed in closer, backing him against the wall.

This was not happening. Not the Viagra conversation with Henry or the worshipful looks on the teenage faces in front of him. And not Max slipping away on him. Again.

If he had a prayer of catching up to her, he needed to go. Now.

Without knocking any of the girls over—barely—he pushed his way free and ran out to the parking lot. He scanned the surrounding area. No pink sweater in sight.

Fuck.

In one direction, he took note of a car dealership, a gas station and a hole in the wall tourist bureau. In the other, a pizza place, a book store and a strip mall. Both sidewalks in either direction were empty.

Which way had she gone?

A bark of laughter caught his attention. Pivoting on his heel, Lucas saw two men leaning against a dark green SUV, sipping coffee.

"I don't suppose one of you guys saw a woman walk by a few seconds ago. Pink sweater, black hair?" Lethal determination.

"Great rack?" One of them joked.

Lucas ground his jaw, not in the mood to screw around. "So you saw her?"

"Yeah, she headed that way." The taller one vaguely motioned in the direction of the strip mall.

Lucas thanked them and took off down the street. This would be the absolute last time she got away from him. Whether she liked it or not, from now on she'd be joined at the hip or unconscious.

Stopping at each shop on the main road long enough to peer through the front window, he searched for any sign of Max.

Outside a crowded bakery, the smell of fresh bread and doughnuts made his stomach rumble. How long had it been since he last ate? He'd devoured a drive-thru burger and fries on his way into Riverbend yesterday, but nothing since.

His stomach rumbled again. Food was next on his agenda, right after he found Max.

After passing half a dozen stores with no sign of her, Lucas wondered if she'd bribed the two men to lie about which way she'd gone...

A flash of pink snared his attention, and he stared through the window of a woman's clothing store just as Max disappeared through a doorway in the back. A changing room or a back door?

Stepping inside, he approached the counter. The sales clerk looked up from a crossword book.

"Hi," he began, his voice purposely low so Max wouldn't hear. "I'm looking for my wife. This tall—" he held up his hand to chin level, "—beautiful blue eyes, sexy smile. Looks great in pink."

The clerk smiled knowingly. "She's in the back trying on a couple things."

"Would it be all right if I went on back? I want to surprise her with something."

"No problem."

Lucas moved as quietly as possible to the changing rooms. After confirming Max was the only one in the back, he tested the handle and, surprised to find it unlocked, shoved the door open—

And found Max naked from the waist up.

Chapter Six

Swallowing past the rough spot in his throat, he slipped inside.

Max grabbed her sweater and hugged it to her chest. With her hands occupied, he snatched her bag off the stool and tossed it into the aisle before closing the door.

"Get out." Her normally round eyes were tiny slits.

Lucas imagined she was more annoyed at being caught off-guard than cornered in a four-by-four square box with only a pink fuzzy sweater between them.

That was for him to worry about. Even without a gun, Max was dangerous, but his mind wasn't focused on defending himself. Instead, it was preoccupied with the slope of her shoulders and how the ill-positioned sweater revealed enough curves to set his senses on edge.

"I said, *get out*," she hissed.

Lucas forced his attention to her face. "No."

"Then turn around."

"And give you the opportunity to jump me again? Sure," he drawled.

"Fine." Max dropped the sweater, and it took way more effort than it should have not to look.

He would have been just fine, except the hostility slowly drained from her face, replaced with something too raw and vulnerable to be misinterpreted for any kind of sexual ploy.

At least that's what he told himself when she slid on a new bra. The one at her feet was ripped, her sweater too, and stained with blood. It was then he noticed the angry scratch that curved down from her side and slashed across her abdomen.

"You okay?"

She angled her body away from him, reaching back to clip her bra and wincing as the material tightened over the scratch. "You're getting better at sounding like you care."

"Maybe I do." He stepped closer to her. "Turn around."

"Why?"

"Just do it, Max."

Watching him in the mirror, she did as he asked, which surprised him. He brushed her hands away, then proceeded to take a full minute to get the tiny clasp to hook properly.

"I hope you're better at taking one off." Her gaze darted away from him, a flush of pink creeping into her cheeks. "That didn't come out the way I meant."

"So let me get this straight. Shoot-outs and car accidents don't shake you up, but lingerie does? Interesting."

Interesting like the pretty lace edging on her bra strap, especially where it curved over her shoulder. He slid his finger beneath the strap, running his thumb over the satin material, up to the exact spot he'd been staring at since moving closer to her—the tempting curve where her neck and shoulder met.

The perfect place to press his mouth and run his tongue across her skin...

Christ, he was having problems. Two of them, he quickly realized, as he caught her reflection and noticed her nipples were hard and pushing against her bra.

If it was part of her plan to distract him, it was working. Because, God help him, he lowered his head. Her hair grazed his cheek, and he turned his face into it, breathing her in.

That should have been enough when he knew better than

to go any further. Instead, it made him need just a little more. Just...

His jaw skimmed her shoulder, and her breath hitched, giving way to a soft moan when he opened his mouth on her.

She shifted just a fraction, her body pressing back against his. His eyes slid shut, and he wrapped an arm around her, pulling her tighter to his chest. He couldn't remember the last time he'd held a woman this close, and Christ it felt good. *She* felt good.

He dragged his teeth across the back of her shoulder, backtracking with his tongue and loving the way she trembled in his arms.

"Lucas," she murmured, the breathy sound of his name on her lips almost enough to mask the worry in her voice.

Almost, but not quite. "I know." He pressed his lips to her once more, lingering for another few heartbeats before finally lifting his head. It took him another minute to let go of her entirely, his fingers sweeping across her abdomen before he finally forced himself to back up.

He turned away from the mirror, telling himself it was to give her room and not because those couple of minutes with Max had been more intimate than any of the women he'd hooked up with in the last few years.

Jesus. Maybe she really had nailed him good last night.

"How are you making out?" the sales girl asked from outside the dressing room.

Max pulled on the gray half-zip hoodie on the hanger next to her. "Fine, thanks. Be right out."

He waited until she tugged the hoodie over her head before he pulled the handcuffs from his pocket and snapped one around her left wrist, then his right one.

Max burned a stare from the cuffs that joined them together, to his face, and back again. He vaguely wondered if the blistering death-glare was hot enough to solder the handcuff to his skin.

"I'm not going anywhere with you."

"Yes, you are. And seeing as we're now stuck with each other, you don't have much say in the matter."

Whatever vulnerability he'd glimpsed earlier vanished beneath the rough-and-tough exterior. "The hell I don't," she hissed.

He shrugged. "If you want to go kicking and screaming, it won't bother me. Of course, it might generate a little too much attention. The kind neither of us can afford after yesterday." He jerked just hard enough to tug her off balance. "And let's not forget you're wanted for murder and the Canadian government would hand you over in a heartbeat."

Strained silence fell between them.

Lucas ignored the sliver of guilt at forcing her into this when only moments ago he'd been ready to undo the buttons on her pants and slip his hand inside. "Are you coming willingly, or do I need to drag you?"

Max scowled up at him. "After you."

In the aisle, she stopped and gestured to the handcuffs. "And what about these? Not exactly inconspicuous," she added, nodding toward the girl at the counter.

"It'll be fine as long as you make it look good."

"You strung up by your balls would look good. Does that count?"

The clerk smiled as they approached, but her polite grin faltered when she noticed the handcuffs. "Is everything okay?" she asked slowly, alarm creeping into her eyes.

"Everything is great. Right, *darlin'*?" Lucas glanced down at Max.

Her spine was straighter than fortified steel, hostility rolling off her, leaving him completely unprepared when she turned in his arms and slid her palm up his chest.

"The best," she purred, winking suggestively.

The abrupt change, right down to the way her fingers

traced an outline around his heart, caught him ridiculously off-guard even though he'd suggested she play along. After six years in Special Forces and three working for the Lassiter Group, he'd participated in dozens of missions that depended on him adapting to changing situations as smoothly as possible.

Never before had an unexpected development played such havoc with his senses, and he was damned if he could figure out what throwing him off this time.

Max ducked under his right arm, wrapped it around her and flattened her hand over his as she faced the counter. "Isn't he sweet? He doesn't want me out of his sight for even a second."

Lucas barely registered the clerk's shy nod and soft smile. The lazy sway of Max's hips and bottom against his lower half had his full attention. Did she have any idea what the sweet friction was doing to him?

Of course she did. She was probably counting on it. Maybe it was some twisted idea of revenge for cuffing them together.

Either way, he didn't move an inch while Max chatted with the clerk ringing up the new clothes, doing his best to ignore the way she played with their linked fingers the entire time. Her hands were soft and warm, and a vision of her running them down his bare chest to his waist had his whole body clenching.

When the clerk finished, Lucas headed for the door, forcing her to keep pace with him. How was it that he and Cara had pretended to be a couple for the occasional assignment and he'd never had a problem mentally distancing himself from it?

At least he had Max where he wanted her—with him. Except now there could be no running away from the unsettling sensation that he was altogether screwed.

God, she was so screwed.

Max shivered in the chilly morning breeze as she tried to determine the most appropriate place to shoot Lucas the second she got the chance. The jerk had cuffed her.

Again.

Either he was desperate to hold onto her for Blackwater, or he was truly convinced she could help him more than she'd been able to help Cara. If Lucas was on the up and up—and being cuffed to him made that a really big *if*—he had to realize that being anywhere near her put his life at risk.

Not that she should have to point that out after his shoulder injury yesterday.

Max deliberately slowed down. "So what's the plan, *lover?*" Her pulse picked up as soon as the word left her mouth.

Tossing around endearments while traveling down the highway was one thing, but after what just happened in the changing room, she was anything but laid back about pretending to be involved.

She exhaled slowly, annoyed with herself for getting rattled by something that wasn't even a big deal. So he'd kissed her neck. No big deal.

Yeah, right.

Lucas glanced across the street, waiting until a car drove past before stepping off the curb. "I'm working on it."

Working on something. Like maybe something to do with whoever he'd been talking to before she'd turned the teenagers loose on him earlier. "So you're from California originally, right? Miss it much?"

He gave her a knowing look. "Minnesota, not California. But then you knew that."

She shrugged. As if she needed to apologize for remaining suspicious. "And now you're living in..."

"Boston." He adjusted the cuff around his wrist, and she hoped like hell it was pinching him.

"Oh, yeah? Go to many White Sox games?"

His lips twitched. "I go to the occasional *Red Sox* game, yes."

"So are you still in the military?" The question might not have been necessary if she and Cara had reconnected under different circumstances and had the chance to talk more about their lives.

"Been out for a few years."

"And what do you do now?"

"Private security."

She paused. "The kind of security that grants you access to information on freelance government operatives? I mean, how else would you know where Cara was the night she died, right?"

He grinned. "I guess it shouldn't surprise me Cara told you what she was working on." He led her around another corner, past a closed arcade and a liquor store.

She glanced longingly at the bottles lining the shelves inside. A nice shot of tequila would go a long way to take the edge off when it came to dealing with Lucas. She could handle the attraction that seemed to crackle between them, or that's what she kept telling herself anyway, but tough guy Lucas was harder to read, harder to anticipate.

Even a beer would go down pretty good right about now. She couldn't even remember the last time she'd truly enjoyed one. Cara had joked about how Max would owe her a beer when she saw the information she'd come across. An hour after that conversation had taken place, Max had gone to meet Cara and was snatched right off the street by Blackwater's men.

She'd run the scenario through her head hundreds of times, imagining that if she'd done just one thing differently that night Cara wouldn't have been killed—butchered, by some sick bastard who got off on torturing women.

And Max had been next on the list, saved only by a Russian's insistence that his deal with Blackwater needed to take place earlier than planned. If all hell hadn't broken loose that night, she would have ended up on that run-down warehouse floor with her friend.

Blackwater himself had nearly succeeded in preventing her

escape, earning a nasty scar that bisected his right eye for his effort. Even if he didn't blame her for his night going to shit, she had no doubt he would have still pinned Cara's murder on her for the damage she'd done with a jagged shard of glass.

Although she'd gone to her commanding officer, detailing everything that had happened, any credibility she'd held on to following her suspension was wiped away the second two eye witnesses stepped forward, along with the murder weapon Max had apparently used to kill Cara.

She didn't have a clue what Blackwater was holding over the witnesses' head or how much he'd bribed them to confess to witnessing Cara's murder, but if not for the heads-up from her partner, Glen, she'd be locked up right now.

Not that her present situation was any more promising.

A loud horn erupted behind her, jarring her into Lucas. He glared at the driver of the car then glanced at her.

"I'm fine," she said before he could ask again if she was okay. She waited until they rounded yet another corner and asked, "Do you have any idea where you're going?"

"About as much as you, I suspect."

They strode past a diner and the mouth-watering smell of bacon, eggs and toast wafted on the air.

Lucas paused and glanced thoughtfully from her to the near-empty diner. "You promise to behave?"

Max held up their wrists. "Are you going to take these off?"

"How stupid do I look?" She opened her mouth, but he was quicker. "Don't say a word."

A smile tugged at the corner of her mouth. "Then don't make it so easy for me."

He rolled his eyes and reached into the shopping bag, withdrawing her pink sweater. He draped it over their wrists, and pulled open the door.

Inside, only a handful of tables were occupied and Lucas led the way to a booth farthest from the door. He slid across the blue vinyl seat, pulling her after him. She bumped into him before quickly wedging her bag between them as a buffer.

"Cozy, huh?"

Max ignored him, studying the black and white prints of past Hollywood stars and musicians that lined the walls.

"Sit still," Lucas insisted.

"I am."

"You're bouncing your leg."

Max ceased the nervous tapping. "I am not."

"Morning. Can I get you some coffee?" A pretty waitress with big brown eyes and a flirtatious smile held up a pot of coffee.

"Please." Eager to continue feeding her caffeine addiction, Max pushed her cup toward the waitress, who ignored it and reached across the table to fill up Lucas's first.

Once both cups were filled, Jane—according to her name tag—pulled a pad from her apron. "What can I get you?" She laughed at herself. "You probably need to see the menu first, huh?"

Lucas shook his head. "That's fine. We'll just have your breakfast special."

"And how would you like your eggs?"

"Scrambled," they said in unison, then glanced at each other.

The waitress's smile dimmed as she noticed just how close they were sitting to one another.

Max waited until their waitress was back behind the long counter that ran the length of the diner. "You do you realize how lame we look crammed together like this?"

He leaned toward her—thank God for her bag—his lips curved in a secretive grin. "We look exactly as we're supposed to, like we're into each other."

"Into each other?" Max echoed, feeling a little lightheaded. A side effect she quickly attributed to not eating anything since lunch yesterday.

"Yeah." Lucas's voice deepened. "Like we can't get enough of each other."

"Well, if anyone actually buys it, it won't be because of your stellar performance." Not until the words left her mouth did she realize how much that sounded like a challenge.

Shit.

She slanted him a quick look, and the calculating glimmer in his eyes made her stomach tug.

He lifted a hand and rubbed his thumb across her cheek, before capturing a strand of hair and tucking it behind her ear. "Are you saying I'm not playing my part convincingly?"

She smacked his hand away, not impressed with how good he was at the role all of a sudden. "You wouldn't need to play at anything if you hadn't lost your mind and cuffed us together."

"Asking for your help wasn't getting the job done."

"Asking? Is that what you call dragging me around at gun point?"

Lucas sighed and took a drink of his coffee.

"You *will* be taking these cuffs off when we're through here."

"Breakfast is served," Jane announced a few minutes later, depositing two steaming plates in front of them. "Can I get you anything else?"

Max glanced up to see Jane had directed that last part to Lucas.

"We're great, thanks." Lucas winked, and Max rolled her eyes, ignoring the pair of them.

She dug into her food, taking a small measure of satisfaction in the fact Lucas had to eat with his left hand to avoid showing off their little accessory. Unfortunately, it also meant he took even longer to eat than she did, and she was forced to wait for him to finish.

She watched him nibble on his remaining piece of bacon

like it might be his last, then it took him another full minute to finish it off, which was no doubt purely for her benefit.

"Finally," she murmured when he pushed the plate away.

"How was everything?" Jane magically appeared at the table and scooped up their empty plates.

"Perfect, we'll take the check now."

Jane set the dishes on the table behind them. "No problem." She cast Lucas a blatantly flirtatious look and scrawled something on her notepad before tearing the receipt off and laying it on the table.

Did the woman not see Max practically sitting in his lap? They were joined by the hip to anyone who looked their way and Jane stood there salivating over Lucas like he was today's special.

"You have a great day, now." Jane sauntered off, bending down to retrieve something off the floor, making sure to angle her ass in Lucas's direction.

Feeling a touch nauseous at the display—Lucas, on the other hand, didn't appear to mind—she glanced over her shoulder just as two RCMP officers walked into the diner.

Max averted her face when the shorter one scanned the room. She waited a beat, then sneaked another peek just as the older, taller officer handed Jane a piece of paper.

A photograph?

Had they tied the truck to what happened in Riverbend and assumed this was the closest town to the wrecked vehicle?

From the corner of her eye, she saw the shorter one head in their direction.

Damn.

Turning her body toward Lucas, she caught a fistful of his shirt and tugged him closer. Surprise registered on his face. "Max?"

"Shut up," she whispered, her gaze darting to his mouth. She had to be out of her mind to even think about it...

Footsteps echoed behind her.

Yeah. Out of her mind, but desperate enough not to care. With one last tug on his shirt, she opened her mouth over his.

She hadn't thought far enough ahead to figure out what would happen when she got to this point. It was only supposed to be a quick kiss to prevent the officer from getting a good look at their faces, but the second her lips brushed Lucas's, she only had one thing on her mind.

More.

More, and soft. God, his mouth was soft, and with every barely-there pass, she felt herself leaning into him until she was pressed up against him as much as her bag allowed. She was half-convinced she would have been in his lap already if they'd been anywhere else.

She tightened her fingers in his shirt, needing something to hang on to as he dragged her bottom lip between his and sank fully into the kiss.

More was right on the money. Loads more.

Lucas slid his free hand up into her hair, his thumb sweeping across her cheek in slow arcs that she felt all the way to her nerve endings. If she wasn't already headed straight for sensory overload, the slow slide of his tongue across hers would have put her on a collision course.

Whimpering softly, she met the lazy pace he set, lingering over his mouth the way she would a dessert that was entirely too decadent, but tasted too good to even think about stopping.

His fingers curled around her nape, the hold both tender and possessive.

"Wait," she pleaded a moment later, needing her heart to slow down a little.

"What was that you told me? Oh right, shut up." He tipped her chin up, deepening the kiss until the feverish rhythm set her whole body on fire.

She looped her arm behind his neck, sliding her fingers up

into his hair. He groaned in approval, his hand trailing down her back and slipping beneath the edge of her hoodie.

As much as she craved to feel his hands on her everywhere, she finally pushed him back enough to break from his mouth. He didn't let her get far though, touching his forehead to hers as they both tried to catch their breath.

That... Holy crap that shouldn't have been... She never meant...

God, she couldn't even think straight.

Lucas teased his mouth across hers once more, doing that crazy soft thing until she made a needy sound, and then drew back.

He exhaled slowly. "I think I like it when you get jealous."

She finally opened her eyes. "You think that kiss was because of our skanky waitress?" He could not be serious.

"It wasn't?"

Apparently he was serious. She slid away from him. "Please."

He didn't look convinced, his cocky smile ruining the buzz humming through her.

"Get over yourself, Casanova."

"So you weren't making some kind of statement?"

She really had hit him hard with that gas can. "The only statement I'm thinking about right now involves ratting you out to the guys sitting at the counter."

His gaze slid over her head to where the RCMP officers were seated, and he frowned.

"One of them was headed in our direction a few minutes ago." She realized then that the sign for the bathroom was just past them on the right.

"That's why you did it," he finally pieced together, sounding a little...disappointed?

That couldn't be right. Clearly the kiss had just messed with her head for a minute.

Just your head?

Ignoring that last thought, she forced herself to meet his eyes. "We need to go."

Lucas stared back at her, his expression unreadable. No desire, no surprise, no disappointment, zip.

Great, now *she* was disappointed?

Jane took her time reaching the table, which probably had something to do with stopping to pick at some invisible piece of lint on her breast.

This time, though, Lucas seemed oblivious, his gaze locked on Max as though he'd find whatever he was looking for if he searched hard enough.

"What?"

He didn't say anything.

More than a little distracted by trying to guess what he was thinking, she failed to notice he'd slipped her wallet from her bag to pay Jane.

"Hey!" Instantly aware of how loud her objection was, she tried again. "I thought this was your treat, *babe*?"

"I'm pretty sure it was dessert that I promised to take care of." He handed Jane enough money to cover the bill, but never took his eyes off Max. "And I have every intention of making it worth the wait." Every word dripped with seductive, sinful promise.

For Jane's benefit, or hers? As if on cue, the waitress sighed and flounced back to the counter.

"After you." He nudged Max out of the booth, adjusting the sweater and lacing his fingers through hers.

Her pulse kicked up the second his grip tightened, and she fixed her attention on the door ahead of them—and not on the RCMP.

And definitely not on Lucas.

She fell into step with him outside, breathing a little easier knowing no one was looking for them, at least not here.

Three blocks down from the diner, Lucas cut across a gravel parking lot, stopping next to a powder-blue Corvette that had passed its prime a decade or two ago.

He reached under the back tire.

"What are you doing?" She watched him produce a key and unlock the door.

"Probably what it looks like. Get in." He opened the door and pulled the *For Sale* sticker out of the window, tossing it into the backseat.

"You're gonna steal this car?"

"No, *we're* going to steal this car, but only if you get that sassy little ass of yours inside." He cocked his head when she hesitated. "Do you really think grand theft auto is going to matter when you're already wanted for murder?"

Since he had a point, she wiggled over the console separating the driver's side from the passenger's and settled in the seat. Lucas slid behind the wheel, flashing a smug and-you-didn't-think-I-knew-what-I-was-doing smile.

When the car didn't immediately start, she glanced at him. "Guess we know why it was for sale."

He tried again and the car rumbled to life. She just wasn't sure if that was a good thing or not. Seeing as she was still cuffed to Lucas, she was leaning toward the *not* column.

"How did you know the key was there?"

"You didn't hear those guys talking at the counter on our way out? About how their buddy's car has been for sale over for a month and that by leaving the key he was just asking for someone to take it for a joyride?"

She shook her head. Maybe she would have caught that if she hadn't been so focused on getting out of the diner without thinking about the mere inches separating her and Lucas.

When they hit the outskirts of town, headed east, she shook her head. "You know this is pointless, don't you? I can't help you even if I wanted to. I don't know who killed Cara. I never saw the guy's face."

His fingers tightened around the wheel, his attention locked on the road. "We'll figure something out."

"Really? You know being some ex-military private security hotshot won't help you any more than it helped Cara."

"Worried about me?"

"Nothing is going to bring her back."

"I know."

She turned in the seat to face him. "Then I don't think I need to tell you that the harder you pursue this, the bigger risk you run of ending up dead too. Or do you think you just got lucky with Snake and Edward Blackwater yesterday?"

"Doesn't matter."

"Maybe not to you, but I haven't spent the last few months trying to fly under their radar to turn around and run straight into their territory."

Lucas jerked the wheel, sending the car to the shoulder of the road, and slammed on the brakes. When he turned to her, his eyes were sharp, unforgiving. "What if the situation were reversed? Do you think Cara would just walk away from your murder because she was scared?"

"I'd be stupid not to be scared. I know exactly what Blackwater and his guys are capable of. I've witnessed it over and over, and I know that whatever proof existed has been destroyed or covered up."

"By who?"

"Probably by the cops who really are on Blackwater's payroll. Maybe even whoever was responsible for mine and Glen's suspension in the first place."

"Your partner."

"Right before our suspension we were supposed to meet with an informant who claimed to have information on cops in Blackwater's pocket. He never showed, but that only made me want to dig deeper. A week later Glen's fiancée was killed by a car bomb meant for him."

She shouldn't have pushed so hard, should have known she and Glen couldn't take on Blackwater all by themselves. When Glen had lost Jillian, he'd fallen apart. Their suspension, coming right on the heels of his loss, had nearly crushed him. Like Cara's death, she would never get the memory of the grief on Glen's face as Jillian's casket was lowered into the ground out of her mind.

"It wasn't your fault, you know."

She met Lucas's eyes, trying not to be moved by the understanding she saw in the dark green depths. "Just like Cara's death wasn't my fault either, right?"

Lucas glanced out the window, and she flattened her hand across her stomach, willing away the horrible ache she couldn't outrun no matter how many miles she put between her and New York.

A cell phone rang, shattering the tense silence. Lucas dug his phone from his pocket, cursing under his breath when he glanced at the screen. He shot Max a look that warned her not to say a word.

"Are you trying to ruin my vacation?" Lucas asked when he finally answered.

Vacation? It was impossible to hear the other side of the conversation, but Lucas didn't look happy about whoever was calling.

"Yeah. Now's not a good time. I'll have to get back to you later." He kept his gaze fixed on the road, but seemed to be watching her from the corner of his eye. "It's complicated and I can't get into it right now."

Max tugged impatiently on the arm left dangling as he used his right hand to hold the phone. "You really need to take these off," she muttered, shrugging when he gave her a sharp look.

Who was he talking to that he didn't want them to know he wasn't alone?

Girlfriend? Wife? Cara used to joke that her brother would

always be a bachelor, but that had been years ago...

Something nagged at the back of her mind, but she couldn't figure out what. She gave up a minute later, after Lucas grew quiet, his expression tense.

"I'll be in touch." He hung up, and she grabbed the phone out of his hand.

"I need to let Sherri know that I'm okay." When he opened his mouth to argue, she added, "Please. She'll be worried about me." And she really needed to tell her friend that she'd find a way to cover the cost of whatever damage had been done to the shop.

Nodding, he guided the car back onto the road. "Did you and Glen end up with any theories on which cops were on Blackwater's payroll?"

"Just a few suspicions, nothing concrete."

"What about your captain? Is he clean?"

She rubbed her thumb back and forth across the buttons on his phone. "I always thought so. Now, I'm not so sure."

Lost in thought for a few minutes, she started to dial Sherri's number just as a white car speared across Max's line of vision. It only took another second for the red and blue lights on the roof to penetrate.

She craned her neck, watching as the car did a U-turn and followed them, lights flashing.

Chapter Seven

Glancing over at the speedometer, she cursed under her breath. "Are you crazy? Ever hear of a speed limit?"

"I was trying to make up for lost time," he argued, easing off the gas.

"If we stop, we're done."

Lucas glanced at the pursuing vehicle in the rearview mirror. "Or they'll just write us a ticket."

"For driving around in a stolen car?"

"They don't know that yet."

"Unless you can guarantee me that someone couldn't have reported it stolen two minutes after we drove away, we are not stopping. It's too risky."

He shook his head. "I'm driving, it's my call."

She looked over her shoulder at the RCMP car closing in on them. Lucas guided the car to the side of the road and turned off the ignition.

"This is insane." She watched the other vehicle pull up behind them.

"So noted."

"And how are you going to explain these?" She jerked her arm up to eye-level in case he'd forgotten the precarious position he'd put them in. Even if they could get away with just a speeding ticket, the handcuffs would not escape notice.

"Don't worry about it."

"The way I shouldn't worry about being Bertha's bitch when this stunt lands me in prison?"

"Bertha?" His lips twitched.

Oh, he was so not grinning at her.

The officer stepped out of his car and approached theirs. The second he reached the rear of the vehicle, Lucas cranked the ignition and punched the gas. Gravel spun from the tires and the cop stumbled back.

He regained his footing and ran for his car just as they zipped around the next bend, leaving him behind them.

Max tipped her head. "What now, genius?"

"Since he's probably already on the radio calling it in, meaning more cars will be closing in on us faster than you can say Royal Canadian Mounted Police, we need to ditch the car."

She surveyed the dense woods they flew past. "Ditch it," she echoed. "Where?"

"Not now, Max."

"Hey, I wasn't the one stupid enough to drive twenty-five miles over the speed limit cuffed to a wanted fugitive."

The RCMP car rounded the last bend, gaining on them.

Lucas whipped the Corvette down a side road on the right. Max gripped the side of her seat as they bounced over the gravel road, clouds of dust mushrooming behind the car.

"This might lead to a dead end." She wouldn't have thought it necessary to state the obvious until Lucas floored the gas pedal.

"You should know that I really hate backseat drivers."

"Then it's a good thing I'm next to you—" The rest was cut off as she sank her teeth into her bottom lip as he whipped them around another sharp turn.

They were driving parallel to the Saint John River now. Waterfront lots and cottages blurred past.

"Lucas!" She braced for impact at the sight the Maple tree that was suddenly in the middle of the road that forked off in either direction.

"Jesus Christ." He wrenched on the wheel, losing the driver's side mirror as they barely scraped by the tree. "Out," he snapped a minute later when the car skidded to a stop around another bend, the thick brush partially concealing the car.

She shoved his phone in her bag and slid it up over her shoulder. She was already scrambling over the seats after him by the time he got the door open.

He gave the area only a cursory scan before pulling her after him. Dead leaves crunched under their feet, their breaths clouding on the crisp air as they tried to get as much distance between them and the approaching siren as possible.

"This way." Lucas led her down a twisting path that took them closer to the water. They emerged beside a toolshed tucked into the woods next to a waterfront cottage.

Breathing hard, Max tugged on the cuffs. "Take these off."

"I can't."

"Lucas—"

He dragged her around to the shed's front door. "I don't have the key."

Not caring if it slowed them down for a few seconds, she dug her heels into the ground. "Where the fuck is it?"

"Probably back with the truck."

She jumped back to avoid being smacked with the shed door as Lucas yanked it open. "You didn't grab it off the floor when you took the cuffs?"

"Didn't have time to look for it."

"You intentionally shackled us together knowing you didn't have the key? That's brilliant." She followed him into the shed, wondering how many critters called the rotting shack home in the off-season.

"I had to improvise." He started moving tools and crates out of the way. "Maybe if you'd cooperated with me earlier..."

She scoffed. "So this is my fault?"

"Pretty much." He grabbed something off the shelf. "I need a piece of wire or something."

They both heard more sirens in the distance and hurriedly dumped boxes over until she found something suitable.

Lucas snatched the wire out of her hand and slid it into the lock on his cuff, circling it around. "Almost..."

"Hurry up."

"Got it." He slid free of the cuff. "Grab the paddles behind you."

Paddles? As in a paddle for a boat? Not a chance. She followed his gaze anyway, shaking her head even before she spotted the peeling wooden paddles that looked like they dated back to the province's original British and French settlers. Not a *fucking* chance.

"I don't think so."

He grabbed both paddles and disappeared outside. "We need to move."

Left with no choice but to follow him, Max shut the shed and caught up with him near the front of the cottage.

"I'm not getting in that canoe." The canoe looked to predate the paddles by at least another century. They'd have a better shot of floating downriver in a bathtub.

Lucas dragged it across the rocky beach. "Fine, you hang out where the cops will eventually look while I'm home free on the other side of the river."

She caught up to him and snatched one of the paddles out of his hand. He pushed the front end of the sickly ash-colored canoe into the water.

"After you."

Max didn't move.

Lucas frowned. "What's your problem? You can swim, can't you?"

"Sure." If sinking like a stone counted.

"Get in then."

106

Holding her breath, she eased into the canoe, trying not to squeal when it started to tip.

"If you move any slower you're going to meet Bertha sooner than you'd like."

Shooting him a dirty look over her shoulder, she made it to the front seat. Lucas shoved them off and stepped in behind her. The canoe pitched precariously to the right, and Max latched onto the sides even though there was a good chance the wood would crumble under her fierce grip.

"Paddle, Max. Faster," he added when it took her a few more seconds to make much progress.

"You should have handcuffed yourself to a member of the national rowing team if you wanted someone experienced."

Awkward at first, they fell into a brisk rhythm, paddling until Max's arms burned and ached from the strain. It gave her a whole new appreciation for athletes who specialized in any type of rowing event.

After an hour or two passed with no sirens heard across the river, they relaxed and drifted with the current.

"So what was that back in the diner anyway?"

Max glanced over her shoulder. "What was what?"

"That kiss."

Her hand slipped and she nearly dropped the paddle in the river. "What about it?"

"You sure made it look good."

"That was your advice earlier, wasn't it? Making it look good."

He didn't respond right away, then, "You sure it had nothing to do with that waitress coming on to me?"

Hearing the laughter in his voice, she sighed. "Sorry, but any fantasy you're harboring of two chicks getting into a catfight over you will have to wait until after Bertha is done with me."

Lucas laughed, and she grinned, her body recovering from

the amount of adrenaline injected into her bloodstream.

"There are some rocks up ahead, once we clear them we'll put in to shore."

No sooner did Max spot the rocks up ahead than the water parted directly in front of them. She heard the bump, felt the boat rock wildly.

She grabbed the edges, tried to compensate but knew it was useless.

The canoe tipped, dumping them into the river.

Icy water closed over Max's head. The water immediately soaked through her clothes, drawing her deeper. The frigid temperature seeped into her bones as she sank, turning her blood cold as she struggled against the current.

Every direction she turned was dark, empty.

Oh god, which way was up?

Her heart pounded in her ears, the frantic pulse releasing a rush of panic that paralyzed her. Suspended in the water, unsure of whether or not she was sinking or floating toward the surface, she kicked her legs, desperate for any leverage that might save her.

Something clamped around her wrist jerking her upward, and her head crashed through the surface. Her mouth opened automatically to draw in enough air.

"I've got you," Lucas said against her ear.

Instinctively, she tried to turn and cling to him, but he locked his arm across her upper body. "I won't let go."

"Prom—promise?" The freezing water sloshed around her face as she tried her best to relax in his hold. His grip forced her to stay on her back as he headed for shore.

That was twice now he'd stuck his neck out to save her ass. She could have easily drowned the two of them if her panic had gotten the better of her.

When her feet scuffed the rocky bottom, she planted her feet too quickly and tried to stand. The water was only thigh deep, but her knees quivered and would have given out if Lucas hadn't been at her side, half-dragging, half-carrying her to shore.

Although she wouldn't have admitted as much to him, she was thankful he was there. His presence held back the hysteria lodged in her throat, all of which was entirely her brother's fault. If CJ hadn't jumped on top of her in the pool during their first swimming lesson as kids, she might have stuck with the lesson past the first five minutes.

Once they hit the beach, she eased away from him, finding the weight of his arms around her a little too comforting. He glanced down at her, his gaze far too perceptive, and she ducked her head.

Now that her heart began to slow, she started to shiver. A gust of wind slashed right through her wet clothes. She might as well have been naked for all the protection the drenched fleece gave her.

She wrapped her arms around herself, sinking on to a large rock.

Lucas caught her arm. "We need to get warmed up." He nodded toward a path that cut across the grassy bank in front of them. "I thought you said you could swim?"

"Yeah, the doggie paddle."

He arched a brow.

"What? You just didn't give me time out there to show you my moves."

"You should have said something."

Legs still a little rubbery, she stumbled up the path. "I wasn't exactly anticipating our little dip."

Lucas stopped, and she followed his gaze to where a blue and white clapboard cottage sat on a cement foundation, tucked under a group of cedar trees.

"Do you think anyone is around?"

"Probably not at this time of year."

Hopefully not at this time of year. Max stopped, spun around. "Where's my bag?"

Lucas carried on ahead of her. "My guess would be at the bottom of the river."

"You lost it?"

"I was kind of busy saving your life."

"My life was in that bag." Her whole life or what was left of it. Identification. Money. Guns.

"So was my gun and cell phone," he reminded her. "And you were trying to drown me."

"Well, I obviously didn't try hard enough."

Everything important to her was sitting at the bottom of the river. All because he'd insisted on fleeing the RCMP in a freaking canoe. Who did that? And so what if it worked and they were likely searching for them upriver somewhere? She was now broke, unarmed and without a vehicle or even a place to go.

God, could the day get any worse?

She glanced down at the first drop of water that hit her hand. Tipping her head back, she felt more drops of rain on her face.

Perfect.

Fallen leaves blanketed the small yard and gravel driveway that disappeared into the woods ahead of them. If no one had been by to rake the leaves, maybe whoever vacationed here during the summer months wouldn't be back until spring.

"Give me a sec." Lucas disappeared around the corner.

Frustrated and freezing, she waited for him, no longer able to hold back the shivers that shook her inside out. True to his word, Lucas reappeared a minute later, probably having scouted the perimeter.

He pulled open the storm door and knocked twice on the oak-paneled interior one.

No response.

On tiptoes, Max peeked through the window beside the door, scanning the dark interior for any signs of movement.

She turned to Lucas. "I don't think anyone is home."

He nodded thoughtfully, then glanced down. He lifted the mat, but there wasn't anything waiting for them this time.

"You didn't think it was going to be that easy twice in one day, did you?"

Ignoring her, he crouched beside an oversized terracotta pot, empty except for soil. "Jackpot." He smiled and held up a key.

Shaking head to foot, she grabbed the key and slid it into the lock. The door needed a nudge to get past the first few inches, and she stepped inside, Lucas following right on her heels just as the rain really started to come down.

The air inside was stuffy and smelled a little like stale cigarette smoke.

"I guess they didn't feel like cleaning up after their last party." Not even a little bit judging by the beer bottles littering the top of the table by the kitchen on the left.

Beyond the kitchen area, more party favors—empty chip bags, food wrappers and overflowing ash trays—were scattered around the couch that faced three large windows that looked out at the water.

"Maybe it wasn't their party." Lucas nodded from the photograph of a couple in their mid to late fifties on a side table to the ripped open box of condoms on the counter by another row of empty beer bottles.

She shrugged, rubbing her hands up and down her arms. "Maybe the couple in the picture are parents or in-laws and not the owners."

Spying a lamp on the table near the door, she reached over and switched it on, brightening the gloomy interior. "At least they still pay their power bill in the off-season."

"They probably keep the basement heated enough so the

pipes won't freeze."

Her eyes widened, but she was almost afraid to hope the place actually had running water if no one was staying here now. There were two doorways to the right of the woodstove and one of them had to lead to a bathroom.

"Where are you going?"

"To see if the bathroom window is big enough for me to squeeze through later." She rolled her eyes, not bothering to look back and see if he actually believed that.

The light in the bathroom worked as well, and the sight of the corner shower nearly made her weep. Which she nearly did when she tried the faucet at the sink and after a minute the water turned warm.

"Thank god."

"Well, that should help get you warmed up."

She turned to find him directly behind her, his approach as stealthy as ever. She wondered if he enjoyed sneaking up on her as much as he did crowding her in small bathrooms.

"You should check and see if there are any clothes we can change into first. I'm going to start a fire."

"Okay."

Lucas didn't move right away, his attention fixed on the floor. She didn't see anything on the slate-gray ceramic tiles at their feet, but the second Lucas glanced at her, she wished he'd kept staring at the floor.

In less than a second his penetrating gaze seemed to slip beneath her skin, and she shivered for an entirely different reason. She never saw him move, but swore he was closer to her than he'd been a moment ago.

"I didn't plan on things turning out this way, Max."

"Good to know you didn't steer us into that rock on purpose."

"I didn't mean just this." He blew out a breath, seeming almost uncomfortable. "I know you've had a rough time and if

I've made things harder on you..."

"Are you apologizing?" At least, that's what it sounded like.

"I'm just saying that if I had to do this whole thing over, I would make a few changes."

"What changes?"

His gaze slipped to her mouth, and her stomach did a fluttery backflip. "I'm going to start that fire." He retreated another step.

"Lucas? Thanks for not letting me drown."

He nodded, his lips slowly curving in a devastating grin that left her staring at the empty doorway long after he'd gone.

Once she was alone, there was nothing to distract her from the cold. She peeled off her boots, leaving them on the floor while she went to check the other room for spare clothing.

The bedroom wasn't very big, the double-sized mattress fitting almost wall-to-wall. Directly to her left were a huge armoire and a small dresser. She checked the armoire first, pulling open the doors and coming face to face with two liquid black eyes.

Holy fuck.

Holding back the scream that shot up her throat, she stumbled backward. It took a moment to register that the previous owner had not in fact murdered her husband and left him to rot in the armoire.

Instead, some dumbass had not only shot and killed Bambi's mother, but decapitated the poor thing and kept her head for a souvenir.

Some men had *way* too much time on their hands.

She quickly shut the armoire doors and turned to the dresser. Inside it she found bed sheets, a couple thick blankets—which she tugged out and set on the floor beside her—some socks, a few T-shirts and drawstring swim shorts that would do.

The door opened, and she glanced into the main room as

Lucas set an armload of wood on the floor next to the woodstove.

Pitching some of the clothes and extra blankets on the chair behind him, she quickly pivoted back around.

"Hold up a second."

"Oh no. I've got first dibs on the shower."

Abandoning his smoldering fire, he trailed her into the bathroom once more. "Oh yeah? Says who?"

"Says the woman who didn't want to take the canoe in the first place."

"You mean the woman who didn't warn me about the rock that caused us to tip?"

Her lips parted, but he held up his hand.

"Just get in there already or you'll be having company."

Carnal images of the two of them beneath the steaming water unfolded in her mind. Heat licked through her veins as he lingered in the doorway looking like he knew exactly what was going on in her head.

She put her hand on the door, torn between closing it and inviting him in. In the end he made up her mind for her.

"Come here." He drew her close, and her breath hitched as his fingers curled around her wrist.

She bumped against him and a wave of need slid through her, running fast and hot. Even drenched, he smelled good, and she thought about pressing her mouth to his jaw to see if she'd still taste the salty river water on his skin.

He lifted her hand higher. "I should take this off."

Yes, he should. Take it all off.

He pulled something from his pocket, and she recognized the piece of wire he'd used to get his cuff off earlier. The pad of his thumb rasped across the inside of her wrist as he turned the cuff around.

After a few seconds of fiddling, he glanced at her. "Isn't this where you ask me if I know what I'm doing?" Something in his tone said he wasn't talking about the handcuffs.

"Do you?"

His eyes clung to hers, his voice rough as he answered, "I guess we'll find out."

The cuff falling away from her skin broke the spell.

"Enjoy the shower." He walked out, closing the door behind him.

Don't do it, man.

Lucas leaned against the closed door, reminding himself that getting involved with Max would be a mistake. He was taking her to Boston, end of story.

After the canoe had tipped and he'd lost sight of her in the water, he'd come a little too close to panicking. That right there told him he was losing whatever objectivity he had possessed before this whole thing started.

He just didn't know if it was Cara's death and doubting Max's role in it that set him on this path, or meeting Max and wanting to believe in her as much as Cara had. It used to be about getting the job done and leaving his personal feelings out of the equation. For whatever reason, it was different this time.

But it didn't change the fact that Joe was expecting him to bring Max in. He wasn't sure if Joe had been suspicious about his whereabouts before he'd called Tess this morning, or if he'd said something that tipped Joe off earlier. And if Joe had suspected something was going on with his team that he didn't know about, he would have hounded his granddaughter Tess until she filled him in.

Either way, three seconds into the call that came through before the RCMP caught up with them, it was clear Joe knew exactly what was going on.

Lucas just couldn't decide if he'd overestimated the odds of keeping his side-mission off Joe's radar or Tess keeping Joe distracted with other things. And now that Joe knew he'd found

Max, he was expecting him to have her back in Boston by tonight.

Since they wouldn't be meeting the plane that would be waiting for them an hour away—not today anyway—he had to find a way to get through another twenty-four hours with Max without doing something stupid.

Stepping away from the door, and doing his best not to think about Max peeling herself out of her wet clothes, he crouched in front of the woodstove. He was still in the same position, annoyed at how much his best sucked right now, when Max emerged from the bathroom.

She took one look at him and the barely smoldering fire and arched a brow. "What, not a Boy Scout?"

Replying involved using his mouth for something other than exploring every inch of her skin not covered by the pathetic excuse for a towel. Did she realize that no matter how hard she tugged, it wasn't going to get any bigger?

The second he felt his cock start to harden, he looked backed at the fire.

"I find the whole being prepared thing highly overrated." At least he had starting thirty seconds ago.

"Is that so?" She crossed to the chair behind him where she'd left the extra clothes.

He watched her from the corner of his eye, the tucked-in fold on her towel in particular, the one that looked ready to come undone. "There's a lot to be said for just going with the flow. If I had been more prepared, you wouldn't be standing there in nothing but a towel."

It was hard to tell in the dim lighting, but he thought her cheeks flushed or maybe that was just from the shower.

"Don't remind me." She gathered up a few clothes.

He stood, but kept his feet planted in front of the stove. "Funny how things work out, huh?"

"Yeah, hilarious."

"At least you didn't end up in the trunk of my car."

She stopped next to him. "I'm sure you'll forgive me if I don't kiss your feet in gratitude."

"There is going to be more than kissing going on if you don't get dressed." If he looked even half on edge as he felt when her towel was one tug from hitting the floor, then she'd be smart to put some space between them.

Seeming to read his mind, she took a step, only it was closer instead of farther away.

"I think we both know that would be a really bad idea."

He caught her hand and just touching her unleashed a rush of bone-deep need. He tugged her closer. "Define bad." Because he didn't need to think very hard to know *bad* would feel really fucking good—the same way her mouth had felt when she'd surprised him in the diner.

He'd barely had time to process her grabbing his shirt before she'd kissed him. Leaned in, slanted her mouth across his and, with a quick catch of her breath, like she wasn't sure if she'd gotten in over her head, kissed him.

In less than three point five seconds he'd been hard for her. If he'd been able to communicate with his brain longer than it took to kiss her back, he would have hauled her into his lap.

"Like we don't trust each other bad."

He curled one arm around her waist, drawing her flush against him. One of them let out a shocked breath at the contact, and if his gaze wasn't already locked on her mouth, he would have tried to figure out which one of them had made it.

"You can trust me, Max."

Her cheek grazed his. "That doesn't mean I should."

"Still don't believe I'm one of the good guys?"

"Either way you're dangerous."

He lowered his head and his lips skimmed her bare shoulder. She gave a little moan of approval.

"You don't sound too worried."

"I can handle it."

He trapped her jaw in his hands. "At least one of us can."

Her lips parted, and he nipped the bottom one then slowly pulled it between his. This time he knew that sharp intake of breath was definitely his, and when she fit against him completely, her hands sliding around his neck, like she needed something to hang onto—and Christ he knew the feeling—he had to tamp down the satisfied groan that vibrated through his chest.

So damn hungry for her, he opened his mouth over hers, taking complete possession. She arched against him, rubbing just hard enough that the slow, sweet friction left him aching to get inside her. Catching her hips, he rocked against her, and she released a deep carnal sigh. He swept into her mouth, stroking deep with his tongue.

Trouble.

With every slide of her lips he knew he was falling deeper into it. He knew he should care, and maybe if kissing her wasn't frying brain cells by the boatload, he would have.

The towel pooled around her lower back and he knew the second it slid down her chest by the way she squirmed against him.

"You're cold and wet."

"Working on it."

She smiled against his lips, and whatever she was going to say was lost to a startled yelp as her legs hit the back of the couch, knocking her off-balance.

He could have steadied her, but he enjoyed the way she clung to him, trying to regain her equilibrium. Not that it mattered when he lowered her to the cushions and followed her down, moving faster than he'd planned, a little too eager to get his hands all over her.

Pain flared across his ribs, and he sucked in a sharp breath.

"What's wrong?"

"It's okay." Already the pain was easing.

She shifted beneath him, allowing him to settle deeper between her thighs. He didn't have a clue if that was her intention, but the moment he fit snug against her, a rush of intense pleasure streamed through him. Irritating his bruised ribs was more than worth it if it meant he could feel her thighs squeeze him again.

Hair damp and tousled and looking like she'd just stepped out of some locker room fantasy, Max stared up at him. Bending to run his mouth along her shoulder, he made his way to her neck, loving how her head fell to the side giving him complete access.

She moaned low and deep and tugged at his shirt until she got her hands beneath it, splaying her fingers across his back. If she wasn't already warming him up, the shared body heat as her hands slid up and down his spine would have gotten the job done.

He traced the hollow of her throat with his tongue before pulling away to peel his shirt off, careful of his shoulder.

"Jesus."

He followed her gaze to the bruise on his side. As far as injuries went, it looked worse than it felt, and he'd certainly had worse. The expression on Max's face bothered him more than anything, and he didn't miss the flash of guilt in her eyes before she looked away.

Maybe Mad Max really wasn't as tough as she looked.

"Touch me."

She shook her head slowly. "I don't want to make it worse."

He caught her hand. "It'll be worse if you don't." And he meant every word.

Maybe they didn't really trust each other, but whatever she'd been through, and he was starting to think it was more than anyone realized, he didn't want to see her hurt by it any longer. He'd glimpsed that easy, sexy grin, heard her moan against his mouth, felt her shudder in his arms and he'd do whatever he could to make it happen again and again.

He brought her hand to his lips and pressed a slow, lingering kiss to her fingertips. "Touch me, Max."

She scooted up a little and he clenched his jaw at the sweet tease along his cock. She tugged her hand free, but instead of running her finger over his ribs, she leaned up and carefully opened her mouth on his skin.

The flick of her tongue set fire to his blood, and he slid down, groaning as her body molded perfectly to his. This time he crushed his mouth down on hers, stark need warring with whatever part of his brain kept insisting he shouldn't rush this.

He cupped her breast, lazily rubbing his thumb across her nipple. She whimpered, so he did it again then inched down so he could draw the tight peak into his mouth. Her back arched with every long, greedy tug.

He swirled his tongue over each hard tip, learning the feel of her, the taste. Her nails raked his arm, and the soft sounds that escaped her quickly heightened his own arousal.

His heart pounded faster than when they'd been running from the police, but the tremor that worked through him was new. If he didn't know better he'd think he was fooling around for the first time, caught in that surreal place between feeling so damn good and praying he wasn't about to screw it up somehow.

He slid a hand between their bodies, tugging impatiently at the towel. Once it hit the floor he caressed the inside of her thigh, inching higher. She squirmed beneath him, tightening her thighs and hugging him closer.

Lightly raking the tip of one nipple with his teeth, he palmed her sex, rotating slowly. God, she was already damp.

"Yes."

He grinned. "Was that yes, or *yes*?" He followed the deliberate emphasis with a soft pump of two fingers that slid

120

deep inside her.

They both groaned, and the slick walls clenched around him. He withdrew, sliding up her cleft in search of the sensitive knot and spreading her wetness across it.

Looping both arms around his neck, she dragged him up to meet her mouth. Bolder than before, she pushed her tongue between his lips, robbing him of any coherent thoughts he might have been clinging to.

As the kiss blew past wild and right into savage, he drove his fingers back inside her. The faster and harder he thrust, the more she strained beneath him. And when he circled her clit again, thumbing the plump flesh in teasing strokes, she lifted her hips, meeting each thrust.

So damn hot. She had barely touched him and he was ready to lose his mind.

The responsive roll of her hips grew more frantic, her mouth moving faster against his.

"Lucas...I...fuck..." She threaded her fingers through the ends of his hair.

Her thighs trembled around him and he buried his fingers deep once more, waiting for that panted moan to slow, then he rubbed her clit. She cried out, her body tensing as she came.

Slowly, she melted back into the cushions, but didn't let go of him, her face tucked against his throat. He already had the top button undone on his pants and his zipper half way down when she pulled back enough to look at him.

She offered him a smile that perfectly suited her stunning blue eyes, which didn't seem quite so haunted. That vulnerability she'd shown him in the hotel room that morning was still there, but softer somehow.

She arched her hips, silently encouraging him to keep going, and so help him, he couldn't think of damn good reason he shouldn't already be inside her and halfway to heaven.

Except that if things went any further between them, he wasn't so sure he could do his job and bring her in.

Chapter Eight

"Lucas?"

Limbs still deliciously heavy from her explosive climax, Max watched indecision run across Lucas's face.

He glanced at something over her head, then straightened. His expression grew tense and he cringed, his hand sliding over his ribs.

"You're hurting," she guessed.

He nodded vaguely and moved to the other end of the couch. Without the warm weight of his body, she felt both chilled and increasingly exposed.

Suddenly self-conscious, she reached for the towel on the floor and wrapped it around herself. "I saw some ibuprofen in the medicine cabinet in the bathroom if you could use something to take the edge off."

"Not this kind of edge." His eyes met hers, the heat in his gaze making her stomach tighten all over again.

He finally stood and she knew she should be grateful one of them had slowed things down. It was the part of her that wanted to coax him back to finish what they'd started that she didn't know what to do about.

She was afraid she was looking for more than just sex, because even with her body riding the sharp edge of release, his hands all over her—and god he knew how to use them—she'd felt...safe.

As much as kissing him in the diner had thrown her world into a wonderfully dizzying backspin, she hadn't truly let go. She hadn't let go in so long she'd been convinced she couldn't anymore—until Lucas had covered her body with his, the drugging weight of him sheltering her, protecting her.

It was almost laughable considering what she'd been through since he had walked into her life. But right this second something in her craved only his arms sliding around her.

She told herself she didn't need it, that she was doing fine on her own, and even if she could trust him, she was still better off on her own.

And what if you're wrong?

Ignoring the small voice in the back of her mind, Max watched the rain spatter on the front windows. Fog was rolling in, making it harder to see across the river.

"I'm going to grab a shower." He didn't move, though, his attention fixed on the fire in the woodstove that was going strong now.

"It's pouring out, Lucas. I've got no dry clothes, no money, no ID and have no idea where I'm even at. I'm not going anywhere if that's why you're still standing there."

She waited for him to look at her to see if she was lying. He only nodded and disappeared into the bathroom.

Once the door was closed, she sagged back against the cushions and closed her eyes. Having grown up with three older brothers and worked in a field dominated by men, she should have more confidence when it came to handling Lucas.

Worried she was going to over-think the last few minutes, she stood and pulled on one of the T-shirts she'd brought out, relieved it fell to mid-thigh. After she arranged her wet clothes on a chair in front of the woodstove to dry, she turned her attention to the pantry.

There were mostly canned goods inside, some unopened condiments, a few bottles of water and packages of pudding, and—she shuddered—sardines.

123

Choosing two small cans of beef stew, she set them on the counter and dug through the cupboard until she found a small pot to warm up the stew. She also came across two more empty beer bottles, a half-eaten chocolate bar and some kind of hard candy someone had spit into an empty glass.

Classy.

Definitely couldn't be the owner's party leftovers.

With the stew heating up, she crossed to the open door, leaned up against the jamb and watched the rain come down in drenching sheets.

She hadn't been lying when she said she had nowhere to go. She'd been so careful for so long, always keeping her next move in the back of her mind, never letting her guard down. But she'd grown too comfortable in Riverbend, telling herself she'd figure something out, but never quiet deciding when, since it would mean she'd have to leave.

And now here she was with nothing but drenched clothes by the fire and no game plan.

How much longer could she keep running? Whatever Lucas was after—revenge, justice, something else entirely—he was right about one thing. Cara wouldn't have run, not for as long as Max had.

Having grown up with her parents on one scientific expedition after another and her older brother in the military and gone almost just as often, Cara had been one of the most self-reliant people Max had ever met.

Being on the run and away from her family left Max lonelier than she'd ever been, but she refused to put them at risk. It didn't matter that her dad and older brothers were in the service—two cops and a firefighter—Blackwater would have found a way to hurt them to get to her if he thought they knew anything.

No, Cara wouldn't still be running. She would have found an angle or a weakness to exploit Blackwater by now.

She heard the bathroom door open behind her and steeled

herself before she glanced over her shoulder. It didn't do a damn bit of good. One glimpse of the towel hanging low and loose around Lucas's hips, his chest bare and his gaze locked on her, and she was grateful she had the support of the door frame.

The man's unwavering confidence echoed in every sure and determined step, and his effortless smile drew her completely. And she wasn't even counting the eyes she'd once believed to be only cold and empty. She knew better now, had felt the heat, the hunger, the sheer want in them every time he'd looked at her earlier.

Lucas had a soul all right, and it burned hot and fierce and touched far more of her than she wanted it to.

She glanced back at the rain, suddenly unsure if she preferred to think he was playing her as opposed to being caught up in something she was afraid to put a name to.

"You're still here." Something hit the floor, his towel maybe.

"Sorry. I know how much you were looking forward to chasing me out in the rain."

He laughed. "Guess I'll have to find another way to amuse myself."

When she felt him behind her, she straightened and turned. Thirty seconds ago she'd been convinced that as long as he got dressed she'd stop thinking about running her hand up his chest.

Apparently not. The plain white T-shirt looked just as good on him and—

She burst out laughing. "Are those—" she tipped her head, "—naked women on your shorts?"

"Hey, you picked them out."

"I must have still been getting over my run-in with Bambi's mom and didn't notice."

He frowned. "Bambi's mom? How much river water did you swallow out there?"

"I'm talking about the deer head in the armoire in the bedroom." She checked the stew, not the least bit surprised that Lucas went to see what she was talking about. "Don't most men usually keep them up some place they won't scare the crap out of unsuspecting people?"

He walked back out of the bedroom. "Am I supposed to have an answer for that because I'm a man?"

She shrugged. "Tracking and hunting just seemed to be an area of expertise for you."

He grabbed a couple bowls out of the cupboard. "Well if I had a choice, I'd take tracking big game over people any day."

"Why is that?"

"Because no matter how big or strong they are, their hooves just aren't capable of swinging a gas can like a pro baseball player."

Despite herself, she felt a smile tug at her lips.

Lucas poured the stew into two bowls and carried them to the table. She moved the garbage and empty beer bottles to the counter before grabbing them each a spoon and water, and sat opposite Lucas.

They ate in relative silence, but it wasn't quite as strained as breakfast. More than once she felt him watching her, but couldn't force herself to lift her head.

"You play checkers?"

Without answering him, she put her empty bowel in the sink and rinsed it out.

"Max?"

"What are you doing?" She turned around slowly. "You're cracking jokes and talking about checkers and passing the time like we're really on vacation. A few hours ago we were fleeing the cops in a stolen car, and that was after you cuffed us together."

He nodded, but offered nothing further.

"You don't think there is anything weird about setting up a

checker board after all that? After what happened earlier?" She blew out a breath.

Lucas stood and crossed his arms, his expression impossible to read.

"We're not friends, Lucas. I've managed to keep myself out of trouble until you came along, and just because we're lying low doesn't mean we need to keep pretending—"

"Pretending to what?"

"Just because I stuck around while you were in the shower doesn't mean I'm going anywhere with you, least of all back to New York, so whatever angle you're working—"

"Angle?" Now he sounded annoyed.

"Isn't that what this whole friendly routine is about? Trying to convince me I can trust you?"

"Contrary to popular belief, I am a friendly guy and you *can* trust me."

She cocked her head. "Who called you earlier?"

He took a beat too long to answer. "My business partner."

"Not your most convincing moment." She moved past him, but didn't get very far.

He snapped his arm out, planting it on top of the table, blocking her. His mouth all but skimmed her temple. "If you're talking about what happened between us earlier, that wasn't pretending."

Rough and loaded with the same dark sensuality she found far too appealing, his words made it a little harder to drag in her next breath.

"If I was just stringing you along, do you think I would have let anything stop me from burying myself deep inside you? I haven't been able to stop thinking about it since you kissed me this morning."

"It was just a kiss," she managed, her voice barely above a whisper.

His lips brushed her temple. "Not your most convincing

moment."

Her eyes slid shut and she held herself perfectly still, wishing she didn't believe him.

He moved away from her, returning to the sink. Still trying to slow her racing heart, she watched him fill the sink up and begin washing their dishes. She wanted to laugh at how out of place it seemed given the last twenty-four hours.

Needing some space, she left him to the few dishes. "Just so you know, I'm not sleeping in the bathroom tonight."

Hours later Lucas was wishing that *he* had slept in the bathroom. Either that or stayed on the couch.

Out there he wouldn't feel the warmth of Max's body, which was pressed close to his, or smell her skin or think the kind of hot, tangled thoughts that were going to get him in trouble.

And all that was before she shifted in her sleep and rolled to her side. Her T-shirt had ridden up and since he knew her panties were still in front of the woodstove, there wasn't a doubt in his mind it was her very fine, very bare ass brushing his hip.

Maybe she hadn't expected him to leave the couch, but since she'd only sighed sleepily when he crawled into bed, he hadn't wasted a lot of time contemplating her objections.

They hadn't spoken much after they'd eaten. Max kept her distance, and he'd kept his, going so far as to try and settle his six-foot-two frame on a couch made for someone five-foot-ten— tops. It seemed like the smartest move at the time, but that was before he'd lain there trying to figure out why he had gone out of his way to make it clear he wasn't pretending when it came to how much he wanted her.

No matter how long he'd stared at the ceiling, he couldn't come up with a reason except that he wanted to be honest with her about something. Something that had nothing to do with Cara or Blackwater or the job he still had to do.

That right there was how he knew he was in trouble. If his attraction to Max was based solely on physical chemistry, he wouldn't be worried about being honest with her about anything. He'd keep his dick in his pants and follow orders.

And he wouldn't be lying next to her clenching his jaw every time she moved, and at the same time hoping each shift would bring her closer.

With another restless sigh, Max rolled to her other side, facing him. He turned toward her, barely able to make out her features in the dark. She released a sharp breath, then another, mumbling something he didn't understand.

He brushed her hair off her face. "You're okay, Max."

She made another sound of distress, but stilled after that, her breathing growing deeper and more even. He lay there watching her until his own eyes grew tired and he drifted off.

It was still dark when his eyes snapped open. Lucas didn't move, trying to pinpoint what had awakened him.

Next to him, Max cried out.

"Hey," he said softly, coaxing her closer.

"No!" She thrashed against his grip, surprising him.

"Max."

"No. Please..." She continued to struggle even when he tightened his hold. "Don't! Stop!" Her voice continued to rise.

Worried he would hurt her if he continued to try and keep her still, he relaxed his grip. "Come on, Max. Wake up."

She screamed, and the chilling sound was like a blow to the chest. He sat up, reaching for the light, and she bolted upright on a cry.

"It's okay. Just a dream." He found her hand, half relieved something had succeeded in waking her.

"Lucas?"

"You're okay. Nothing but a bad—"

She threw her arms around him, tucking her face against his throat. "Not just a dream." She struggled to catch her breath. "Always the same...always so real," she sobbed, her body trembling.

"Tell me," he coaxed, wishing like hell the sick feeling in his gut had nothing to do with her nightmare.

Max shook her head. "I can't save her. No matter how hard I try, I can never save her."

Christ. He squeezed her tight, not wanting to hear what he knew was coming, but he suddenly couldn't stand the thought of Max suffering alone. "You did everything you could."

"No." It was only a whisper.

His throat felt wet and he knew then she was crying.

"I couldn't get to her, Lucas. They had me, and I tried so hard to get to her, and then—" she shuddered, the words coming between broken sobs.

Oh, Jesus. He'd assumed she'd been there that night, but this...

"—and then I knew it was too late. I couldn't watch her die, but they made me." Her whole body shook, her arms locked around him like he was her only lifeline in a raging storm. "They made me watch what that bastard did to her, made me watch her being cut over and over. I couldn't save her."

His throat burned, and for a painful minute he wasn't sure who was holding on tighter.

Finally her shaking began to ease. "I tried not to let her see how scared I was, but what he did..."

It was impossible to get any words out, so he held her until she slowly calmed. Even then he wasn't ready to let go and tugged her down beside him, keeping one arm wrapped around her. They lay that way for a long time and he wasn't sure which of them was more afraid of her falling back asleep.

"I'll be back." Her arms tightened around him briefly, and then she climbed off the bed.

Not liking where his thoughts began to drift the second he was alone, he got up, trailing her into the living area.

She stood at the sink, an open bottle of water in her hand. He didn't bother asking if she was okay. He knew she wasn't. Neither one of them were.

She didn't look at him when he stepped up beside her, but held up the bottle of water. He took a long drink, letting the cool water slide down his throat as though it could wash away the hurt and guilt Max's nightmare had awakened.

He handed the bottle back and their fingers brushed. It shouldn't have meant anything, but he felt the connection like a brand on his skin. His body reacted like she'd just slowly sucked one of his fingers into her mouth, leaving him in a bizarre state of sadness and arousal.

The latter frustrated him, that even after the nightmare, he couldn't keep from wanting her. He could have told himself that thinking about Max, about brushing up against her just to feel that shock of sensation flood his system, meant he wouldn't think about Cara's death.

But the truth was nothing he did now or next week or next year was ever going to bury what he'd just learned deep enough. He'd carry it with him, always, the same as he did the other scars he'd earned over the years.

Acknowledging that made some of the pressure weighing on his lungs ease up a bit. Too bad it didn't make it easier to put some space between him and Max. Giving her room, even a handful of feet was harder than it should have been.

He leaned against the counter feeling his guilt rise as he studied her face, noting the smudged mascara under her eyes. He wasn't sure how a dunk in the river and her shower afterward hadn't taken it all off. Industrial strength make-up maybe.

She looked tired and emotionally wrung out, and while he may not have put those nightmares in her head, he'd dragged her out of hiding and forced her to face the past she'd been running from. Without the attitude and cutting one-liners she always seemed poised to deliver, it was easy to see that everything had taken its toll on her, and all he wanted to do was kiss her and make it better.

Christ, he was an ass. She was standing there, toying with the bottle in her hand, looking unsure of herself and all he could think about was kissing her. And not some sweet, I'm-here-for-you kiss. No, his imagination had cruised over that and jumped right to the part where she had her tongue halfway down his throat.

Ass.

He exhaled and glanced at the floor. Max put the half empty bottle in the fridge and then stared out the window above the sink. Outside the rain had slowed, only gently tapping the glass now.

She finally looked at him, and his pulse jumped ahead a few beats. God, she was beautiful. Blond hair, black hair, smudged make-up or nothing but a heart-stopping grin on her face. Just...beautiful.

Inside of five seconds he was right back to wanting to kiss her again. She moved toward him and his heart pounded in his chest, the beat growing faster and wilder with every step she took.

Pushing up on her toes, she leaned into him, her lips grazing his cheek in a brief kiss that still managed to lock his feet to the floor.

"Thank you," she murmured. "You didn't need to do that."

"Hold you?"

When she nodded, he grinned, trying to lighten the mood. "Wasn't exactly a hardship." Not like this was, with her body tucked close and her mouth right there. He tried to satisfy the need to touch her by brushing her hair over her shoulder. "You should try to get some sleep."

They both should, but he doubted it would come easy for him unless he stuck to the couch.

"We should," she agreed. "I'm just not tired."

"I'm not—"

Her lips teased across his jaw.

"—tired either," he managed, holding himself still in case he'd somehow imagined she'd kissed him a second time. Or a third time, this one whispering across his mouth.

Dumbstruck or simply afraid to chase her off, he was slow to respond, his body already tuned in to anticipating where her mouth would touch next.

Exquisite, light kisses ignited his blood, and when she caught his face in her hands and sealed her mouth over his, he nearly spontaneously combusted on the spot.

He ran his hand down her back and beneath her shirt. Every attempt to try and reign himself in failed spectacularly. Max didn't seem to mind though, each silken slide of her tongue pushing him right into the fast lane.

Groaning against her mouth, he knew without a doubt they weren't stopping this time. They weren't even slowing down. It was almost as if they'd released the pause button, only his internal temperature was running a hundred degrees hotter now.

Seemed like they only needed to share the same oxygen and he was hard and hot for her. So fucking hot.

Max tugged at the drawstring on his shorts, working them down over his hips. She closed her hand around him, pumping her fist the length of his shaft in slow, greedy pulls. He had her shirt off in between the hoarse groans that rumbled up from his chest.

The T-shirt hit the floor and his gaze trailed over her full breasts, her hard nipples, and he drew his thumb across each tip.

She moaned against his lips, meting out equal torture with her hand. He rocked his hips, pushing his cock harder into her grip and telling himself the whole time that he wasn't going to explode in her hand.

God, it was too soon. They'd barely gotten started and he was losing his mind to the carnal rhythm. He should have been fine, *would* have been fine, but there was more than heat consuming every cell in his body. There wasn't a name for it, just a feeling, and his brain was too close to overload to waste a single circuit trying to puzzle it out.

But it was real and overwhelming and so damn good.

So damn right.

Something was wrong, Max thought. She just wasn't sure if it was because things where moving too fast or not fast enough.

So help her, she hadn't planned on this happening again. What he'd done for her in the bedroom, the way he'd held her so carefully, so protectively, affected her almost as much as the nightmare.

The kiss hadn't been any more intentional than what followed, but when it was over, she hadn't been able to tell herself to let go of him. Lucas had turned her life upside down, so why did it feel like she was actually living it for the first time in months?

Living it. Craving it.

Craving him.

He pressed an open-mouthed kiss to her neck, lingering there, drawing out the slow slide until she could barely feel him moving. She dropped her head back, moaning at the sweet suction that had her squeezing her legs together—right up until he cupped her sex, lazily stroking his fingers along her cleft.

There was no holding back her hiss of pleasure. She bit her lip, and he slid down to her opening where she was already wet for him. Wet for him since the second she felt his rough jaw graze her cheek.

He broke from her mouth, dipping down to circle her nipple with his tongue.

Oh god. Please...

His lips closed around her and he pulled her deep into his mouth, sucking slow and long.

"Lucas—" Whatever she'd been about to say evaporated on her lips as he thrust two fingers inside her.

Electrifying pleasure shot through her. She released her hold on him, grabbing the edge of the table she came up against. She hadn't even realized they'd moved at all. She'd been too wrapped up in what he was doing with his mouth.

After one more hungry tug at her breast, he slanted his mouth across hers. His hand worked between her thighs, sliding in and out, and the first hot edge of release skated across her nerve endings.

She moaned against his mouth, pulling him closer, happy to drown in the kiss that was dragging her under. She felt him everywhere, filling her up with his tongue and his fingers, his body rubbing up against hers. All she could think about was the next touch, the next slide of his mouth, the next thrust into her sex.

Without drawing back, he lifted her onto the table and wedged himself between her thighs.

"I—" More than once she tried to ease away from his mouth only to be coaxed back every time. "We need..." Something. God help her she wasn't so far gone that she couldn't think. She knew things, damn it. Guns. Drugs. Bad guys. Good guys.

Hot guys.

Insanely intense hot guys. One in particular that she needed to feel inside her.

"On the counter behind you," she murmured finally, then caught the tip of his tongue between her lips, sucking him back into her mouth.

He groaned. "Already got one."

Jesus the man was slick. It was one of the first things she'd noticed about him, and there was no other way to describe how he'd snagged a condom from the ripped open box on the counter when he'd barely taken his hands off her.

"And when did you figure out you were going to need one."

"When that kiss in the diner damn near knocked me on my ass."

Hearing the kiss had been just as mind-blowing for him made her even hotter. She heard him sheath himself, then felt the full head of his cock slide along her folds.

Her inner muscles clenched in greedy anticipation.

Mouth on hers, he pushed up inside her in one smooth thrust. For a crazy second everything stopped. Stopped breathing, stopped moving, stopped thinking. Only the riot of sensation continued, coiling around her, through her, tighter...tighter.

He felt so incredible inside her, she looped her arms around him, tucking her face against his throat and kissing him there. And then he was moving, filling her up over and over, his cock so hard and getting so deep.

He wrapped an arm around her back, anchoring her, and then he started pumping his hips, each thrust becoming faster, harder. His body pressed her back against the table, his strong arms keeping her up just enough to create the perfect angle.

Fierce satisfaction glittered in the eyes watching every move she made, every harsh catch of breath and arch of her spine. Then he tilted her hips just a fraction and she cried out.

A smile that bordered on feral curved his lips, his pace almost punishing. And god she loved it. She slid her hands down his back, to his ass and pulled him even tighter. He growled in approval, pounding into her.

She arched up seeking the release that hovered just out of reach, and the friction hit in all the right places.

Yes.

The shattering climax went on and on, and she hauled him to down to meet her mouth. She poured herself into the kiss, crying out when he used her wetness to get impossibly deep.

Lucas groaned and drove into her over and over, his body

finally shuddering and pressing her flat on the table.

Their crazy kiss slowed, but he didn't move and she didn't want him to. Wanted instead to keep him close for as long as she could.

"Warm enough?"

Max nodded, not looking away from the flames licking the woodstove's glass door, content to stay snuggled up in a blanket on the couch.

They hadn't turned on any lights, as if they both knew it would change what had just happened between them. The sun would be up in another couple of hours and then she could worry about what came next.

For now she didn't move an inch, listening to Lucas's heart pound strong and sure in his chest. He ran his hand up her back, and even through her T-shirt the lulling sensation made her eyes grow heavy.

"Why did you become a cop, Max?"

Frowning, she opened her eyes. "Aren't men supposed to be the quiet ones after sex?"

"Maybe I'm just trying to kill some time before I roll you beneath me and get back to the sex part." His voice, low and sexy and combined with the image he'd just put in her head, made her body stir.

She lifted her head. "I thought you already did your homework?"

"Humor me."

Ducking her head, she traced random circles across his chest. "Being a cop runs in the blood I guess. I don't really remember wanting to be anything else."

"Not even a pop star or ballerina?"

She snorted. "I grew up with three older brothers. Hard to dance in a tutu to the likes of AC/DC."

He laughed. "They turned you into a complete tomboy, huh?"

"I think it was easier for them that way. Except CJ. He would go through these stages when he would try and make me play with girl toys." She tapped her finger on his chest, focusing on the memories and not the long ago pain that surfaced with them.

"He used to buy me these play makeup sets even though the only way I'd touch them was if I could use them on him too."

"And he let you?"

"Right up until the two oldest walked in and saw thirteen-year-old CJ sporting the latest in Scandalous Scarlet lipstick." She laughed, thinking of the horrified look on CJ's face.

"I suppose that was the end of the makeovers?"

"Nope. Though he stuck with just hair and nails after that."

Lucas held up her hand, running his thumb across her fingernails. "And did he give you a tutorial for these?"

Her smile dimmed. "CJ died when he was nineteen." She swallowed past the sudden tightness in her throat. "You probably already knew that, but he is definitely the reason I still do my nails whenever I want to feel girly."

"Is he the reason you started hating Blackwater? Because CJ died of a drug overdose?"

"I also hated CJ's idiot friends who supplied the drugs that night."

He played with a strand of her hair, running it back and forth across his thumb. "How old were you?"

"Sixteen."

"And probably wishing you were already a cop so you could do something about it."

Surprised by how perceptive he was, she only nodded.

"So what did you do about it?"

"What makes you think I did anything?" She was pretty

sure that kind of information wouldn't have been in any file he had on her since she hadn't gotten caught. When he merely waited, she shrugged. "Just slashed some tires on the car belonging to the guy who bought the drugs."

"Good for you."

For some reason his approval felt good. "I never told anyone about that until now."

He looked a little taken aback by that, but quickly smiled, though, the gesture a little forced. "Your secret is safe with me." He glanced at the woodstove. "I should throw some more wood in and then we should try to sleep for another couple of hours."

Giving him some space, she moved to the opposite end of the couch. Deciding it was best to change the subject, Max asked, "So how did you get into your line of work?"

"According to Eli and Caleb it was all a matter of the right time and place."

Awareness sliced across her mind, and she sat up straighter. "Have you all worked together long?"

"A few years." He shoved a piece of wood into the fire and shut the stove.

Careful not to draw too much attention to herself, she stood. "Caleb must miss his sister a lot."

"Yeah—" Lucas went perfectly still, as if realizing his mistake.

He carefully stood, and she was more than ready for him.

Chapter Nine

Lucas dodged to the right as something whistled past his head.

A piece of wood hit the wall next to him.

"Max—"

A kick to the back of the knee threw him off balance, but he kept himself upright—barely—and spun to meet the punch she threw. He caught her wrist, twisting to snap her arm behind her back. "Hold on," he began.

She drove her heel down, and he cursed, but somehow managed to keep ahold of her.

"You lying son of a bitch." She jammed her elbow back, catching him in his sore ribs.

White streaked across his vision, and he released her, pressing his arm to his side as though it would ease the pain. "Just listen for a second."

"So you can lie to me again?" She laughed, the sound harsh and unforgiving.

Her next punch found its mark. His head snapped to the right and he tasted blood on his tongue.

Instinct warred with the need to hold the woman who had only moments ago been curled around him, giving him the kind of peace and contentment he hadn't felt in months, maybe even years.

Reflex had him avoiding another blow, but he didn't

retaliate, just stayed out of her reach.

"Who are you?"

"I'm not her brother but I am... I was her partner."

She shook her head. "You're lying. Her partner's name wasn't Lucas."

"My last name is McAllister. Cara always called me Mac."

She started to shake her head, but he cut her off.

"It was Caleb's fault, actually. When she came to work for the Lassiter Group he decided to mess with her and tell her my name was Mac. He knew it drove me crazy. Cara already knew who I was, but played along and it just stuck."

"Then why not tell me who you were from the start?"

"You did have a knife to my throat at the time."

"So you made up some crap about being her brother?"

"Seemed like a good idea at the time," he admitted.

Max glared at him. "Do not take another step."

He stopped, hands held up. "The truth is I wasn't sure you wouldn't kill me either way."

"Like I killed Cara?"

"Yes. No," he corrected. *Shit.* "I know you didn't kill Cara, but I couldn't take the chance I was wrong, not then." He mentally judged the distance to the door in case she decided to run for it.

She took a step in his direction instead. "No." Her brows drew together. "Her partner was ex-Special Forces."

He nodded, wondering just how much Cara had told her. "That's right."

"So you're telling me that with all the training you've had, the threat of a little piece of metal—"

"It was not little."

"—made you lie when you probably could have disarmed me before I did much damage?"

"I was having an off day."

"Or..." She made a sound of disbelief that he didn't like one little bit. Her eyes narrowed. "It was never about me helping you nail Blackwater, was it? You came to bring Cara's murderer in, didn't you?"

He lunged forward to grab her a heartbeat before she tried to bolt. He'd like to think she wasn't crazy or desperate enough to run into the night in only a T-shirt, but he believed in covering his bases.

He pressed her up against the wall. Not hard enough to hurt her, but to at least prevent her from hurting him. "Yes, I lied. And yes, I had every intention of bringing you in."

Sensing where he was headed, she snorted. "But now you've conveniently changed your mind, right? Aren't I lucky?"

He decided to ignore the rhetorical question. "When I went to Riverbend it was on nothing more than a hunch. I wasn't even supposed to be there. My boss thought I was on vacation."

"Wow," she mocked. "So I'm not the only one you've lied to? And here I thought I was special."

"I didn't tell him the truth because a few weeks ago he ordered us to let it go." Ordered *him* to let it go.

"Fuck orders." She tried turning around, but he didn't give her enough room to pull it off, not when he could still feel the fury rolling off her. "No. There's no way. Her team wouldn't just cut her loose like that, wouldn't let someone get away with what they did to her."

"So you're the only one allowed to run, to pretend it's out of your hands?"

"I didn't have a lot of choice." Her voice dropped, and for the first time she sounded like she was second-guessing herself.

"I'm giving you one, Max." He loosened his hold.

She turned around, her gaze cutting into him. "And how do I know that this time you're telling me the truth?"

"You don't." He knew there wasn't anything else to say. If he'd been through what she had, he wouldn't want to put his faith in anyone but himself either.

"Where were you?"

He frowned, confused by the question. "When?"

"The night Cara died. You say you're her partner, so where were you that night? Where were you when they grabbed her, when they roughed her up, trying to figure out who she worked for?" She shoved him back, and he let her. "Where the hell were you when they chained her up and took a knife to her?"

Every word drilled into his chest. They were questions he'd hammered himself with over and over again, but coming from Max reminded him of how it felt the night he'd realized what happened to Cara.

Eyes bright with unshed tears, Max gave him another shove, but he held his ground this time. "Partners back each other up, Lucas. Or Mac or whatever the hell your name is. Why weren't you there backing her up? Why..." She dragged in a sharp breath and tried to get past him, but he pulled her close, keeping her between him and the wall.

Struggling not to cry, she pushed at his chest. "You should have been there. Someone should have been there. Someone—"

"I fucked up, Max." Emotion swelled in his throat. "She shouldn't have been on her own. I should have been with her. I wanted to be there and if I could have found a way to take her place I would have." He clenched his jaw until it ached, but the pain didn't come close to the guilt and hurt that had been swallowing him piece by piece for months.

One tear ran down her cheek and he watched it slide down to her chin.

"Those nightmares you have are my fault," he finally managed. "Cara said that you could help, that your suspension was a load of crap, that you were a good cop. I told her we should wait a little longer. I didn't think we needed you and she disagreed. Said it wasn't my call to make."

"She always had a mind of her own," Max murmured, her palms softening against his chest.

"We were at Blackwater's party that night, posing as potential buyers, hoping to identify some players for a big deal that was going down. The evening was pretty much a bust so we split up and were out of communication for a bit. Next thing I hear, she found something you needed to see. She planned to meet with you and bring you back to our hotel for a full briefing."

They both knew what came after that.

The last of the fight went out of Max and she leaned into him, her head tucked under his chin.

"I should have stayed with her, should have insisted she wait for me, but we trusted each other's gut, you know?" He closed his eyes, "I should have been there. If I had maybe—" He tightened his arms around her, holding on even though he was certain he was the last person she wanted to be near.

"Maybe you'd be dead too," she whispered, tipping her face back to look at him.

Shiny blue eyes met his. He could tell she wasn't ready to trust him, but the earlier accusation was gone, replaced by an understanding of the shared grief both of them were still working through.

"It wasn't our fault," she said a few minutes later.

"Which one of us are you trying to convince?"

She gave him a sad smile. "Both, I think."

"You need to come with me, Max." He wiped away the evidence of her tears. "I won't let anything happen to you."

He wished he hadn't said a damn word the second she pulled away from him.

"I need some time to think." She headed back toward the bedroom, and he stayed where he was, wanting to give her some space and needing some of his own.

When he felt her hesitating in the doorway, he glanced in her direction.

"You want me to trust you, Lucas, but you're not exactly

reciprocating. You're worried I'll run and you plan to stay on the couch for what's left of the night so there's less chance I'll slip by you."

No chance, he thought, but wisely kept that to himself. "Night, Max."

Max was awake long before she heard Lucas get up and walk around the main room. He cursed under his breath, and she assumed he'd noticed her clothes were gone from the chair by the woodstove.

She gave him another few seconds and met him in the doorway, knowing he'd come to make sure she was still there.

"You snore, you know."

Relief crossed his features first, then annoyance. "No, I don't."

She shrugged and walked past him, determined to regain all the ground she'd slowly been losing in the last three months. From the pantry, she grabbed one of the prepackaged puddings, then found a spoon to go along with it.

Every move she made, she felt Lucas watching her intently. She wasn't any more certain of her next move than before having sex with Lucas had blindsided her, but she knew she couldn't do it alone.

Glen would be there for her in a heartbeat and so would her family, but they'd already suffered enough. Just by knowing her, defending her, their own hard-earned reputations were dragged through the mud, and knowing that hurt more than anything anyone said about her.

Whether she liked it or not, she needed Lucas. At least to help her get to New York. She believed that he was Cara's partner and that he did want justice, but she also knew there was more to it than that.

"Why did your boss order you to stop digging into Cara's

145

murder?"

"Until the night she died, Blackwater wasn't as important as the primary objective."

She took a bite of the pudding. "Which was?"

Lucas scrubbed a hand over his face. "We were looking for a biological weapon stolen from a Czech scientist a few months ago. Blackwater was brokering the deal, but no one knew when or where."

"So that's why you and Cara got yourself invited to Blackwater's party. You were hoping to get added to the shortlist."

"It was a long shot from the start, but Eli, another one of our team, called in a few favors from some shady people that lent a lot of credibility to our cover."

Max finished off the pudding and grabbed the bottle of water she'd left in the fridge last night. Her fingers closed around it and immediately her thoughts turned to what had happened between her and Lucas. Even though everything had changed afterward, her face grew warm as she tipped the bottle back to take a drink.

She chanced a glance at Lucas and was relieved that nothing on his face hinted at knowing what she was thinking about.

He ventured closer, choosing the same spot as last night to lean up against the counter. Okay, so maybe he did know what she was thinking.

Shaking off the memories best forgotten, she crossed her arms. "I still don't know how you think I can help."

His expression grew solemn. "I need you to walk me through everything you can remember about Blackwater and the people in the warehouse that night. We've got photographs and intel at headquarters that might help you identify someone besides Blackwater. Maybe then we can figure the rest out."

"Okay," she said slowly.

He nodded, his lips curving in a grateful smile that made it all too easy to remember how she'd ended up naked and on the table last night. Positive her cheeks were flushed, she fiddled with stuff on the counter while he got dressed.

She was the first one out the cottage door after they grabbed some food and locked up. It was easier to breathe outside and there was no way for Lucas to box her in. He hadn't said a word about them getting naked, but the long, loaded looks he aimed in her direction whenever he thought she wasn't paying attention said it all.

It would have been just fine if she didn't feel that tug low in her belly every time she noticed him watching her. Letting things go so far between them when she hadn't known the entire truth was bad enough. Giving in a second time would be disastrous. Almost as disastrous as sleeping with a senior detective in the middle of a huge case and watching him take all the credit for the bust.

Thinking of Wade and the crap he'd undoubtedly been saying about her since her suspension hardened her resolve to clear her name and prove to him and everyone else she was a good cop.

Dark, heavy clouds hung low in the sky, promising more rain in the not so distant future.

Max fiddled with her hoodie and fell into step beside Lucas as they followed the leaf-covered driveway up to a winding dirt road. "So what's the plan?"

"Lover?"

Confused, she frowned.

"The last time you asked me that, you called me lover." His shot her a teasing grin, and she caught herself wanting to grin back at him.

"I was just playing along."

"And last night? Were you still just playing along?" He was still smiling, but his tone hinted at something deeper.

Something that made her heart pick up speed even when

she knew she couldn't let anything like that happen again. Aside from the fact that trust was an issue for them, the sex had thrown her into a dizzying backspin and changed things between them. There just wasn't in any point in figuring out what that meant when she planned on parting ways with him at the earliest opportunity.

Maybe Lucas knew what he was getting into with going after Blackwater, but her own determination to see the dealer brought down had already come at a high price. Whether or not Lucas had lied to her, she didn't want him to end up dead too.

Her stomach wrenched painfully at the thought.

"Max?"

The concern in his voice only made it that much harder to pretend last night hadn't meant anything to her. "Oh, does your ego need a little boost this morning?"

"Not quite." He continued to stare at her, his gaze probing a little too deep.

"What?"

"Last night," he began, but she sidestepped to cut him off.

"There's really nothing to say. We both got carried away last night, and it's not all that surprising considering how much adrenaline was drop-loaded into our bloodstream in a twenty-four hour period."

His lips twitched. "So the sex was about adrenaline?"

Apparently it only sounded like a reasonable explanation in her head. "I don't think we really need to fixate on it. We're both adults and we had sex. End of story."

Lucas didn't press the subject, surprising her, and they feel into an awkward silence that only grew more uncomfortable as they traveled along. After nearly an hour they reached a paved road, but with little traffic they could flag down for a ride.

Finally a red pickup truck stopped, and the driver offered them a ride to the closest gas station after Lucas lied about their car breaking down. Unfortunately, the closest gas station ended up being nearly a half-hour drive, during which she was pressed up against Lucas from shoulder to knee.

But that wasn't the worst part. Lucas had stuck with their original story of being a vacationing couple and held her hand whenever he got the chance, his grip solid and warm. Only when the lazy rub of his thumb across the top of her hand left her insides all tangled up, did she finally tug her hand free.

Thinking about her plan to eventually slip away from Lucas was the only way she could distract herself from how good he felt next to her. As it was, by the time they were dropped in front of a small brick structure with two gas pumps out front and hopefully a pay phone inside, Max was about to melt right out of her skin.

Inside the store they found a guy in his mid-forties behind the counter, reading the paper.

"Morning," he called out as they walked inside. "Another dreary day, but better rain than snow I say."

Still a little chilled from the walk, Max shivered hearing the word snow.

"Do you have a pay phone?" Lucas asked, taking a look around.

"Sure. Down the small hall at the back, opposite the washrooms."

"Great." Lucas took a step, paused.

She waited for him to say something about going with him, or at least give her a look warning her to stay put, but he headed for the phone without a backward glance.

Deciding it was better to hear his side of the conversation than none at all, she trailed behind him. A thickly frosted cinnamon roll sat with some other baked goods on the end of the counter, and she eyeballed it as they passed.

She leaned up against the wall, watching Lucas dig out his wallet from his side pocket and use a credit card to place the long distance call. At least one of them had money, which meant that cinnamon roll was hers when he finished the call.

Lucas looked a little relieved at whoever answered the phone, but his expression quickly changed and he paused, listening.

He cursed under his breath. "We don't need to wait—" He snapped his jaw shut, listening again. "That's not necessary. Max is working with us on this."

Whatever the voice on the other end of the phone said, Lucas didn't appear happy to hear it.

"Don't tell Caleb, Joe. Not yet." Lucas glanced at his watch. "Eli can't get here before then? I can try renting a car—" He flashed Max a quick look. "Fine. We'll find a place to lay low and call you back with the location."

All traces of his earlier laid-back mood had vanished by the time he hung up. Max turned and headed back to the counter, grabbing two cinnamon rolls, along with something to drink on the way.

"Just passing through?" The man behind the counter asked.

Lucas wandered over to the far aisle, browsing the shelves and leaving Max to answer. "We're from Ontario actually. Just visiting some family in the area."

The owner began bagging the items. "My son lives in Toronto. Just landed himself a new promotion and bought a house in the suburbs. He and his wife are expecting a baby and are about to make me a grandpa."

"Congratulations." Lucas dropped a couple of T-shirts on the counter with a logo Max only got a peek at before they were added to the bag on the counter. "Is Miss Maddy's Bed and Breakfast far from here?"

"About twenty kilometers or so. You stick to the main road for about ten to twelve kilometers and then take a left. It's a big old farmhouse, you can't miss it. Maddy has done the place over really nice."

"Great." Lucas handed over his credit card.

Max noticed him staring at the newspaper on the counter

and she followed his gaze to the headlining article about the incident in Riverbend and whether or not it was connected to yesterday's car chase involving two suspects.

Max tensed, but kept her smile in place, shooting a quick glance at Lucas.

He looked thoughtful for a second, then gave her slow, sexy grin. "A little alone time and a break from your family is just what we need."

"They're not that bad," she managed for the owner's benefit, trying not to stare at Lucas's mouth.

He glanced at the owner. "It's like visiting with The Addams Family, but I'd do just about anything to make her happy."

If she thought the sincerity in his voice was too much to process, Lucas looping an arm around her waist and pulling her close was probably enough to knock her brain offline.

He ducked his head, his mouth drifting lazily across hers. The kiss was over before it really got started, but the tease of his lips, soft and slow, lingered long after he'd turned back to the counter to collect their bag.

"I'll give Maddy a call and let her know to keep an eye out for you two."

Max trailed Lucas out of the store, looking forward to the twenty kilometer walk as much as she was to pretending that kiss hadn't made her crave a longer, deeper one.

"I take it we have to wait at this bed and breakfast for your team?"

He nodded. "Yeah. Seeing as we made the front page of the local paper, probably better if we're not hitching our way into town to rent a car."

"So I take it hot-wiring cars is not one of your strengths."

He pulled one of the cinnamon rolls out of the bag and took a bite. "One stolen car per assignment is my limit."

She took the second roll he held out.

"And twenty kilometers isn't that far," he added.

Glancing down at her non-hiking boots, she failed to work up much enthusiasm. "Maybe for some people."

"At least it's not raining."

She punched his arm. "Are you trying to jinx us?" The words had no sooner left her mouth than the air thickened into a wet mist followed by a drizzle, and she shot him a dirty look.

Three and a half hours later they reached the bed and breakfast, both of them soaked to the bone. A woman in her late sixties—by Lucas's guess—with hair dyed a bright fire-engine red and sharp, intelligent eyes waited for them on the huge porch that ran the length of the farm house.

Haunted came to mind as he surveyed their temporary safe house even though there wasn't any peeling paint or broken windows. Still, the place gave off an eerie vibe that sent a shiver zipping up down his spine. Clearly all the updating had taken place on the inside.

He and Max exchanged speculative glances as they walked up the steps that creaked under their weight.

The woman smiled in welcome, but there was an edge to it that hinted at a steel backbone beneath the simple white apron and heavily applied make-up.

"Welcome. I'm Miss Maddy, the proprietor. Let's get you inside and out of this horrible weather." She paused. "No bags?"

"This was an unscheduled stop actually. We're taking a time-out from some overbearing family members we're visiting."

"The Addams Family, right." She grinned, apparently having heard all the details from the gas station owner. She squeezed herself between them. "I haven't had any guests in a few weeks. The last couple who stayed with me had an unfortunate accident. I tried to warn them... Oh, but I should stop myself before I really start to ramble. You two need to get settled."

Unfortunate accident?

Brow arched, Max met his gaze.

"I'm sure you'll both just love it here," Miss Maddy continued. "This used to be my great, great-grandmother's home. She was a fisherman's wife, spent a lot of her time alone with her fourteen children and such. My grandmother inherited the place and then my mother. When it passed to me, my Earl suggested I turn the place into a B&B. Earl always had good ideas like that, a thinker he was."

Max smiled at Miss Maddy, the innocent curving of her lips certainly not meant to entice him, but damn if he wasn't thinking good and hard about her lush mouth. She'd finished off her cinnamon roll a while ago, but he'd bet he could still taste the sweetness on her lips.

His body tensed, revisiting the memory of how her body had strained beneath his last night, and his thoughts quickly turned to getting rid of their hostess, backing Max into a corner and peeling the wet clothes off her piece by piece.

"Perhaps, I'll just save the tour for later and get you two...ah...settled."

"Do any of your rooms have twin beds?" Max asked.

Miss Maddy frowned and Max hurried to add, "He snores."

"I don't—" Lucas began.

"Want to keep me up. I know." Max smiled sweetly. She turned to Miss Maddy after warning him with a subtle jab of her elbow.

He decided to keep quiet in case she started talking about erectile dysfunction again. Once was plenty.

Miss Maddy slipped behind the desk in the foyer. The inside had definitely been redecorated, the warm earth tones and solid wood furniture off set by cheery colors that made him feel at home.

"I don't have twin beds, but I could offer you adjoining rooms if you prefer."

"One will be fine," Lucas insisted, handing over his credit card before Max said another word.

"Oh, the room at the very top has a pull-out sofa bed."

Max smiled. "Perfect."

Seeming pleased that she'd satisfied her guests, Miss Maddy finished registering them and selected a key from the cupboard behind her, then waved for them to follow her upstairs.

Lucas gestured for Max to precede him. He regretted the thoughtless decision the moment he had Max's sweet ass swaying in front of him, right at eye-level. Christ, she was killing him and she probably didn't even know it.

She'd blown him off this morning, and at the time he thought it was the right call. Maybe it still was.

Joe hadn't wanted to hear anything about Max willingly working with them, and after his solo mission, he didn't need to give his boss another reason to rake his ass over the coals. Getting further involved with Max would put him on Joe's shit list. Might even earn him Eli's top spot.

Except that near kiss in the gas station—and if her tongue wasn't in his mouth, it wasn't an actual kiss to his way of thinking—felt different somehow. He didn't want to go deeper than that, and Max's ass really wasn't helping him to forget the whole damn thing.

Ahead of them, Miss Maddy opened the door at the end of the hall. "This is Passion's Penthouse."

Lucas stopped in the doorway, resisting the urge to shield his eyes at the overpowering shades of pink. Pink walls, pink carpet, pink ruffles on the pillows, even the furniture, which he guessed was a nice wood of some kind, had been painted pink.

He swore his testosterone levels dropped just taking one step over the threshold.

Max glanced at him then averted her face, but not before he saw her grin.

"This is actually my favorite room in the house," Miss Maddy added. "A lot of memories." She glanced longingly at the bed, and Lucas prayed she wasn't about to share any of *those* memories.

"Well, I'll leave you two to unwind. Dinner is at six o'clock, but I'll bring you up a snack shortly. And there are nice fluffy robes in the closet so you can put your wet clothes in the basket right outside the door. I'll see that they're cleaned and brought back later this afternoon."

"We don't want to put you through too much trouble—"

"I insist," Miss Maddy cut in, her words laced with just enough sugary bite to make him rethink disagreeing.

"You two enjoy." Miss Maddy smiled and left, closing the door behind her.

Relieved to be alone, Lucas removed his soaked shoes and socks. He glanced at the bed, but opted for the pink rocking chair since he was still wet. The phone on top of the roll-top desk in the corner caught his eye.

Max checked out the bathroom. "There's a claw-foot tub in here."

"Let me guess. It's also pink."

"But pink is your color," she teased, reminding him of the pink sweater that hadn't survived their little adventure.

Needing to call Joe back and preferring to talk without Max overhearing anything that might make her skittish, he padded into the bathroom and turned on the tub faucet.

Max leaned in the doorway behind him, arms crossed. "Calgon calling?"

He snorted. "It's for you." He took a step toward her, letting his gaze slide the full length of her body. "Although that tub is plenty big enough for two."

She cocked her head, looking like she was thinking it over just long enough to make his whole body clench. "I think I'll pass."

He stopped in the doorway, fully aware he was crowding her. "As long as you're sure."

Her attention slipped to his mouth. "I am."

"Okay then," he murmured against her ear as he passed. "You know where to find me if you change your mind."

She closed the door without a backward glance.

Damn.

With Max secure in the bathroom, he grabbed the phone and moved as far across the room as it would reach before dialing headquarters. Not surprisingly, Joe answered, but before Lucas got more than a few words out, the bathroom door opened wide enough for Max to toss her clothes out.

"Would you put those in the basket for me?"

He glanced down, noticed the silky purple panties peeking out from under her shirt. He swallowed just to make sure his tongue hasn't gotten stuck anywhere after the sudden image of Max sitting on the edge of the tub, sliding her panties down her legs ran through his head.

"Lucas?"

"Sure, no problem," he finally answered, and Max shut the door once more.

"Lucas?" This time it was Joe saying his name.

"Hang on a sec." He lowered his voice, picking up the clothes without giving the underwear another thought— mostly—and tossed them in the basket outside the door.

"What took you so long to check in?"

"We're in the middle of nowhere with no vehicle and trying not to draw any more attention to ourselves that necessary."

"Just keep it that way. Eli ran into a little problem, but should be there by tonight."

He glanced at the door, wondering how he was going to keep Max from rethinking her decision to help him in the meantime, and he'd seen that brief fight-or-flight glimmer in her eyes this morning, right around the time she hadn't wanted to talk about the flat-out incredible sex they'd shared.

She hadn't entirely abandoned the idea of ditching him just yet. He just wished he knew whether their sleeping together was working for or against the odds of that happening.

And thinking about sex when Max was on the other side of the door, probably slipping into the tub, her skin wet and warm from the water...

"What's going on with you, Luc?"

The question succeeded in making Lucas turn away from the door. He pressed the heel of his hand to his right eye where he could feel a headache building.

"I'm good. It's just been a crazy couple of days."

"And the target is cooperating?"

Hearing her called a target bothered him for some reason. "*Max* is fine." He wasn't sure he could say the same about himself. He glanced again at the door then, hearing Joe sigh, became annoyed with his own lack of focus. "I've got it covered."

"I know you've had your doubts about the extent of Walker's involvement—"

"She didn't kill Cara, Joe." He was confident of that much. "And she was there that night. She might be able to identify someone who can lead us to the weapon. She mentioned a Russian being there at the time of the deal but thinks he was killed. If we can figure out who he was working for, we might have something to work with."

"I'm sure any cooperation on her part will work in her favor with the DA."

Lucas struggled to keep the anger out of his voice. "We can't turn her over to the NYPD, Joe. Blackwater will get to her."

"Our priority is the weapon, Lucas. Not protecting a dirty cop."

"She has nothing to do with his dealings."

Joe sighed again. "Then how come the guy she was engaged

157

to marry, a fellow cop, thinks she's guilty? He's gone on record as stating that's the reason he broke it off."

He shook his head, unable to remember having read that in the brief notes he had on Detective Wade Cummings. "When was this?"

Joe ignored the question. "I know you took Cara's death hard, Lucas, but if you can't follow orders then I need to know that right now. Eli is on his way and you two will escort Walker here to see if she has any useful information, and then she'll be turned over to the proper authorities. Is any of that going to be a problem?"

He clenched his jaw. "No."

"Good. What's your location?"

Lucas returned to the desk where he found a piece of custom stationary—also pink, go figure—and rattled off the address so Eli would be able to find the place.

When he hung up, he sank onto the edge of the bed, not caring that he was still wet. By following orders Max would be transferred into police custody and he couldn't shake the feeling he needed her to nail Blackwater and find the weapon. Needed more than her just identifying a dead Russian.

Didn't he? Or was he letting what happened between them—sex that Max had insisted wasn't worth talking about—cloud his judgment even further?

The bathroom door opened a short while later and Max breezed out, her body wrapped in a towel. She snagged one of the robes from the closet and slipped back into the bathroom long enough to change.

"You didn't take very long."

"It was hard to enjoy a good soak when I knew you were out here still wet and probably not very comfortable."

She padded past him without meeting his eyes. An unsettling vibe ticked in his chest. Had she somehow overheard him?

Max collapsed on the bed, massaging her feet and ankles. He noticed she wore the same dark polish on her toes, which had somehow escaped his attention yesterday.

Grinning, she snatched up the remote control. "I think I even saved you some hot water."

Lucas stood there another minute, searching her face for some hint she'd been listening at the door.

She sprawled on her stomach, her knees bent and ankles linked in the air. If she had overhead anything, she didn't seem too concerned. An act? Or had his brief conversation with Joe just reminded him that he couldn't let his personal feelings get in the way of doing his job? Personal feelings that made him want to keep her close, to trust her completely.

Stripping out of his shirt, he headed into the bathroom. The mirror over the sink was still clouded with steam and the smell of some fruity soap lingered on the air. He turned the shower on full, peeled off the rest of his wet clothing and climbed in.

Hot water sluiced down his back, slowly warming him.

A knock at the door had him pulling back the curtain, and he watched Max grab his wet clothes.

"Thanks."

"No problem," she echoed, her gaze drifting down over his shoulders to his chest. "Uh, how are your ribs?"

"Fine." If he didn't count the lingering soreness from their little trek to Miss Maddy's B&B.

"Good." She lingered another minute, then slipped out, leaving him with the impression she'd wanted to say something.

Alone, he closed his eyes and stepped back under the water, but instead of turning the water as hot as he could stand, he turned the dial in the opposite direction. Once he was satisfied he wasn't going to emerge from the bathroom with a raging hard-on, he looked for the soap, but the tray was empty.

Pulling back the shower curtain, he scanned the

countertop, but didn't see the soap.

"Max?"

No response. She probably couldn't hear him with the television on. He stepped out of the shower and snagged the extra towel from the shelf over the toilet, wrapping it around his waist.

"Hey, Max, what did you do with the soap?"

No response.

He opened the door wider and stepped into the room. "Max?"

Fuck.

She was gone. Again.

Chapter Ten

"It's good to hear your voice, Max."

Leaning against the wall opposite Miss Maddy's registration desk in the foyer, Max smiled at the sound of Glen's voice. "You too. How is everything? Your suspension was lifted I take it?" When her partner hadn't answered his home number, she took a chance and called in to the precinct.

Not until she heard his voice did she feel relieved that she'd talked herself into calling him. If she stood a chance of repairing the damage Blackwater had done, she would need a little help, someone with access to information she didn't have. As long as she was careful and didn't tell Glen any more than she absolutely had to, it would keep him off Blackwater's radar.

"If that's what you call sitting on my ass behind a desk, but at least I'm back to work," he paused. "Shit, I'm sorry, Max. I can be an insensitive asshole some days. You okay? I'd ask where you are..."

"But I probably wouldn't tell you," she finished for him. "I don't want you to have to lie for me, especially not now." Her chest felt tight even though she was happy that he could focus on work. He deserved that much after losing Jillian. "How are you?"

"I'm sleeping and still remembering to eat, if that's what you mean." He kept his tone light, but underneath she heard the slight catch to his voice.

They'd been partnered together three years ago, right after

Wade had earned his shiny new promotion and decided he didn't want to get married after all, but most days it felt like they'd been working together longer. Glen seemed to know what she was thinking and often tried to talk her out of whatever risky idea she was entertaining.

He'd wanted her to hide out at his family's cabin upstate, and she'd thought about it until she realized it was the last thing he needed. Having a partner wanted for murder was enough for him to deal with. He didn't need to get caught helping her.

"You sound tired."

She smiled at how well he knew her. "Exhausted actually, but I'm alive and that counts for something, right?"

"What happened?" Glen demanded.

"Too much to get into right now. I'm headed back to New York." She waited to feel that initial panic that always snuck up on her whenever she started to think about going home, but this time it passed quickly, reaffirming that her decision was the right one.

"Are you sure it's safe enough? You're not thinking of turning yourself in, are you? You know the evidence is stacked against you. They even have your prints on the murder weapon, Max."

Blackwater had certainly pulled out all the stops to guarantee she went down for Cara's death, hadn't he? "I can't sit and wait for someone else to clear my name."

"I just don't want you taking unnecessary risks."

Max glanced up at the ceiling thinking of Lucas. Nope, no unnecessary risks for her.

"I've tried digging into the witnesses' backgrounds, trying to figure out what Blackwater could be holding over their heads, but haven't turned up much so far. I'm not giving up, though."

"What about Burton? Anything new there?" She'd met Captain Ralph Burton nearly eight years ago through her oldest brother, and spent the last six working under him.

Burton had always been fair and alternated between bouts of offering wisdom and encouragement and being a general pain in her ass. All of which made it harder to face the possibility he could be in Blackwater's pocket and had played a role in their suspension.

Glen sighed. "No. He's been quiet for a while. No late meetings or out of the ordinary calls or disappearances. I—" He broke off and she heard him talking to someone in the background.

Her stomach prickled and a moment later she asked, "Was that Wade?"

"In all his dickhead glory. Guess I got lucky today since he usually never has anything to say to me." Glen sighed. "He's putting off a weird vibe so maybe we should keep this short. When will you be back?"

"In a few days but I don't want you getting too heavily involved." If anything else happened to him because of her... Maybe it had been a mistake to call him after all.

"Don't shut me out, Max. Not now."

Max closed her eyes, recalling the way Glen had fought back the tears as they lowered Jillian's body into the ground. "I don't want you getting hurt."

"I want to nail that bastard as much as you do," Glen snapped.

Maybe more than she did, but that only gave her one more reason to keep him out of it. "I know. I'm working with someone—"

"You know I'll always have your back, Max."

"I know."

He said something to someone else in the background, then lowered his voice. "Can you trust whoever it is?"

Wasn't that the million-dollar question? "Yeah, I can." She hoped she sounded more confident than she felt.

A door slammed overhead followed by running feet

pounding the floor.

Max rolled her eyes. "I should go. I'll call you when I'm back."

"Stay safe, Max."

"I will." She missed the sound of Glen's familiar voice the second the line went dead.

Max replaced the cordless handset just as Lucas barreled down the stairs. He'd wrapped a towel around his waist and water still glistened on his chest. Her stomach tightened at the picture he made standing there, arms crossed, looking too damn hot for his own good.

"Something wrong?" Max met him at the bottom of the stairs.

He paused, shrugged one shoulder casually. "I was just wondering what you did with the soap."

She arched a brow. "The soap?"

"Yeah, I couldn't find it..." he trailed off, glancing away.

"You ran down here like your ass was on fire for soap?" She folded her bottom lip between her thumb and forefinger to hide a smile.

He relaxed against the wall opposite her. "I figured I might run out of hot water waiting for you to come back up. It's an old farmhouse, right?"

"Right," she readily agreed, earning a speculative look from Lucas. "Old farmhouse." She started up the stairs ahead of him, glancing back over her shoulder. "And the soap was in a dispenser right by the faucet."

"Oh."

She continued up the steps, half wishing she'd ducked into a closet just to see how far he would have gone in the towel. "And just so you know, if I had planned on taking off, I wouldn't do it wearing just a robe."

Upstairs, Lucas released a long sigh and eyed the bed thoughtfully.

No freakin' way. "Hey, you get the hide-a-bed, remember?"

His lips curved arrogantly. "You were the one who wanted separate beds. The way I see it, you should get the hide-a-bed."

"Arm wrestle you for it."

He laughed, then realizing she meant it, straightened up. "Arm wrestle. Seriously?"

She fought a grin. "Worried you can't take me?"

His lips twitched, and he laughed harder. She crossed to the sofa table, removed the pink African violet in the center and dragged it to the middle of the room.

Setting her elbow on the polished pink surface, Max flexed her hand then crooked her finger at him. "Unless you're too scared."

Lucas immediately sobered. "You're really serious."

"Come on, tough guy, I don't have all day. Show me what you got."

Grinning like he had it in the bag, Lucas approached the table. He leaned down and fit his palm tightly against hers. He didn't seem to notice when she curled her wrist the tiniest bit forward to give her an edge.

An edge quickly sacrificed when he lightly rubbed his fingers over the back of her hand. A hot, feathery sensation rippled under her skin.

Okay, so maybe this hadn't been her best idea.

"Winner gets the bed, agreed?"

Max nodded. "On three. One, two—"

"Just one more thing," he interrupted.

"Quit stalling."

Lucas leaned closer, amused eyes locking on hers. "I just wanted you to know that I'm going to enjoy every inch of that king-size mattress."

"Three." Max leaned forward, getting her upper arm and shoulder lined up above her elbow as much as possible. The move would draw his arm a little closer to her, giving her the advantage.

For endless seconds their tightly clasped hands hovered over the center of the table. His eyes widened as though he hadn't expected that much resistance from her. She concentrated on pushing into his hand, forcing him to widen his fingers.

Surprising him was more important than getting his arm down, and the second he got cocky again, Max reached her free hand under the table and ripped his towel off.

He instinctively released her hand, groping for the falling material.

Waving the towel like a victory flag, she grinned. "I win."

Lucas spun around, treating her to a fantastic view of his ass, and seized a pillow off the bed. He fired it right at her head.

A little distracted by how aroused he was, she was too slow to block the fuchsia-colored missile. The pillow caught her square between the eyes.

"You cheated."

Max threw the pillow back. "You forfeited, so I win. And just so you know, I'm going to enjoy every inch of that king-size mattress."

"Over my dead body," Lucas growled.

Dead wasn't the word that came to mind when she ran her gaze over his body, lingering on his smooth chest and sliding much lower.

"Max." The rough edge to his voice gave her half a second to brace herself.

He threw a second pillow, and then lunged for her.

Laughing, she darted around the sofa table, determined to make it to the bathroom. She would have made it too, except the stupid robe she wore snagged on the corner of the table.

Lucas caught her around the waist and tossed her onto the bed. She scrambled to get up, but he quickly trapped her beneath him, pinning her arms overhead.

"I said, you cheated."

"So?" She tried to wiggle out from under him.

He shifted, applying more weight to keep her still, and his arousal nudged her inner thigh through her robe. His gaze snapped to hers, and he moved again, inching higher to rub against the center of her.

Fiery threads coiled tight low in her belly. "Not fair." She absently tugged at his grip on her wrists, feeling herself sink a little deeper into the mattress.

"You weren't worried about that a few minutes ago." He didn't look away from her as he bent his head and slid his mouth over hers.

Fireworks exploded in her stomach, sailing outward until her whole body was in a slow burn. Need, pure and unrestrained flared through her. She parted her lips, inviting him to deepen the kiss.

He caught her lower lip between his teeth and slowly pulled it into his mouth. Between one long drugging kiss and the next, he released her hands and traced her jaw with his thumb.

Moaning, she dragged her hands up his back, holding him close as his tender caress pushed her heart into a full-out, knock-down pace that would have taken her to the floor if she wasn't already on her back.

So much for keeping her distance and pretending last night had been a one-time thing. What had even possessed her to believe she could put the whole thing out of her head when every nerve ending begged for his touch?

His tongue swept across hers possessively, and the slight tremble that slid up her backbone turned into a full-body shiver when his hand moved beneath her robe and found her breast.

Max arched against him, deciding she didn't care why he could make her feel so damn good. She just didn't want him to stop.

With a teasing bite, he left her mouth to trace a sensuous path down her throat. He laved at the soft hollow, sucking at her skin in deep, hungry pulls. She breathed deep, hoping a little more oxygen would make it easier to believe he wasn't taking a piece of her inside himself with every taste.

His thumb brushed her nipple and her back bowed off the bed. He groaned and slid his body against hers, settling hard and heavy against her sex. Once more his mouth returned to hers, and the deep stroke of his tongue heated her insides with a delicious, meltdown intensity.

"I thought we weren't going to do this again," she murmured.

"*You* thought we weren't going to do this." He pushed her robe apart and bent to slowly suck her nipple into his mouth. "I can't keep my hands off you long enough to *not* do this."

"I drive you crazy wanting me, do I?"

Lucas lifted his head and the fire in his eyes softened. "You have no idea."

Afraid to read too much into that, she dragged her palm along his rough jaw. He turned his face into her hand and pressed an open-mouthed kiss to its center. The slow, wet heat was both carnal and inexplicably tender, and whatever Lucas saw on her face made him glance away.

"Max," he began, his tone cryptic.

A knock sounded at the door, followed by Miss Maddy's voice. "I brought you two a little snack."

Lucas rolled away from her and sat up.

Choosing to believe she hadn't somehow revealed just how much his touch undid her on every single level, she sat up and tugged her robe closed. She stared at his back for another beat, wondering what he'd been about to say, then tried for a smile.

"I think I'll get the door so you don't give the poor woman a heart attack." She reached down and handed him the towel, then stood just as another brisk knock came.

"Coming," Max called out, unable to stop herself from watching Lucas drape the towel around his waist and disappear into the bathroom.

Running her hands over her face and hoping she didn't look as warm as she felt, she opened the door. Miss Maddy stepped inside carrying a tray weighed down with two thick wedges of chocolate cake covered in inch-thick frosting and two tall glasses of milk.

She shuffled past Max and set the tray on the sofa table without commenting on the room's new arrangement. "Settling in?"

"We are, thank you." Her attention strayed to the cake, and her stomach rumbled at the thought of devouring her piece in one bite.

"It's an old secret family recipe," she confided.

"I'm sure they're delicious." Wondering if the milk was cold enough to bring her internal temperature down, Max picked up the closest glass and took a long drink.

Miss Maddy arranged the napkins and forks on the table. "Chocolate is an aphrodisiac, you know."

Max choked on her milk, which quickly turned into a coughing fit when she couldn't catch her breath.

Lucas poked his head in the room. "Max?"

"Oh, she's fine," Miss Maddy answered, slapping Max's back like she had a chicken bone lodged in her throat.

Still draped in just the towel, Lucas ventured farther into the room.

"I'm—fine, really," Max managed between coughs, inching away from Miss Maddy's cast-iron fists. "Really, I'm good now."

The old woman dusted her hands together and winked at Max. "Don't forget what I said now." The door shut firmly behind her.

Lucas arched a brow. "What was that all about?"

"She brought cake." Bad enough she couldn't seem to get sex off her mind to begin with, she didn't need to share Miss Maddy's wisdom with the man at the center of every sinful thought running wild in her head.

"I'm starving." Instead of grabbing up his own piece he leaned forward and stole the bite off the end of her fork.

"Hey."

His mischievous smile tugged at her heart, and she picked up her plate, ordering herself to focus on the dessert and not the six-foot-plus male standing inches away.

She took a bite, giving a little sigh of pleasure as her taste buds drowned in the rich chocolate flavor. She broke off another piece with her fork and all but inhaled it.

"What?" She paused as she finished off the last bite.

"Hold still a sec." He ran his thumb across her bottom lip, sliding it back and forth. "You had some frosting there."

The last bite of cake seemed to stick in her throat. "Thanks."

His hand dropped back to his side and he pivoted around. "I'm going to finish my shower. Try not to eat all the cake."

"I was raised not to make promises I can't keep."

He laughed and closed the bathroom door, leaving her with the cake, something that wouldn't come close to satisfying her real appetite.

Max was asleep on her side by the time he finished his shower and emerged from the bathroom. Her face was relaxed, peaceful. He leaned in the doorway, watching her for awhile. Every now and then a ghost of a smile would curve her lips.

Was she dreaming about him, about the same insanely wild and hot things he was driving himself crazy thinking about? Things like her body curled around him, on top of him, her spine arching as she took him deep inside her. Or all that silky hair teasing the inside of his thigh as she went down on him.

Yeah, that one in particular was burning a hole right through the back of his head and making him contemplate another cold shower.

Christ. She wasn't even his type. He preferred to date easygoing women who had their lives figured out, who had steady, predictable non-life-threatening jobs. Predictable worked for him. Predictable with no strings and zero complications worked the best.

There wasn't a predictable bone in Maxine Walker's body. If she felt the least bit threatened, she'd run and do her best to ditch him in the process. Which meant he had no business screwing around with her and giving her another reason to bolt. Except they weren't just screwing around, were they?

He hadn't paid the least bit of attention to his predictable, no strings, zero complications policy where Max was concerned, and the worst part was he couldn't drum up even a little bit of regret.

Sitting on the edge of the bed, he brushed aside the strand of black hair on her cheek. She was so much more beautiful than he'd first realized, more...everything. Predictable was suddenly looking boring and unsatisfying next to the woman lying next to him.

Reluctant to awaken her, Lucas carefully stretched out beside her. She murmured something, then rolled against him. He breathed deeply, inhaling the combination of fruity soap and Max's own natural scent. Draping one arm across her waist, he drew her closer, relaxing more than he had in days.

As his eyes drifted shut he couldn't recall the last time simply holding a woman while she slept had felt so right.

Darkness greeted Lucas when he opened his eyes awhile later. The clock on the bedside table read five fifty p.m.

He turned on the light, and nudged Max's shoulder. "Time to wake up."

She groaned, but she didn't open her eyes.

"Max, it's time for dinner."

Groggy, she cracked open one eye, then scowled at him. "I'm sleeping," she mumbled before turning onto her stomach and burying her face in the pillow.

"Dinner is supposed to be in ten minutes." Tempted by the sight of her thigh peeking out from under the robe, he forced himself to get up.

"Ten more minutes."

He laughed and checked the hall, picking up the basket with their freshly laundered clothing. "Ten more minutes and we'll be late."

Her sigh lasted forever. "Fine." Looking sleepy, she grabbed her clothes and shuffled into the bathroom.

Dressing quickly, he waited for her in the hall and they walked down to the foyer together. He tried not to stare—at her eyes, her mouth, the small half-moon scar on her chin—and was clearly failing judging by the curious look she slanted him more than once.

Thankfully she never called him on it, and he didn't have to scramble to come up with a reason for gawking at her that didn't involve admitting how pretty she was.

Jesus, how old was he? Eighteen?

Miss Maddy was waiting for them in the foyer and ushered them into the dining room. She gestured for them to take a seat, and Max slid into the chair opposite him.

Candles flickered in the middle of the table, casting a soft glow around the room decorated in rich shades of burgundy and emerald green. A door to the left swung open as Maddy disappeared through it, delicious smells wafting from what he assumed was the kitchen.

"Bet you never expected to wind up here with me when you rolled into Riverbend."

"You mean Passion's Penthouse didn't cross your mind when Blackwater's men walked through the door waving your picture?"

Miss Maddy strode back into the room. She held out a small cylinder to Max. "This fell out of your pocket in the laundry, dear. I forgot to put it in the basket earlier."

"Thanks." She slid it into her pocket and took the glass of wine Miss Maddy offered her.

When their hostess poured Lucas's wine and retreated to the kitchen once more, Max met his gaze. "Just mace."

He laughed and relaxed in his chair, determined to enjoy dinner. Eli would arrive before long and this surreal break from reality would be over.

Tonight Max's hair had a soft tousled look, her lips on the sexy, pouty side and her eyes—damn they just kept sucking him in. He didn't know how long they just sat and stared at each other. The silence wasn't awkward or tense, but natural, as though they'd known each other for a long time.

"Dinner is served." The swinging door flew open again and Miss Maddy glided into the room carrying a silver platter. She deposited the tray with a flourish, lifting the dome to reveal two large lobsters.

Lucas eyeballed the red crustaceans staring back at him with black glassy eyes. Any second he expected an antenna to twitch before the damn thing scuttled across the table and snapped at him with one of its monstrous claws.

Max, on the other hand, admired the lobster the way he would a juicy, charbroiled burger.

Miss Maddy darted back into the kitchen, returning seconds later with another tray. This one carried two small bowls of melted butter, two wooden cutting boards and two miniature mallets.

A time or two he'd enjoyed prepared lobster rolls, but had never eaten lobster meat straight from the shell. It was hard to work up an appetite when the damn thing wouldn't stop staring at him.

Unruffled by the lobster's empty stare, Max snagged one of

them and set it on her cutting board. At their elbows, Miss Maddy set two side salads and finally puttered out of the room, leaving them alone.

Mallet poised in midair, Max paused. "You don't like lobster?"

He'd like it a whole lot more if it wasn't watching him. "Just taking my time." He took another drink of his wine for courage and then reached for the remaining lobster. His fingers grazed the still warm shell and he forced himself to grab it.

Picking up the mallet, he mimicked Max's actions until he had separated the claws, legs and tail from the body. Miss Maddy returned just long enough to cart away the excess and hover over his shoulder as he dipped his first bite in the butter and popped it into his mouth.

The rich flavor all but melted on his tongue. Still chewing, he dug another piece of meat from the tail.

Miss Maddy nodded approvingly. "Just watch out for the poop shoot, dear."

Poop shoot? The last bite of lobster caught in his throat. He coughed, reaching for his glass of wine, but Miss Maddy was on him in a heartbeat.

The first slap snapped his teeth together, and he bit the tip of his tongue. If she'd been beating him with a frying pan, he was sure he wouldn't have been able to tell the difference.

Across the table, Max smiled knowingly.

"Thanks," Lucas mumbled when he finally stopped gasping for air.

Seeming satisfied that she wouldn't need to perform the Heimlich, Miss Maddy trailed back into the kitchen.

"The claws are the best part," Max said between mouthfuls.

"No poop shoots there, right?"

She laughed and shook her head.

God, even the soft sway of her hair against her cheeks was sexy.

He finished off another glass of wine and refilled both their glasses. Already a pleasant warmth crawled through his system, and he knew he'd just about reached his limit for the evening.

"So did you always want to work for the government, or did you secretly want to be a rock star when you grew up?"

"Is that who you told those kids I was yesterday, some musician?"

She gave him an I'll-never-tell smile. "Don't change the subject."

"I went into the military after my parents died. My brother was headed off to college on the other side of the country and I didn't have a clue what I wanted to do with my life."

"How did you meet Caleb?"

"We were on the same Special Ops team. He got out before I did, though. He went to work as a private contractor then approached me with a job offer when we ran into each other while I was on leave a few years back."

She cocked her head. "How many times have you been shot?"

"Shot or shot at?"

Taking a sip of her wine, she shrugged, but her expression was anything but indifferent.

"A few," he ventured, testing the waters. He'd never talked about the gritty side of his line of work with anyone outside of his team. Even though Max wasn't unfamiliar with violence, he found himself not wanting to talk about the kind of things that had gotten them both to this point.

He leaned back in his chair. "So aside from your family, is there anyone else back in New York wondering what's happened to you?"

"Like..."

It was his turn to shrug. "Friends. Girlfriends..."

"Boyfriends? Is that what you're getting at?" A smile played across her lips. "Don't tell me it was just my professional background that you investigated?"

"Things get missed." Things that he was realizing he wouldn't like hearing. Would *hate* hearing actually.

Max polished off the last of the wine in her glass. "No boyfriend. No one in a long time."

"Not since you were engaged," he guessed.

She pursed her lips, and for a second he wanted to kick himself for going there. "So you did do your homework. But to answer your rather personal question, no. No one serious since Wade the asshole." She played with the stem of her glass. "Anything in particular you'd like to know aside from the number of ways I dreamed of castrating him?"

"Ouch."

Lifting a shoulder, she leaned forward. "Since we're on the subject of exes," she prompted.

Lucas reached for the second bottle that was already a third gone. "More wine?"

"Changing the subject twice in one night?"

He was saved from answering as Miss Maddy bustled back into the room bearing cheesecake. Although they both insisted they were too full, the woman talked them into sharing a piece.

Lucas offered the first bite to Max. Her lips slid over the end of the fork, and he couldn't help but imagine her lips sliding over him the same way. His cocked hardened at the thought.

Max closed her eyes on a deep sigh, then licked her lips. "Mmmm. That is fantastic."

Her mouth against his would be fantastic, and if they were naked at the time it would be even better.

He broke off another piece and offered it to her. They only made it halfway through the cheesecake before she insisted she couldn't take another bite, and the only bite he was interested in taking involved baring the sweet curve of her shoulder, or maybe the inside of her thigh.

Too uncomfortable to sit, he was relieved when Miss Maddy motioned for them to go. Max walked ahead of him, laughing as she raced up the stairs. He wasn't sure why Miss Maddy insisted on accompanying them upstairs, but he ushered her into the room ahead of him too.

"Such a gentleman." She smiled approvingly. "My Earl was a real gentleman too."

Max leaned against the desk as Miss Maddy pulled back the covers on the sofa bed she must have set up while they were eating. He didn't pay much attention to her—he was too occupied with watching Max.

Her eyes flared when she realized he was staring at her. She sucked at her bottom lip, trapping it between her teeth. Lucas swallowed a groan. If Miss Maddy didn't finish up in the next ten seconds he might have to toss her out.

"Did I tell you two that this was my Earl's favorite room?" Miss Maddy stared at the bed with another wistful expression on her face. "I guess it was fitting that his last night on earth be spent in that bed. You kids sleep tight." She spun on her heel and left them, closing the door soundlessly behind her.

He looked at Max and together they glanced at the bed.

"You know, Lucas, I was thinking. You were right about my cheating. It's only fair that you have the bed to yourself."

"And what happened to enjoying every inch of the mattress?"

Grinning, Max moved closer to the sofa bed. "Earl happened, or died rather."

The sight of her smile left him a little dazzled, and every attempt to remind himself that Eli could be rolling up any time, ended with, so what? They could figure it out tomorrow, or in a little while.

He didn't really care as long as he got to put his mouth on Max now.

He'd been thinking about the taste of her since that first bite of cheesecake. Thinking and anticipating, and if he didn't make it happen soon, he was going to lose his freakin' mind.

Since he couldn't easily reach her with the bed between them, he fluffed one of the pillows. "Do you want the left side or the right?" He could take the big bed and they both knew it, but he didn't want to and he was hoping like hell he wasn't misreading the wicked glimmer in her eyes.

"No hogging the covers."

"Scout's honor." Before he could crawl across the sofa bed, she disappeared into the bathroom.

He dropped onto the springy mattress, his eyes never leaving the bathroom door. Seconds ticked by. He pushed to his feet, too anxious to sit still. How was it he had taken part in countless ops that required waiting until the right moment to strike, and he couldn't manage to keep his butt planted for more than twenty seconds to wait for Max?

Taking a breath, he perched on the edge of the mattress just to prove he could, which was all well and good until the bathroom door finally opened, and he almost fell off the bed.

The pale glow of the room's only lamp illuminated every inch of her naked body, catching every delectable curve and made him hot all over.

"Wow," he mumbled, deciding he was better off staying on his ass for another second or two.

She took a slow step toward him. "I think I had a little too much to drink."

He shook his head. "Or maybe just the right amount."

"Why doesn't it surprise me to hear that?" She offered up a secretive smile, and he noticed something in her hand.

"That's not mace, I hope."

Max glanced at her hand. "Miss Maddy left us a little present in the bathroom."

"Oh, yeah? I like surprises." Especially when they involved

Max naked and walking toward him without a hint of insecurity.

"Then I'm betting you'll like this one."

She stopped in front of him, and he settled his palms on her hips, tugging her closer. Her skin felt warm and soft, and he pressed his lips to her abdomen. He heard her swift intake of breath before she leaned into him. Opening her hand, he saw a small bottle of oil and a rolled up pink scarf.

Max slid into his lap, wrapping her legs around his waist and fitting snug against his cock. His eyes crossed for a moment, all the blood in his body rushing straight to his groin.

Her lips brushed his ear. "It would be a shame to let this stuff go to waste, don't you think?"

It took longer than it should have to process her words. Maybe if he couldn't feel the warmth of her sex straight through his pants.

"I agree." He caught her around the waist and rolled her beneath him, slipping the bottle and scarf from her hand. "I think it's time you let someone else be in charge, Mad Max."

Chapter Eleven

Someone else?

The meaning of the words seemed to hover just beyond Max's comprehension, her body buzzing from a little—okay, a lot—of wine. She was pretty sure it wasn't the alcohol, though, that left her skin hypersensitive. The faintest sensation of his breath teasing across her neck sent scorching waves rippling over every inch of her body.

It had been so long since she'd indulged in anything that hindered her response to a threat, but right now the only threat was losing this moment with Lucas.

Maybe it was crazy to think they could pretend nothing else mattered but how they felt right this second. Maybe she was down-right insane to believe the way he'd been looking at her at dinner—the way he was looking at her now—meant he felt it too, that fierce pull between them that was more than adrenaline or circumstance.

It couldn't be love. It was too intense, too crazy, too temporary. They could steal a few hours, but tomorrow...

Her heart squeezed and she blocked it out, focused on the hot slide of his mouth up her neck.

It didn't matter what this was or if it was all in her head. It felt real. He felt real, and she'd never wanted to be with anyone as much as she did Lucas. Wanted him badly enough she'd left all her inhibitions—and her clothes—at the door.

All it took was meeting his eyes, falling deep into the

glittering green depths to know the only place she needed to be was here.

He opened his mouth over hers, taking it so agonizingly slow their lips moved only millimeters at a time. Seeming to savor every pass, every graze of teeth and tongue, he made love to her mouth and all she could do was hang on for the breath-stealing ride.

So lost in the kiss, so hot and aching and a little bit wild from it, she whimpered when he broke from her mouth. He brought her hand to his lips, running his tongue across the inside of her wrist. She shut her eyes, willing to offer up any part of her for his thorough exploration.

Silk encircled her wrist, followed by a tug that succeeded in penetrating her lust-drenched thoughts. She glanced from the band of silk to Lucas, trying to work something through.

This was not at all what she had in mind when she came out of the bathroom. She had only wanted to show him a few of the goodies Miss Maddy had left in a basket in the bathroom. The silk scarf in particular had made her smile thinking of Lucas's earlier response to all the pink.

By the time she pieced together his intentions, he had wrapped the silk around her other wrist, binding them together.

The thought of being at his mercy—at anyone's—was sobering, and she pulled at her bonds.

Sensing her rising anxiety, he quickly returned to her mouth, stealing both her words and her breath, dragging it out until she felt half out of her mind.

"You're safe with me, Max." He tenderly traced her jawline, his lips whispering across hers. "Trust me."

"Lucas," she pleaded, intending to tell him she couldn't do it, couldn't sacrifice any more control to him or anyone, but the words stuck in her throat.

Because of the wine? Or the way she felt about him?

Lifting her up, Lucas settled her in the middle of the mattress and pushed her arms above her head.

181

His fingers trailed down the inside of her arm. "You are going to play nice, aren't you?" He blew a warm breath across her nipples, bringing them to tight, aching peaks.

Dragging in a lungful of air, Max watched him through heavy eyes. "Define nice."

He smiled suggestively, tilting the bottle of oil towards the light. "This should be interesting."

"Maybe you should be the guinea pig then."

"What? Not too fond of being tied up?"

She parted her thighs just enough to tempt him with the view. "I'd rather it be you."

"No doubt." He laid his palm on her belly, then gently raked his fingers downward through the curls between her legs. His fingers traced her damp seam.

Max dropped her head back against the pillow. She widened her thighs to give him better access. The tip of his forefinger just grazed her clit before he pulled back.

Snapping her eyes open, Max glared up at him. "Tease."

The corners of his mouth lifted in a cocky grin. "What are you gonna do about it? Shoot me?"

"I'd be tempted if I still had my gun."

"Guess I should be thankful you lost it in the river, huh?"

Max tried to sit up. "*I* lost it?"

Lucas slanted his mouth across hers, silencing her, and the molten conquest left her damn near boneless. It was hard to drum up a lot of protest when he was so good at kissing her completely senseless.

Slowly, he drew back, his green eyes a heady mix of desire and control. He opened the bottle, poured a few drops into his palms and rubbed them together. "Now where should we start?"

She tried once more to convince him to release her. "How about with you?"

He shook his head, urging her to lay back. "Relax. This won't hurt a bit." He massaged her thighs, inching higher in light, circular motions that echoed deep in her muscles.

Maybe this wouldn't be so bad. She couldn't remember the last time a man had touched her with such precise intimacy, his intent to please evident in every lazy stroke—maybe never. And not once with a look of such hunger, such determination to satisfy her every desire.

Just shy of her sex, he changed directions.

"You're going the wrong way," she whispered as the deep kneading proceeded toward her feet.

His hand stopped at her ankle. Back and forth his thumb caressed the sensitive flesh above her heel. "I don't think so."

She closed her eyes and sank deeper against the pillows behind her. Now this she could handle. Each feather-light caress relaxed her until her bones softened to butter. He replaced his hand with his mouth, and the seemingly innocent kiss unleashed a ravenous yearning deep in her core that had her hips swaying upward.

"Not bad, huh?"

Max opened her eyes and watched the delicious curve of his lips as he brushed his mouth across her knee. He edged closer, one hand kneading the muscle on the underside of her leg while his lips tantalized the top.

She squeezed her thighs together, the ache intensifying with every sweep of his mouth over her skin. When he was even with her hips, she arched toward him.

"Not yet." He replaced her hands above her head.

She hadn't realized she'd moved them until her fingers had tunneled through his hair.

Lucas continued to knead and caress, slowly, worshipfully. His fingers drifted through the damp curls between her legs. One finger parted her silky flesh, swirled across her clit once, twice, a dozen times.

Pleasure streamed through her system.

He reached above her for the bottle he'd set aside, his lips closing over one aching nipple in passing. He tugged it deep into his mouth, and she moaned softly.

She yanked on her bonds, unable to lie still while he ruthlessly teased her. "Untie me, Lucas."

He ignored her, rubbing more oil onto his hands and spreading them across her belly. Every soothing pass found more pleasure points that left her blissfully mindless. He blew a breath across the oiled skin and warmth radiated outward.

"I don't hear any complaints so far." Lucas moved up from her navel, molding her flesh to her ribs as he inched closer to her breasts.

Both taut peaks ached for his undivided attention. He palmed her breasts, teasing her nipples until the carnal sensation was almost more than she could stand.

"Please," she breathed.

His teeth scraped the tips as he laved the surrounding flesh with his tongue. She writhed against him, the feel of his mouth pushing her need for him well beyond desperate.

"Am I driving you crazy yet?" He ran his hands up to her neck as he pressed his mouth to the corner of her lips.

"I already passed crazy, along with wild and out of my ever-lovin' mind."

His hands fell away from her. "Maybe we should slow down then."

"No!"

He laughed, and began retracing his steps in reverse, trailing past her breasts and stomach to her thighs. Nudging her legs wider, he moved down her body, sliding his fingers along her folds.

Her inner muscles clenched and she was pretty sure she could have blacked out when he bent his head and pressed his mouth to her center. Every inch of her body seemed caught on the edge of release, trembling with every deep lick of his tongue.

"I want to touch you. Untie me." Her voice sounded too

breathless.

"Not yet." Lucas swirled his tongue across her clit, flicking softly, then pulled the sensitive knot between his lips and sucked.

"Lucas!" She flexed her hips, unable to stop herself from grinding softly against his mouth.

He drove his fingers inside her, and she cried out, locking her wrists around his neck. The exquisite rhythm he set only intensified the slick friction between his tongue and her clit.

Moaning, she squeezed her legs around him, release wavering at the edge of her senses. She couldn't take much more, yet she didn't want it to end.

Abruptly he pulled back and sat up.

"Don't," she pleaded, her voice almost hoarse. He couldn't stop now.

Without apology, he flipped her onto her stomach. "We can't forget your back now can we?"

"Enough, Lucas. I want—"

"This isn't about what you think you want, Max." Brushing her hair aside, his lips trailed up her neck. "It's about what you need. What only I can give you."

He poured more oil onto her back, his palms smoothing it over her skin. The heat between her legs continued to throb as he worked the muscles in her back. Just as relaxation began to dull the sharp edge of need still running close to the surface, his finger traced the curve of her bottom right down to her sex.

"Damn it, untie me, Lucas. Now."

"Or?" He ruthlessly circled her clit.

"Please," she whimpered.

He pumped his fingers into her from behind. "Soon." His breath rushed across her cheek, coming nearly as fast as her own.

Sensation after sensation knotted together until it felt like just the right tug would unravel her completely. And he knew it, knew how to take her right to the edge every single time, only to drag out the pleasure again and again.

He pulled away and she heard him stripping off his clothes. The sound of something thumping against the door reached her ears. His shoes?

Then it didn't matter. His body slid overtop of hers, his chest warm against her back. She closed her eyes as his cock nudged her, gliding down her wet seam. On a groan he buried himself inside her.

Bone-deep pleasure snapped through her and she lifted her bottom, meeting his thrusts as he rocked them to a frantic beat. She fisted the blanket in her fingers, clinging to what little leverage it offered.

She turned her head and he lowered his mouth to hers. With the first push of his tongue into her mouth, his entire pace ground to a halt. He withdrew and thrust so slow she could feel him inch by inch filling her up, stretching her, becoming a part of her.

Taking things down a notch should have given her a moment to catch her breath. Instead, she was drowning in him, in the long, deep kiss. Her hands might have been bound, but the rest of her felt free, unleashed.

Lucas slid from her and rolled to his back. Reaching for her, he untied her wrists and dragged her across his body. His fingers tunneled into her hair, guiding her down.

He pressed his lips to her jaw, her cheek, her eyelids, her forehead. "I trust you, Max."

Too moved by his words, by the emotion behind them, she slanted her mouth across his and slid down his hard length, taking him deep inside her.

He groaned, gripping her hips and pushing her up to ride him. Careful of his ribs, she only had to rock a few times to propel the both of them right to the edge. Fisting a hand in her hair, Lucas pulled her down once more just as she came.

Delicious spasms gripped her and she clenched her inner

muscles around him. He drove up into her again and again, rocketing her higher with every thrust, until he shuddered hard, his ragged moan hot against her neck.

Breathing hard, she collapsed on his chest. It took her a minute to try to roll off him, but he put an end to that when he locked one arm across her lower back and yanked the blanket up over them.

The sun was just creeping over the treeline visible through the window on the east side of the building when the bedroom door flew open.

Miss Maddy barreled into the room, pink rollers still in her hair, cast-iron frying pan in her hand. "There are men in the house. They have guns. I hit one in the head. I think I might have killed him."

Max leaped out of the bed, darting into the bathroom to grab her clothes and hurriedly dragged them on.

Oblivious to the fact he was completely naked, Lucas crept into the hall and glanced down the stairs. A second later he closed the door and wedged a chair under the knob.

"Blackwater's guys?"

Lucas yanked on his clothes and shoes. "We have to assume it is."

"How did they find us?" She didn't wait for Lucas to answer since they could waste time speculating later. "Plan?"

He nodded to the window.

"Good." Miss Maddy nodded. "You two go. I'll hold them off."

Max snorted at that. "She can't go out the window, Lucas." The woman might appear spry for her age, but she was hardly up for scaling the roof. Max wasn't even sure *she* was up for it.

"The attic," Miss Maddy said. "There's an access panel in the closet."

Max listened at the door as Lucas helped Miss Maddy into the attic.

"The keys to my Caddy are in the ignition if you need to make a run for it to get help."

Lucas nodded. "Did any other guests arrive last night?"

Max didn't hear Miss Maddy's reply before he shut the panel and closed the door.

"So we're on our own then?"

"Looks like it." He listened at the door, then motioned to the window.

Max hesitated. "You think she's safe up there?"

"If it is Edward Blackwater and company, then it's you they're after. They'll be too busy tracking us to bother with her." Lucas pulled the screen inside and set it on the floor then shoved the window open. "After you."

She grabbed the sill and pulled herself up, realizing she'd gladly take a canoe and white-water rapids over walking the narrow ledge of a roof any day. Climbing a tree was one thing— a catwalk on a steep roof was entirely different.

Knowing time wasn't on their side, Max edged out onto the ledge, doing her damndest not to look down. Lucas crawled out behind her, and the wood creaked under the added weight.

Nightmarish images of the wood trim giving way beneath them froze her in place for a moment. The cold bite of the air she dragged into her oxygen-starved lungs finally managed to get her moving again.

Inch by agonizing inch, they moved along the ledge.

At the corner, Max griped the eave above her head and dropped down onto a flatter part of the roof. Immediately to her right, the remainder of the roof sloped at a precarious angle. Had it not been for Lucas's presence she might have risked a slower pace, Blackwater's guys behind them or not.

Near the edge, she paused, scanning the ground for any sign of movement. Only a plump chipmunk scampered among yellow and orange colored leaves below.

Max pivoted to mention the lack of ladder waiting for them to Lucas, but the words wedged in her throat as the shingled roofing gave way beneath her feet.

She clawed for something to grab onto and caught only air. The pain of the fall barely register as she slid down the steep section of roof, the gritty texture scraping her palms as she fought to catch herself.

Her feet and legs plunged over the edge first, and for a second she thought she might be able to perch on the edge.

Gravity had other ideas.

The rest of her body carried over, but she snagged the plastic eaves trough to stop her fall.

Blood thundered in her ears as she dangled from the roof. The weathered plastic groaned and trembled under her weight. The ground seemed to reach up for her, waiting for her grip to falter.

Breathing fast, she tilted her head back, afraid to yell for Lucas and bring Blackwater's men running. Had they heard her?

She gritted her teeth against the burning strain in her arms. Oh god, she was going to fall.

Lucas's hand closed around her wrist.

"Cutting it close, aren't you?" She hissed at the pain that flared along her arm as he started to pull her upright.

"Not now, Max." Slowly, he yanked her up enough she could hike her leg over the edge and haul herself up.

Trembling from both the spike of adrenaline and near-fall, she crumpled beside him.

Lucas cradled her cheek. "You scared the crap out of me."

"Sorry, I'll try not to let it happen again."

Looking like he wanted to say more, he settled on squeezing her hand. "Watch your step this time, huh?"

On the far side of the house they climbed down the

latticework that somehow managed to hold their weight.

Lucas jumped the last couple of feet and grabbed her hand, pulling her along. They rounded the corner and Max immediately spotted a garage and Miss Maddy's dusty rose Caddy. "There."

He followed her gaze. "Keep your head down and don't stop moving."

She rolled her eyes and whispered, "Gee, thanks for the tip. I've never done this before."

His lips cracked in a fleeting grin, and then he pulled her after him. He released her hand, but instead of sticking close to her as she rounded the rear of the Caddy, he moved toward a sedan peeking out from the opposite end of the farmhouse.

Keeping her attention fixed on the side door she half-expected to fly open any second, Max slid behind the wheel. Across the driveway, Lucas opened the door to the parked sedan.

What the hell was he doing?

A moment later, he ran toward her. He tossed the keys to the sedan into the back seat as he jumped into the car next to her. He hadn't even gotten the door shut before the B&B's side door opened.

Fuck.

Edward Blackwater and another man Max vaguely recognized from the warehouse that night stood on the step. She'd cranked the ignition just as the two men charged toward them.

The Caddy turned over on the first try, and she jammed the gearshift into reverse.

"Buckle up." She floored the gas pedal.

A bullet pierced the windshield, thankfully missing them, but spidered Lucas's half of the glass.

With one hand on the wheel and the other stretched across the back of the seat, Max whipped the Caddy down the driveway and onto the road.

God, she hoped Miss Maddy stayed hidden until the men either hotwired their car or abandoned it.

"How did they know where we were? There's no way it could be a coincidence."

Lucas didn't say anything right away, then glanced at her. "Who did you call?"

"Me? You were on the phone too. And yes," she added, "I know you called your boss yesterday."

Frowning, he glanced out the window behind them. "It doesn't change the fact that Blackwater is determined to get ahold of you. He could have had you killed at any time, yet he went through a lot of trouble to make you look guilty of Cara's murder."

"He wanted to make sure other people were looking for me too."

"But why go out of his way to track you down?"

She winced. "That could have something to do with his face."

"His face... Christ, you did that?" She wasn't sure if he sounded worried or proud.

"Yeah." She checked her rearview mirror compulsively. "Or maybe he's worried I can identify someone important who was there that night."

"Like the Russian." Lucas shook his head. "We're missing something. Were you telling me the truth that morning about the Russian's money?"

The road directly behind them was still deserted, but she eased up on the gas only when they hit a winding turn. "Yeah. But I just assumed that Blackwater must have found it by now."

"How big was it? The case," he clarified.

She frowned. "Briefcase sized, maybe a little smaller."

"Son of a bitch."

Max took her eyes off the road long enough to glance at him. "What?"

"It wasn't money. The kind of funds involved in a deal like this would have been too much to carry in a case that size. The money would have been transferred electronically."

"It was the biological weapon you and Cara were looking for, wasn't it? The one stolen from a Czech scientist."

"Maybe. Maybe that's why Blackwater wants you. He thinks or is hoping you know what happened to it."

A red mid-sized car turned onto the main road ahead of them, cutting them off. She jerked the wheel, but couldn't avoid sideswiping the other vehicle.

The jarring collision slammed Lucas into the door.

"How many busted ribs are you looking for?" she snapped. "Put on your damn seat belt."

The passenger side mirror exploded, and gunshots peppered the back end of the Caddy.

"Stay low." Lucas pushed her down in the seat, then waved to the right. "Turn down there."

Swearing, Max took the turn too fast, and the car skidded on the shoulder of the road. More shots scraped the paint off the side of the car.

The tires spun in the dirt and the wheel suddenly wrenched loose of Max's grip, and they swerved into a ditch.

Pain slashed across her temple as her head connected with the window.

She fumbled with her seatbelt as Lucas threw his door open. There wasn't time to wait for the world to right itself completely before she scrambled out after him, taking his hand.

The Caddy's back tire had blown out from a bullet, leaving them no choice but to run.

Struggling to keep focused on the uneven terrain, she couldn't compensate fast enough to stop her ankle from rolling as they ran. Crying out, she tripped, but used her fierce grip on

Lucas to keep from hitting the ground. They hit the woods just as the sound of car doors slamming echoed behind them.

How many were there? Was there a third car they needed to worry about too, or was Snake on his own?

Pain dulled by the adrenaline pounding through her system, she kept pace with Lucas as they headed into the thickest part of the surrounding forest.

"Any ideas?"

"I'm thinking."

"And?" Max pressed, leaning into him when he paused for a second to scan the area.

"You'll be the first to know."

A bullet whistled past Lucas's head, splintering the tree branch next to him. They scrambled down an embankment, the sound of rushing water growing louder as the trees thinned to their immediate right and the ground dropped off next to the river.

Another bullet cracked into the tree, just missing Max.

Lucas urged her closer to the edge of the treeline, and turned to glance behind them. Another gunshot sounded, and he staggered sideways, clutching his side.

Oh god.

She lunged to reach him, but he went down hard, rolling backward until he disappeared over the edge and plunged into the water below.

"Lucas!" She skidded down the damp earth, scanning the narrow channel of dark, choppy water.

Panic iced her blood. Where was he?

Another gunshot—a warning one—hit the ground a few feet from her hand.

"Do not move."

She recognized Snake's voice, but didn't so much as glance over her shoulder as she pushed off and jumped into the river.

Lucas thought he heard his name over the rushing water around him. He tried to turn himself around, but his limbs wouldn't cooperate beyond keeping him afloat. The freezing water pulled at him, but nothing compared to the fire that blazed across his mid-section.

Where was Max?

Jaw clenched, he tried twisting around, searching the water for her even as he struggled to keep himself upright.

More gunshots echoed on the air. Were they shooting at Max? The fast moving current sucked at him, and he almost missed the dark blur that shot past his peripheral vision.

The water splashed higher around him, and more than once his face became submerged. The agony in his middle made the rest of his body slow to respond. He slipped beneath the surface again, but was dragged upward a moment later by an awkward tug on his shirt.

Max.

Relief gave his useless limbs enough strength to keep himself buoyant as she struggled to get them to shore. The current carried them part of the way, and out of range of the gunfire.

By the time they reached a shallow inlet, every breath Lucas drew felt like taking a scalding baseball bat to the chest. His feet finally touched, but he could do little except try not to fall face-first into the water as Max herded him toward the shore.

On the beach, Max collapsed next to him, worry etched on her face.

He tried for a reassuring smile. "Trying to drown me once wasn't enough for you, huh?"

Ignoring his attempt at humor, she lifted his shirt to check the wound. He hissed out a breath, trying to judge how bad it was by the look on her face.

Really bad, he decided a moment later when he swore her eyes became suspiciously shiny.

She blinked a few times and scanned the area around them. "We can't stay here."

He knew she was right, but wasn't sure how far he'd get when just lying there made every part of him hurt like a bitch. "How bad, Max?"

Instead of answering him, she checked the wound again, applying pressure this time.

It took more than a minute to make his voice work through the pain. "Not so bad."

"Christ," she murmured, not even seeming to hear him, and he instantly recognized the look on her face.

"Not your fault," he managed. "But how bad?" he pressed.

"Bad enough you need to get to a hospital. Not enough to be a wuss about it, though."

Lucas squeezed his eyes shut. "Damn it."

"You're gonna be fine," she insisted. "We just need to get you out of here." Sliding her arms under his, she gave him the leverage he needed to stagger to his feet.

"It's not that." He leaned against her, gritting his teeth until his jaw felt ready to snap. "I hate needles."

"Needles? You've been shot, we're likely miles from any clinic or hospital and have men after us, men who clearly have no problem taking you out, and you're worried about a little needle or two?"

Or five or ten. "I can always count on you to put everything into perspective for me."

By sheer determination, and a hell of a lot of support from Max, he remained upright. One step at a time, they crossed the rocky beach, moving into the woods in hopefully the direction of the road they'd left earlier.

After less than five minutes, Lucas lost his footing. Somehow Max got him propped against a tree, and he slid the ground.

"You need to go. Send help back for me." Even though he

knew better, knew just how bad off he was, he still couldn't seem to keep his eyes open.

Max crouched next to him. "I'm not leaving you here. You'll be defenseless."

"We don't have much of a choice. You can't carry me out of here, Max. If you don't go—"

"Blackwater's men will kill you if they find you."

He shook his head. "They won't."

"I'm *not* leaving you."

"You know it's the only way." Even when it meant sending her off, unarmed, with Blackwater's men still in the area and gunning for her. "Please, Max."

"Lucas," she murmured, cupping his face. "I can't."

"Yes, you can. You don't even like me, remember?"

That almost earned him a glare. "Don't be a jerk."

"I need you to go, Max. Now."

She finally nodded. "I'll find the road and flag someone down. I won't be gone long."

"Sounds like a good plan, lover."

A weak smile curved her lips, and she leaned in, pressing her mouth to his. He kept her there as long as he dared, savoring the kiss that managed to dull his pain, if only for a few seconds.

"Stay safe," she whispered against his lips, and then finally stood and disappeared into the woods.

Chapter Twelve

Christ, his chest ached.

Lucas opened his eyes, and immediately squeezed them shut against the overhead florescent light.

Where was he?

The familiar disinfectant smell that reminded him instantly of a hospital was somewhat reassuring. At least he was still alive. Alive and hurting. Goddamn, it was like someone had thrown him in front a stampeding herd of cattle.

Tuning out the pain as much as he could, he tried to focus. How had he gotten here?

Max.

His eyes snapped open, his gaze sweeping the room for her. There was no sign of her, but Eli Vale sat in a chair opposite the bed, his dark blond head tipped back, attention fixed on the ceiling.

Sensing Lucas's eyes on him, Eli glanced in his direction. A broad grin cut across his face. "Decided to rejoin the living after all, huh?"

"So it would appear." He tried to move and immediately sucked in a breath at the pain that flared up his side. "Where's Max?"

Eli's shoulders stiffened and he stood. "I was kind of hoping you'd know. What the hell happened, man?"

She was gone.

An icy slab of apprehension settled on his chest, his fear that something had happened to her only making his pain that much more intense.

"You haven't seen her since she brought me in?" He must have already blacked out by the time she'd come back with help.

Eli shook his head. "Two hunters found you unconscious, in the woods. They dumped you in the back of their truck and drove like mad to get you help. You're damn lucky you didn't bleed out on the drive."

"When?" He fought the hazy fog that continued to weigh down his thoughts.

"Two days ago. You've been drugged up most of the time, in and out of consciousness and mostly incoherent. You came way to close to buying the farm, dude."

Lucas closed his eyes. By some crazy twist of fate he'd survived, but had Max? She went for help, so if she didn't make it back to him before the hunters stumbled across him, what the hell had happened to her?

He needed to find her. Now.

Sharp, red-hot pain knifed across his chest when he tried to sit up.

"Whoa. You're not ready to get back up in the saddle just yet."

Lucas forced air through his teeth, determined to get upright. "I need to find Max." Before Blackwater and the RCMP or anyone else looking for her did.

"Jesus, the woman put a bullet in you. Let someone else track her down."

The unrestrained hostility in Eli's voice was exactly why he couldn't sit back and let someone else handle it. "She didn't shoot me. Or kill Cara," he added.

Not even pretending to be convinced, Eli put a hand on his shoulder. "Look, it's completely understandable that your memories are a little jumbled after what you've been through. You need to rest, Lucas."

Knowing Eli was just looking out for him was the only thing that stopped him from telling his friend to back the fuck off. Instead of taking his frustration out on Eli though, he concentrated on getting upright.

"My memory is just fine. Max didn't shoot me. She saved my life. I probably would have drowned if she hadn't jumped in after me." Lucas paused as his brain processed his own words.

Max wasn't a fan of water, could barely swim and yet she'd jumped in after him. The realization did wonders to improve his mood, easing the pain in his chest long enough he made it to his side. He needed to find her, needed to make sure she was okay.

"Let's say she didn't shoot you," Eli conceded.

"She didn't. It was one of Blackwater's guys."

Eli frowned. "How the hell did they find you?"

"I don't know." He closed his eyes, inwardly bracing for the pain that was going to snatch his breath the second he tried to sit up. "What happened to you the other night? You didn't show."

"No shit. Those back roads are crazy to follow in the dark. Got lost and turned around more times than a blindfolded kid playing pin the tail on the jackass. The police were already at the B&B when I rolled up that morning, talking to the woman who owned the place. It was hard to tell how much progress they were making, though, when she wouldn't put down the frying pan she was carrying."

Relieved to know Miss Maddy managed to get out of the attic without hurting herself or anyone else, Lucas focused on the present. He finally made it upright, panting the whole way. His pain level had jumped from nine-point-five to twelve out of ten, easy.

"You're not going to do her any good if you collapse. Tell me what you want me to do and I'll do it."

"How'd you find me?"

"Tess did. The gunshot injury was reported to the RCMP and local police. I imagine they'll want to talk to you once the nurse lets them know you're awake. I believe you're a person of interest regarding a certain high-speed car chase to boot."

"Don't sound so impressed."

Eli grinned. "Just sorry that I missed riding shotgun. Joe is making some calls, but if he can't find a way to get you off the hook legitimately, then we'll have to get creative. Which means you need to rest up."

Still too weak to put up much of a fight, he let Eli help him lie back. "She'll go back to New York. Tap some contacts there. I need to find her."

Exhaustion pulled at him, and he rested his eyes for just a moment.

He wasn't sure how much time had passed when he resurfaced again—an hour? A day?—but Eli was no longer in the room.

Instead, it was Caleb who lounged in the chair next to him. Seeing his friend's face, the slate gray gaze mirroring Cara's so closely, Lucas welcomed the wave of grief that rose up, letting it temporarily drown out his other pain.

Caleb took a minute to notice he was awake, leaving him slower than usual to flawlessly mask his emotions. "Hey."

"Got stuck babysitting me, huh?" Lucas tested the pain by shifting a little in the bed.

"Eli's running interference with the local RCMP."

"Any news on Max?"

Caleb leaned forward, looking first at his hands and then Lucas. "You should have told me what you were up to, and if not you, Tess damn well should have."

"Great, like you needed another reason to give her a hard time." Caleb and Tess's arguments were practically legendary, both of them too damn stubborn for their own good.

"I would have had your back, Luc," he said quietly. "I'll always have your back. No matter what." He glanced at the floor. "You weren't to blame for what happened to Cara. I never thought you were. I just..."

"You're just damn lucky you didn't die before he had a chance to say that," Eli finished, striding into the room.

Ignoring Eli, Caleb held Lucas's gaze. "We cool?"

"Yeah." He released a breath, taking Caleb's outstretched hand and letting his friend help him into a sitting position. When he could breathe without the pain blurring his vision, he glanced at Eli. "What did you find out?"

"I've only had feelers out for half a day, but so far no one has heard anything about Blackwater catching up with her or taking her out. That doesn't necessarily mean anything, though. Maybe word just hasn't gotten out yet."

"Or maybe he doesn't know where she is either." She wasn't dead. She was fine. He needed her to be fine.

And he needed like hell to find her.

"Oh," Eli continued. "There was one little detail that you might be interested in hearing. Seems there was a nurse checking up on you when you came out of surgery. The doctor asked for her assistance and she split. No one has seen her since, nor does anyone seem to know who she was."

Max.

Lucas smiled despite wanting to shoot her for risking a run-in with the RCMP. She couldn't have stuck around though, or Caleb and Eli would have seen her by now. Which meant she was likely on her way back to New York.

He was torn between hoping that was her plan, which would make it easier to find her, and wishing she'd put as much space between her and Samuel Blackwater as possible.

"Oh, man, are you in it up to your balls, or what?"

Lucas frowned, glancing back and forth between Eli and Caleb. "Huh?"

201

"I know that look, dude." Eli stood at the end of the bed. "You've got it bad for her, don't you?"

Scowling, he nodded toward the door. "Take a walk while I get decent." He tugged at the top of his hospital gown. "I assume one of you guys found me some clothes."

"Damn." Eli whistled. "Real bad."

Caleb grabbed some clothes from the cupboard across from the bed. "Sure you don't need some help?"

Lucas shook his head, waiting until the door closed to change—a painstaking process that took him way too long. He was sweating right through his clean shirt and hurting all over by the time he finished, and that was with Eli checking on him twice.

As much as his body wanted nothing more than to crawl back into bed, he couldn't afford to waste any more time here.

God, he needed to get to Max before Blackwater.

He didn't know when finding Max became more about helping her get her life back and less about Cara's death and Blackwater's dealings, but somewhere along the way that's exactly what happened.

Probably right around the time that the connection between the two of them deepened into something he wasn't ready to let go of.

Not today. Maybe not ever.

Ten days.

Ten days since Lucas had been shot. Ten days since she'd run through the woods after flagging down a car only to find he'd vanished. She thought at first she'd gotten lost and misread the markers she'd left to find her way back to him, then she'd seen the blood.

For ten minutes she'd searched the area, terrified Snake or Edward Blackwater had found him and tossed his body in the river. Only when she crossed paths with two hunters who, after berating her for running around the woods during deer season without an orange hunting vest, mentioned an injured man being found earlier.

Relief had nearly broken her, and seeing her distress, the hunters had offered her a ride to the closest hospital where they were sure Lucas had been taken.

That had been ten days ago, and after making sure he was okay, she had contented herself with only calling the hospital to check on him. As much as she wanted to see him, to stay right there next to him, she wanted him safe and alive more.

Being anywhere near her, especially with Blackwater more determined than ever to get to her could only end up hurting him more. Until she found a way to nail the drug and arms dealer, she would keep her distance. Maybe that way she could keep him safe.

More than once he'd risked himself for her, and she refused to let him do it again. He was better off far away from her. People kept getting hurt when they got involved with her—Glen, Jillian, Cara and now Lucas.

Bringing down Blackwater on her own seemed impossible, but she wasn't willing to spend another day looking over her shoulder, wondering if he'd finally caught up with her. If she didn't find a way to clear her name, Blackwater would win. She couldn't let that happen. Couldn't let him ruin everything she'd worked so hard to build.

Her father had been so proud of her the day she'd graduated from the academy, his eyes shining with unshed tears when he'd said that CJ would have cheered the loudest for her. How could she let memories like that be shadowed by the pity and scorn her family would have been living under since she'd run?

They didn't deserve to be whispered about behind their backs. Glen didn't deserve to be tainted by the same brush that marked her as dirty.

She'd fix it. All of it.

It had taken her days to hitch her way back to New York, but she was finally ready to make some kind of move. One that started with getting back inside the warehouse.

The only problem was the number of guards Blackwater had watching the property and her lack of familiarity with the warehouse beyond the few details she could remember from the night Cara died.

With very few people on the streets she could trust, she had no choice but to ask Glen for information, and she'd been careful never to stay on the phone for too long. She wanted to be a hundred percent certain her location at the B&B hadn't been tracked through her conversation with Glen, but if Lucas was right and Blackwater suspected she knew where his missing weapon was, he'd undoubtedly find a way to tap Glen's phone at the precinct.

She and Glen had only spoken twice since her return, but she'd agreed to meet him in a couple hours after learning he was continuing to investigate the witnesses who had claimed she killed Cara. Seeing as he stubbornly refused to listen when she insisted he stop digging into it during their brief phone conversations, she was counting on a personal visit convincing him.

Shivering from the late October cold snap, Max tucked her chin into her borrowed jacket as she hit the last block leading to her cousin's apartment. She had finally gotten in touch with Sherri and apologized for the damage to her shop and for scaring the crap out of her friend by not letting her know she was okay sooner—the latter of which Sherri wasn't going to forgive her for anytime soon apparently. She'd had Sherri call Max's cousin Ashley, who lived in France part of the year, and ask about a friend subletting the place.

With Sherri personally vouching for the mystery tenant, Ashley had agreed and made arrangement for keys to be left, which Max had picked up three days ago. Although no one had any reason to be watching Ashley's place, Max had been careful to make sure she wasn't being followed.

Her stomach rumbled as she dug the key out of her pocket and let herself into the apartment building. By the time she climbed the three flights of stairs, she swore she could feel every single hour since she'd left Lucas in the woods bearing down on her.

Letting herself into the apartment, Max surveyed the stark white walls and open concept design, wishing she was in her own cramped cluttered apartment instead. Although here she could appreciate the security that came in knowing there were very few places an assailant could hide in plain sight if they managed to follow her home.

Drawing a weapon she'd stolen from her father's lockbox—and getting in and out of there without being noticed hadn't been easy—she did a sweep of the apartment to confirm she was indeed alone, then unzipped her jacket and left it on the table.

She grabbed a bottle of water from the fridge and scanned the notes she'd been making, trying to figure out a way to get into the warehouse that didn't involve strolling right up to the front door.

She dug Cara's lip gloss from her pocket and rolled it back and forth in her palm, staring at the pages in front of her until she couldn't ignore her hunger any longer. Two pieces of toast—even if they were slathered in strawberry jam—were a far cry from the lobster dinner she and Lucas had shared.

God, she hoped he was doing okay. No matter how many times she tried reassuring herself that they hadn't known each other long, she couldn't pretend she wasn't thinking about him—missing him—so much it made her heart hurt.

Worried, tired and more than a little convinced she'd foolishly given more of herself to Lucas than she counted on, she headed for the shower. Her most recent recon of the warehouse had ended with running smack into a wino, one in the midst of taking a swig from his pint of rum, the contents of which had been splashed down the front of her in the process.

The wino hadn't been impressed.

Setting her gun on the back of the toilet, next to the shower, she stripped down and hopped in, letting the hot water wash away both the rum and whispers of doubt that she wasn't going to beat Blackwater.

When she finished and changed into a clean shirt of Ashley's, she glanced at the bed, wondering if she had time for a quick nap.

Something in the hallway creaked, and she pivoted around, snatching her gun off the bed. Pulse pounding, she crossed to the door and checked the line of sight to the kitchen.

The hallway was empty.

Trusting her gut and not the voice that wondered if she suffered from chronic paranoia, she started down the hall, then paused, sensing movement directly behind her.

Spinning to meet the threat, she lead with her fist, not hearing the sound of her name until her hand had already connected with Lucas's face.

Goddamn it.

Lucas's head snapped back, but the pain that flared across his jaw wasn't as bad as his side when he twisted to dodge the blow. With his hand pressed to his still healing side, he backed up, giving her plenty of room.

He would have called out her name earlier, but thought he'd recognized one the guys who walked into her building a few minutes ago as one of Blackwater's. If the guy had ID'd Max and got in ahead of Lucas, he hadn't wanted to give the guy any kind of heads up.

Apparently, though, he was the only one who needed advance notice. Christ, she had a good throwing arm.

"Lucas?" Max asked.

Shaking off the pain, he straightened. "Surprised to see me I take it."

Max stilled, an unreadable expression clouding her face. "What the hell are you doing here? And why didn't you knock? You scared the crap out of me."

As far as reunions went, this wasn't how Lucas had envisioned this one going down. Her arms around his neck maybe, her mouth on his—definitely. An aching jaw and a gun between them? Not a chance.

"I think you can put that down now."

She glanced at the weapon in her hand. "I could have shot you, you ass." Her words were laced with more worry than anger, so he chanced pressing his luck and got right into her personal space.

Her gaze landed on his jaw. "You okay?"

"Yeah. Good thing you hit like a girl."

She rolled her eyes, and he pulled her close, opening his mouth over hers. At least now he knew he hadn't imagined how good kissing her felt, or how much he'd missed her. He'd known her staying away from the hospital had been the right call, but every moment since then he'd been so worried about her.

Who cared that she was strong and resourceful and determined? He'd wanted her close so he could see with his own eyes that she was okay. If anything had happened to her...

She murmured a little protest against his lips, and he forced himself to give her a little room to breathe, but didn't release her entirely. He wasn't ready for that yet.

Eyes closed, she held onto him, her free hand cupping his face and erasing anything negative Joe might have said about Max when his boss had cautioned him against going after her.

Max finally drew back, her attention sliding down his chest.

It didn't take a lot of imagination to know she was thinking of his gunshot wound. "Max—"

"I should get some ice for your face." She turned and

walked away from him.

Lucas followed her into the kitchen, wanting to tell her...what exactly? How much he'd missed her, was glad to see her, that the last ten days had been the longest in his life?

Max motioned for him to take a seat, and turned to grab something from the freezer. Ice probably. If he hadn't glimpsed that little flutter of panic in her eyes a heartbeat before he'd kissed her, he would have insisted he didn't need anything but her to make him feel better.

Sensing she needed something to keep her hands busy, though, he kept quiet.

"How did you find me?"

"You were spotted near Blackwater's warehouse last night." He'd been both relieved and angered to know someone had spotted her. Relieved that she was safe, and angered that she hadn't been careful enough to avoid notice entirely.

Any one of Blackwater's snitches could have ID'd her and followed her back to the apartment. One of them had probably come too damn close to exactly that tonight.

She pulled an ice pack from the freezer. "How come you haven't gone after the weapon?"

"Big warehouse and lots of places to check without knowing where to start."

Her fingers faltered as she folded the pack up in a dish towel. "So you need me," she guessed, something in her tone rubbing him the wrong way.

"Need you to tell me where it is, yes."

"So you can go in and get it," she finished, finally meeting his gaze.

"That's the plan." Among other things. Things he didn't want Max anywhere near when they went down.

She pressed the pack to his face, and he closed his hand over hers. "I want in."

"That's not part of the plan."

Her eyes narrowed at the corners, but she didn't pull away from him. "You wanted my help."

"Coming back here to handle Blackwater on your own wasn't exactly what I had in mind."

Anger flared in her eyes. "I was just supposed to cooperate and do everything that you told me to, right?"

Why did it seem like answering such a straightforward question was so incredibly complicated?

He set the ice on the counter. "How about we start over."

She shook her head. "I need to get in touch with Glen. I don't want him anywhere near that warehouse when you guys make your move."

Lucas frowned. "Why would he be near the warehouse?"

"I'd like to think he's steering clear of it, but just in case he's following leads he thinks will help me, I need to give him a heads up."

"Are you sure you can trust him?"

She crossed her arms. "You tell me. I'm sure you've probably investigated him by now. Right?"

He nodded, not feeling the least bit apologetic for doing his job.

"Look, I realize that I can't be sure about anything anymore—"

Now why did it feel like he was suddenly being lumped in with that?

"—but Glen has been looking out for me too long not to give him the benefit of the doubt."

"Fair enough." He let it go for now, really wanting to get back to the part where she was in his arms and tucked against him. Safe.

All too soon they would need to talk about the case's location inside the warehouse, but for a few more minutes he just wanted to indulge in being close enough he could reach out and touch her.

Max reached for the phone, and he did his best to be patient while she left a short message for Glen to meet her an hour sooner if possible.

He'd strategically placed himself behind her, and when she hung up the phone, she turned around and nearly ran into him. Her eyes drifted up, studying him through thick dark lashes.

He cupped her cheek. "So did you miss me at all, Max?"

A soft, sexy smile—the one he'd been dreaming about— touched her lips. "Wouldn't you like to know?"

He grinned, murmured, "Hell, yeah," against her lips, and slid his mouth over hers.

Each time he kissed her, he expected the feeling to be less powerful, less consuming and each time he was never so happy to be disappointed.

Much too soon she pulled away from him. "We should go. Glen will be waiting for us."

Deciding it would be good to meet this guy in person, Lucas nodded. "But when we get back, there are a few things we need to settle between us."

"Us," she repeated. "Like the weapon's location?"

"Us. As in you and me." No matter what happened with the weapon and Blackwater, he wasn't leaving her again until he knew where they stood.

Max tried hard to concentrate on the menu in her hand and not think about what Lucas planned on saying when they got back to her cousin's apartment. Not even the inviting smells wafting out of the run-down diner's kitchen, a place she and Glen had stumbled across after a stakeout a couple years back, managed to tempt her to think about food over the man opposite her.

Every time she looked at him she felt her insides slide

together in a warm wave that made her want to get as close to him as she could. But as much as she wanted him here, she couldn't help but wish he hadn't found her and was far away from New York.

Her gaze drifted to his chest, and she fought the urge to run her hand over him to make sure he really was okay.

"So you say the pancakes are good?" Lucas's voice pulled her mind from the guilt still swirling in her stomach.

"The best in the city," Glen finished, sliding into the empty seat next to her.

Before she could get a word out, his arms went around her, squeezing the air from her lungs.

"Glad to see you're in one piece." Glen nodded to Lucas, his practiced cop smile revealing only polite curiosity. "Who's your friend?"

Setting aside her menu, she made a quick introduction that didn't fully satisfy Glen.

"Lucas..." Glen trailed off meaningfully, not missing the fact she hadn't mentioned his last name.

"McAllister," Lucas finished, setting his own menu aside and staring just as intently at Glen.

"How about we put away the testosterone until recess," Max suggested.

They both glanced at her then back at each other, both equally guarded and just a little bit suspicious.

Glen took a sip of the coffee the waitress had left for him as he continued to size up Lucas like he would a suspect during interrogation. Before she could tell him to knock it off, he looked at her. "I'm glad you called actually. There's talk that Blackwater has a new deal going down. Something big, apparently."

"Who's your source?"

Glen didn't even pretend to contemplate answering without waiting for her to nod that they could trust Lucas. "It's one of

211

Wade's informants."

"Wade Cummings? The narcotics detective Max was engaged to?"

"His informant thinks it might have something to do with a deal that went bad a few months back," Glen continued.

Max sat straighter in her seat. "Like the night Cara was killed."

"Or," Lucas interjected, "Blackwater knows Max is back in town and wants to find a way to draw her out."

Glen nodded. "We can't rule out the possibility."

"Not when it's personal after what she did to him."

Frowning, Glen glanced at her for an explanation. "What does he mean?"

"She gave Blackwater that scar over his eye," Lucas answered before she could get a word in.

Surprised by that, Glen shot her an incredulous look, and then went right back to his conversation with Lucas. "She did that?"

"*She* happens to be right here," Max said through her teeth, not bothering to hide how annoyed she was that they were talking like she wasn't even in the room.

God, it was like they'd gone from testosterone archrivals to estrogen allies in less time than it took for them to take a piss. "Are you two finished?"

Both heads swiveled in her direction, neither one of them missing the hard edge to her voice.

Slanting her a mildly apologetic look, Lucas focused on Glen. "Do you have a time and place this is going down?"

"I'm working on it, but there's no guarantee I'll hear before the deal is over."

Lucas dug into his pocket and pulled out a card. "You can use that number to get ahold of us."

Her partner took the card, glancing between the two of them at the barest emphasis Lucas had put on *us*. "If this deal is meant to draw you out, Max, you know you can't be anywhere near Blackwater when it goes down."

"If you can't tell me you're absolutely certain it's some kind of trap, I'm not sitting on the sidelines."

Lucas crossed his arms. "There's no way to know that, Max."

"Then I guess we all understand each other."

His expression darkened. "The only thing we all need to understand is that Blackwater wants to get his hands on you, Max. You can't just waltz straight into the lion's den and expect to come out unscathed."

"If you didn't want me involved in any of this then maybe you should have left me in Riverbend."

"Max—"

"Don't *Max* me. It's not your career or your life that Blackwater screwed with. You don't have people you worked with, people you trusted, friends, thinking the worst of you, that you're one of the bad guys."

"I know this is hard for you," Lucas began.

"Then don't sit there and expect me to stay out of it when we both know you wouldn't if our positions were reversed." Glen stood up. "I think that's my cue actually. I'll be in touch as soon as I hear anything else." His gaze moved to Max, and she swore he was trying not to grin. "At least you're finally involved with someone who makes as much sense as I do."

"We're not involved," she and Lucas said in unison.

Glen nodded toward the door. "Well, while I'd love to stay and mediate for you two, I want to see if Burton disappears mysteriously when he hears about this potential deal." He quickly drained the last of his coffee. "You two play nice."

Nice apparently equaled quiet in Lucas's book, Max soon realized.

He hasn't said more than a few syllables on the walk back

to Ashley's. She wanted to think he was preoccupied with staying focused on their surroundings and making sure no one followed them from the diner, but she couldn't entirely ignore the vibe that warned her there was more to it than that.

A vibe she'd felt since Wade's name was mentioned.

As much as her ex was a total asshole, she'd always been convinced he was a good cop. Now she didn't know what to think. His name being tied to a tip about a deal she had a vested interest in brought to mind a few questions.

Like had Wade realized who Glen had been talking to the day she called him at the precinct?

As soon as they were inside, Lucas stripped out of his jacket and got right down to business. "I need you to tell me exactly where the case is, Max. Any detail you can remember about where you saw the Russian stash it, any marker or anything at all would be helpful."

"Or you could just let me go with you."

"You're not trained for that kind of thing and you know it."

She did know it. She also knew she wasn't crazy about sending him in there when she knew how scared she'd been the night Cara died. Scared enough to screw up a detail that she might not remember clearly until she was back inside the warehouse.

"So I'm not a covert operative. That doesn't mean I can't follow orders."

He snorted, and she ignored him, focusing on what else she did know.

"You're the one with the highly trained team. You mean to tell me you guys aren't good enough to cover my ass in a situation like this?"

He took a step toward her, intentionally invading her space as though she'd be intimidated into backing down. "I don't want your ass anywhere near a situation like this."

"If there really is some kind of deal in the works, do you

really think we can afford to waste time arguing about it?"

Something flickered on his face, and she cocked her head, waiting.

"You know something, don't you?" When he didn't answer, she ran the possibilities through her head and guessed. "You already knew about the deal."

He finally nodded. "I was the one who set it up."

Chapter Thirteen

Running her hands through her hair, she pivoted away from him, then spun back around. "You wouldn't have spent so much time trying to find this weapon only to give it back to him. Why set something up?"

"To get him and his men far away from the warehouse, making it easier for us to go in and get the case."

"I need to tell Glen."

He cut her off before she reached the phone. "If Glen knows it's a bogus deal, he could end up tipping off whatever cops are in Blackwater's pocket."

"Like Wade?" She shook her head, working through everything aloud. "But if Wade is working for Samuel Blackwater, why pass on any details about the deal? He'd want that stuff kept under wraps, especially after the way things went down the last time."

"Maybe he plans to feed bad intel down the line and have the cops preoccupied elsewhere. Could be he's hoping you really will show up. Or hell, maybe Wade Cummings is just pissed at Blackwater and doesn't give a shit anymore."

"So where does that leave us?"

"Me," he corrected. "Not us."

"Convenient how you get to decide what constitutes each *us* thing."

Lucas sighed. "Are you going to be stubborn and not tell me

where the weapon is?"

Really hating how he made it seem like she wasn't using her head, she threw her hands up. "It's in a floor grate. Southwest corner, near a painted Greek numeral or a symbol similar to that. I think. Happy now?"

"Come here."

She shook her head, tempted, but determined to will away the horrible feeling in her stomach that she had somehow signed his death certificate by telling him. "I need a little space and you probably need to call people and coordinate things."

When he didn't disagree, she assumed she was right on the money.

"I'll leave you to it then."

Not surprisingly, he didn't prevent her from heading to the bedroom. She tried not to pace as she waited for him to finish, or wonder if Wade and Lucas had more in common than she'd realized—and at the same time wished like hell she hadn't come so dangerously close to losing her heart to him.

God, who was she trying to kid?

It was already his.

Feeling a little overwhelmed by that realization, Max flopped back on the bed. She pressed the heels of her hands to her eyes, trying not to panic a little. She truly had gone and fallen for Lucas, the very same man who was doing his best to keep her out of the loop.

Maybe he was right to. Maybe she'd been insane to return to New York on her own thinking she knew enough to expose Blackwater somehow and get her life back.

Seemed like the only thing she'd been doing consistently since Cara's death was overestimating herself. She hadn't been able to disappear or get rid of Lucas. She certainly hadn't been able to prevent Lucas from getting hurt or execute any kind of plan that involved clearing her name and exposing Cara's murderer.

No matter how much she doubted herself, though, Lucas leaving her out of his plans still felt like a betrayal.

She sensed Lucas in the doorway long before he knocked on the doorframe.

"Look, I know you're pissed at me."

She didn't let him go any further than that. "Good, then we can skip the part where I pretend I'm not really mad at you and jump right to me asking you to leave."

"I'm not going anywhere."

Of course it wouldn't be that easy. It was apparently too much to ask that she feel sorry for herself on her own terms. "You got what you came here for, Lucas. Don't you have a weapon to retrieve?" She raised herself up on her elbows.

Indecision crossed his face, and for a moment she thought he really was going to leave. Her heart constricted at the thought even knowing she might be better off if he did. At least then she wouldn't be left wondering where they stood.

Without a word, he shut the door and approached the bed.

"Still worried I'm going to run?"

"You might strongly consider it if you knew what I was thinking right now."

She was rather proud of herself when she let every dark and sexy nuance of his voice roll right off her—mostly.

"You and I are far from done with each other, Max."

He stood at the foot of the bed, watching her, and for no reason that she could actually put her finger on, she wondered if she should be worried about that closed door after all.

"We're not?"

He shook his head, placed a knee on the bed. "Not even close."

"Now see, that is where you and I disagree." She almost sounded convincing, though she wasn't so sure she looked it by the time his other knee hit the mattress and he hovered over her.

"So I was wrong to think there was more than just adrenaline-based sex between us?"

She winced. He would have to go right for her weakest argument. "Even if there is more, now isn't the best time to get into it."

"Because you think I don't trust you."

"Because I *know* you don't trust me," she corrected. "But that's only a part of it."

She planted her hand on his chest, applying enough force to make him rethink whatever was going on in his head, and she bet it had something to do with kissing her judging by the way he kept staring at her mouth.

"I do trust you, Max. I just don't trust you won't get hurt if you're a part of the retrieval team."

"Hurt like you were?"

He nodded, and she shimmied up the bed, away from him.

"How come you're the only one who gets to worry about one of us getting hurt? Why don't I get to make the same call?"

"You did, the second you came back to New York alone." He closed in on her, backing her up against the headboard. "Unless you weren't trying to protect me by not contacting me as soon as you could."

He wasn't even done talking and already she felt like she was being set up somehow.

"Maybe my boss was right," he continued. "Maybe you've had an ulterior motive all along."

"You don't believe that." And he certainly wasn't looking at her like she had some hidden agenda. Not unless he suspected it involved something very naughty.

Lucas caught her hips, tugging her down beneath him. "You're not exactly giving me a lot to work with, Max."

If she gave him much more, she wasn't sure she'd be able to put herself back together if things ended badly. And if she didn't know better, she'd swear he figured that out with no

219

more than a good, long look.

Awareness brightened his eyes, and he curled his fingers around her wrists.

"Forgot your handcuffs this time?"

Whatever playfulness she might have glimpsed in his eyes earlier, evaporated. "No one is putting cuffs on you. Not Blackwater. Not the police. No one." His tone dared her to disagree with that, with the unspoken vow that he'd do whatever he could to protect her.

He was right, though. She had done the same to him by keeping him in the dark, and she knew she would probably do it again in a heartbeat if it meant saving him somehow.

Lucas gently cupped her face. "I'm ninety-nine percent sure I'm falling for you, Maxine Walker, and it has nothing to do with justice or revenge or retrieving any kind of weapon."

All the air left her lungs in a shallow exhale that left her shaking inside.

His forehead rested against hers. "Tell me you believe that?"

"You're only *ninety-nine* percent sure?"

He laughed. "The other one percent is too damn scared, but it'll come around." He opened his mouth on her neck, pulling at her skin.

"Maybe it should be scared. I got you shot."

She felt him smile against her neck. "You know this isn't all about you, right? Blackwater's guys deserve a little credit for that one."

"But if I had just agreed to go with you sooner—"

His mouth moved over hers, and she felt his impatience in the kiss, the slide of his lips, short and purposeful and more than a little untamed.

"This falling for me thing," she began.

"So you were paying attention."

She nodded, just not sure what to say now that she'd

brought it up. Not sure how to get the words out that she was right there with him.

"It wouldn't have happened if you had kept your hands to yourself, you know."

She tipped her head back, watching him.

"If you hadn't teased me in the truck or kissed me like that in the diner—"

Sensing a pattern, she finished, "Or seduced you in the cabin and later begged to be tied up."

"And then you started looking at me like..." he trailed off, seeming to choose his words carefully.

"Like what?"

He raised his eyes to hers once more and the burning intensity there made every nerve ending hum. "Like I was all you needed."

"Maybe you are." She wrapped her arms around his neck and drew him close.

Their lips came together slowly, as if they were both exploring something new, something just as scary as it was amazing.

His hand slid beneath her shirt and shivery tingles broke across her skin as he trailed upward, stopping just under her breast.

"*You* are all I need, Max." He kissed her again, deeply, then moved on to her jaw, her neck, sending delicious waves rolling down her spine and setting every part of her below the waist on fire.

Every part of her, period.

Lucas moved his hands lower, drawing one leg around his waist so he fit snug against her. Only the denim separated her from his fingers when he slid a hand between them and teased the inside of her thighs.

Moaning, she squeezed her legs together in hopes of capturing some of the sweet friction he worked that had her quickly panting against his mouth.

Just as eager to please him, she felt him tense as her fingers skimmed the edge of his waistband, but by the time she rubbed him through his pants, his hand closed over hers, increasing the pressure as he groaned against her lips.

He murmured something that sounded like, "Fuck," and jerked her shirt over her head, tossing it behind him.

A wicked smile curved his lips as he openly appreciated her breasts. He drew a finger along her shoulder, slowly pushing her bra strap down.

God, she couldn't take her eyes off him as he slipped a hand beneath her and unclipped her bra on the first try.

Her bra was gone and then the warm weight of his palm settled over her heart, firm and possessive. "Do you have any idea what you do to me?"

She shook her head. "Maybe I should see for myself."

He cursed softly, as if reading her mind, and moved onto his back.

Remembering his injury, she hesitated. "Are you sure you're even allowed to do this?"

A mix of desire and amusement glittered in his eyes. "That depends. Are you pulling out the whips and chains to get even with me?"

"Crossed my mind, but I figured I should save something for a rainy day."

He laughed and pulled her down, settling her against his uninjured side. "I'm fine, Max."

"Good." She leaned in, running her mouth along his jaw. "No more lies or half-truths between us?"

Lucas brushed the hair from her face. "No more lies."

Not waiting for her to test how sore he was, he pulled her tight against his side and had her jeans halfway down her legs before she caught her last breath.

Luscious tension curled through her as he slipped a hand

between them and caressed her sex straight through her damp cotton panties. Moaning, she closed her fingers around his zipper, and with a drawn-out tug that had him holding his breath, she worked it down.

His cock tented his boxers, and she drew a line from peak to base. His hips jerked and a harsh moan rumbled up his throat, the sound so primal, needy, she reveled in the power she possessed to please him.

"I want—"

She pressed her mouth to his, cutting him off. "This isn't about what you think you want. This is about what you need, what only I can give you," she whispered.

The corners of his mouth kicked up. "How long have you been waiting to say that to me?"

"At least the last five minutes."

"And what exactly is it you think I need?"

She tugged his pants past his hips. "I'm sure you'll figure it out."

God, she was killing him.

Lucas closed his eyes, dying a little more every second she traced his cock through his boxers. Just thinking about where this was headed, about the feel of her taking him into her mouth, had his entire body stretched taut.

Like she was unwrapping a gift she wanted to savor, she worked his boxers down, removing them along with his pants. Wiggling the rest of the way out of hers as well, she tossed them on the floor with the others.

She ran her fingers down his abdomen, circling the base of his cock.

Mother fuck—

He fisted one hand in the blankets, wishing he had something to brace the rest of his body against.

Max flicked her tongue across the broad head, and then

kissed him there. A long, wet hot kiss that promised he was going to enjoy every freaking second of whatever she had in mind.

Riveted by the sight of her tongue sliding up him, he tucked her hair behind her ear, guaranteeing he didn't miss one second of what she was doing to him.

She curled her fingers around the base of his shaft, pumping slowly as her mouth sank down to meet them. His hips surged upward on a wave of searing pleasure, and Max grinned wickedly.

Leaning over him, she took him deep, drawing the slow suction out. Rocking to the rhythm she set, Lucas realized he could just reach her and hooked the edge of her panties with his finger.

He couldn't remember enjoying stripping a woman out of a piece of clothing as much as he loved tugging the soft material down Max's legs as she went down on him. When the panties hit the floor, he smoothed a hand down her backside, continuing to watch his cock slide into her mouth.

She whimpered, leaning into the fingers he pushed against her slippery opening. The next time she sucked him deep, pulling at him with her tongue, he pumped his fingers inside her.

The soft sound she made vibrated along his cock, and both her mouth and her sex squeezed him, intensifying the pleasure coursing through him in knee-buckling waves.

Alternately teasing her clit and thrusting into her slick center, Lucas pumped his hips until release echoed inside him, spinning closer with every stroke of her tongue, every soft gasp from her lips.

But it wasn't enough. He needed to possess her completely.

Dragging her toward him, he covered her mouth with his and rolled her beneath him. The pain in his side dulled his pleasure for only a second, and then he was taking her mouth fast and deep and forgetting everything but how good it felt with

Max.

Everything about her excited him, tempted him, unraveled him.

Gripping her hips, he thrust inside her, pumping his hips over and over. She moaned against his neck, pleading with him not to stop—as if he could.

She felt so incredible, her arms pulling him tight, the slick walls of her sex greedily clenching around him. Again and again, he drove into her, the building tension so intense he almost didn't want to come. He would happily spend the rest of day fucking her slow and hard and every variation in between, if it meant she was right here with him, riding the edge and holding onto him for every moment of it.

Thrust after thrust fired him closer to his own climax, and when he felt himself on the brink, he locked gazes with Max, hoping she saw in his eyes everything he felt. All the desire, the need and the love he felt swelling in his chest.

Her thighs squeezed around him, and she threw her head back, breaking away from his mouth as she came. One last thrust that seemed to go on and on hurtled him into blissful oblivion.

He groaned her name and buried his face in her neck as deep, radiating contentment tunneled through him.

Lucas tuned out whatever Max said and dragged the pillow over his head with one hand as he reached for her with the other.

He felt only emptiness next to him, and finally raised his head in time to be treated to a view of Max's ass as she streaked out of the room.

"You've got ten minutes until Eli gets here," she hollered out. "And no, you're not getting into the shower with me."

"You just had one."

"It doesn't count when I don't have the opportunity to wash."

A huge grin spread across his face as he thought of the shower they'd taken in the morning. After which, he'd dragged her back to bed, indulging every wicked thought that crossed his mind at the time.

The time for the deal with Blackwater was set for a few hours from now and with everything ready to go with the warehouse, he and Max had well and truly indulged in each other.

The only thing they hadn't talked about was what came next once the entire Blackwater situation was behind them. He'd tried to broach the subject more than once but the woman got awfully creative when she was avoiding a particular topic.

He suspected it had something to do with the fact she was still wanted for murder. She'd confessed to spending months just thinking about her future one day at a time, so he got that it might take some time for her to think long-term again.

"Get up," she yelled again from the bathroom, and he laughed.

If all went according to plan, twenty-four hours from now they'd have the case and Blackwater in custody. Even if the charges didn't stick, Lucas knew more than a few players on the international black market, like the ones left in the lurch three months ago, wouldn't risk Blackwater being offered a deal to name names.

Someone would take him out.

Eight minutes later they were waiting outside for Eli.

A black SUV with tinted windows rolled up, but instead of Eli stepping from the vehicle, Edward Blackwater emerged, his gun locked on Max.

"My father would like a word. With both of you," he added as if he somehow anticipated Max would insist on going alone.

Taking a step closer to Max, Lucas scanned the street but found no sign of Eli. *Shit.*

Blackwater Junior inclined his head toward the back door of the SUV that opened from the inside.

The odds of walking away from the situation dropped dramatically the second they got into the vehicle, but he couldn't risk Max being shot.

She preceded him into the SUV, hesitating for only a heartbeat when she spotted Snake already inside. When Lucas was seated next to her, Edward shut the door and the driver pulled away from the curb.

"Weapons, please. Slowly," Edward advised.

Max unstrapped her ankle holster and handed her weapon over to Snake. Max's expression betrayed nothing but casual indifference, and he admired how easily she could appear unruffled when they both knew Blackwater would kill her the moment she became of no use.

Lucas carefully reached in and withdrew his from his shoulder holster and handed it over.

Had the drug and arms dealer figured out no one had the weapon, that it was all a ruse? Or was finding Max merely a bonus and he had every intention of making the meeting in just a handful of hours. Maybe he did believe the deal was authentic and had no use for Max anymore, leaving Lucas to wonder if they were being taken to Blackwater, or to an execution point?

They left Manhattan behind, taking the Lincoln Tunnel to New Jersey. Were they being taken right to Blackwater's home? Lucas's suspicions were confirmed a while later, when the SUV left the main road and turned onto a private estate.

Before they got out of the car, Snake gave Max's thigh a meaningful squeeze. Lucas didn't need to react, and he probably wouldn't have been as quick as Max, who didn't give Snake the chance to block the vicious jab.

Cursing, Snake grabbed a handful of Max's hair, jerking her out of the car.

Fury ripped through Lucas and he lunged across the seat, but Edward Blackwater already had his gun to Max's head.

Fuck.

"You are both supposed to arrive alive, but that doesn't mean I have a problem putting a bullet in either one of you."

Max's expression after Edward's comment was the same as that night in the woods when Lucas had said something similar. *Bring it on.*

Snake cast another leering glance at Max, before taunting Lucas. "Maybe I'll let you watch the two of us have some fun later."

"Didn't realize you wanted an audience when I shove your dick down your throat," Max quipped.

Any other time Lucas would have grinned at her bravado, but not when it made Snake snarl at her like he was going to enjoy hurting her.

The bastard gave her a hard shove toward the mansion in front of them then glanced back at Lucas, as if daring him to do something about it.

As tempting as it was to tell the guy he'd be eating through a tube before he put his hands on her, Lucas kept his mouth shut. Blackwater's crew didn't need any more leverage.

"Let's go." Edward waved him out of the vehicle, and they headed up the brick path leading right to the front door.

Lucas noted five guards on this side of the house alone. Past intel had indicated only six for the entire property. Something clearly had Blackwater good and spooked.

Tonight's deal, or something else entirely?

Snake led them into the house past pricey pieces of art and other window dressing that was probably supposed to depict Samuel Blackwater as some kind of patron of the arts.

They were shown into an office at the back of the house as though they had an appointment. The man of the hour himself was waiting for them behind a large mahogany desk.

Samuel Blackwater turned from the window. His small, dark eyes were lost in his portly face and salt and pepper comb-over that might have been in style a decade or two ago. And that was if the jagged pink scar across his eye could be overlooked.

Too old school to consider a better plastic surgeon?

"Nice to see you again, Detective Walker."

"Oh, the feeling is mutual."

Snake pushed her into the closest chair, leaving Lucas to stand.

"I believe you have some property of mine."

Max frowned. "Oh, was I supposed to hold on to that sliver of glass I cut you with as a keepsake? Sorry."

A cold smile cracked Blackwater's lips. "I don't think I need to remind you how I punished the last woman who chose not to cooperate."

"You married her?"

Damn, that one almost made Lucas crack a smile.

Blackwater on the other hand didn't look impressed. He leaned across the desk. "My staff was scrubbing your friend's blood and pieces of her off the floor for weeks."

Max didn't so much as flinch. "You must have a very attractive benefits package."

Blackwater nodded, and Snake produced a knife, pressing it against her throat. "Let's try this again. Do you have something that belongs to me? Yes or no? And I promise you will regret lying to me."

"Screw you."

With a barely perceptible nod from his father, Edward swiveled and shoved his gun against Lucas's temple.

"No!" Her gaze snapped back to Blackwater's. "You're right. Let's start over."

It wasn't the first time Lucas had found himself in a bad situation, but the uncertainty that came with Max sitting opposite him, a knife to her throat, made his gut ache until all he could think about was ripping Snake's arm from his body.

Nodding for his son to lower his weapon, Blackwater crossed his arms. "Continue."

"There was a case. The Russian had been carrying it around," Max said.

"That's right. It wasn't recovered with his body."

"He hid it."

Blackwater frowned. "He told you where?"

She shook her head, her gaze touching briefly on Lucas. "I saw where he stashed it."

Shit. She wasn't seriously going to tell him?

"In the warehouse," Blackwater guessed, and both Edward and Snake turned their full attention on her.

"In a floor grate in the north east corner of the building."

After a jerk of Blackwater's head, Edward spun around.

Max deliberately waited until he reached the doorway. "Of course it's no longer there now."

Blackwater came around the desk, and Lucas guessed his intention too late to prevent him from backhanding Max. Her head snapped to the side and blood trickled from her split lip. Only the feel of Edward's gun digging into the base of his skull kept Lucas in place.

Ignoring him altogether, Blackwater kept his attention fixed on Max. "Where is it?"

She blew out a breath, wincing at the blade digging deep enough to draw blood. "I sold it. Sort of anyway. I think they screwed me on the currency exchange because I blew through the twenty grand in less than a month."

Visibly sputtering, Blackwater's face turned an ugly shade of red. "Twenty grand?" he echoed.

"I needed money to get out of town."

Looking uncertain, Blackwater leaned down, placing a hand on each armrest and getting right in Max's face. "Who did you sell it to?"

"Some European guy. Austrian maybe or Czechoslovakian."

Just as quickly as Blackwater's face had flushed, all the color drained away. Jesus, he actually believed her. And the story Max was spinning was apparently worrying him.

Knowing that didn't mean a damn thing except Blackwater had no reason to keep them alive, Lucas stayed where he was.

"What about the flash drive?"

Flash drive? Lucas frowned, glancing at Max for any sign she knew what he was talking about.

"I don't know anything about a flash drive," she managed. "Maybe one of your high-paid janitors found it when they were scrubbing the floor."

The nervous glint in Blackwater's eyes retreated, and he nodded to Edward.

"On your knees." Edward jammed the gun into Lucas's skull. "Now."

"No!" Max strained against the knife, causing more blood to slide down her throat. "Just wait. I don't know anything about a flash drive."

Forced to his knees, Lucas held Max's gaze, willing her to keep it together. "We're okay."

"It belonged to your friend." Blackwater cocked his head, waiting. "She stole some information from me and I want it back."

Max shook her head, all traces of her earlier attitude slashed away, and the vulnerability on her face made Lucas's chest ache worse than any gunshot wound. "Cara never said a word about any flash drive."

"My son is going to count to five, Detective."

"Damn it, no. I don't know anything about a flash drive."

"One."

"Stop, please!"

"Two."

"Don't." She tried again to pull away from Snake and cried out at the cut of the blade.

"Three."

"No." A tear escaped and tracked down her cheek. "Please, just wait. Cara never gave me anything. I never saw any flash drive. I swear it."

Looking thoughtful, the drug and arms dealer studied Lucas. "And what about you, Mr. McAllister?"

"Do you really think you'd be sitting here all cozy in your office if there was evidence somewhere that could lock you away?"

"You make a good point." Blackwater glanced at his watch, then out the window. "Unfortunately, my ride is here and I have another meeting I need to prepare for shortly, so we'll have to continue with our little chat later."

"You want them downstairs?" Snake asked, finally withdrawing the knife from Max's throat.

Blackwater paused in the doorway. "For now. I'll be in touch if that changes." He disappeared out the door.

Snake motioned for Max to stand. "I guess you and I get to spend some quality time together." He circled her, his smile somewhere between disturbing and homicidal, and Lucas couldn't wait to smash the expression off his face.

"And if you're a real good girl," he continued, "I'll let you play with my Albino friend."

Max smiled sweetly. "You do know that having pet names for your penis is so junior high, right?"

This time Snake only sneered at her.

Edward grabbed the back of Lucas's jacket. "Up."

"Please wouldn't hurt," Lucas muttered, getting to his feet.

The half-anticipated elbow jab to Lucas's spine hurt like a bitch, but he knew it meant the gun was no longer pointed at his head.

Pivoting, Lucas drove his own elbow into Edward's lungs, then nailed him in the jaw with a punch that snapped the asshole's face to the left. The gun hit the floor, and Edward dove for it.

Lucas beat him to it, twisting around, his finger on the trigger.

"Don't be a hero," Snake warned. He'd switched his blade for a gun—one he had against Max's head.

No, he realized, the blade hadn't been exchanged for the gun at all. Max had gotten it away from him and had pressed it to Snake's thigh, right next to his femoral artery.

Lucas didn't have time to make a decision before the large bay window shattered and he felt himself thrown backward by an explosion.

Chapter Fourteen

Max slowly opened her eyes. Her head felt like someone had shoved it into a speaker at a rock concert and then plunged it into the river immediately afterward. All around her there were pieces of glass and wood littering the floor, like something had barreled right through the office window.

What the hell had happened?

She lifted her head and saw Lucas dragging himself to his feet just as a groan came from somewhere behind her.

Awareness returned at the same moment one of her ears popped and unfiltered sound rushed in.

Rolling to her side, Max spotted the gun lying on the carpet between her and Snake. She scrambled for the weapon, her fingers closing around the grip a heartbeat before Snake's. Glass scraped her palm and bit into her knees as she backed away from him, her breath hissing out.

Snake didn't move. Not so brave when he wasn't brandishing a machete, was he?

Lucas slid a hand under her elbow to help her up. "You okay?"

"More or less." Her gaze swept the room, landing on an unconscious Edward Blackwater. "What the hell was that?"

"I don't know." Lucas crossed to the gaping hole in the wall where the window used to be.

Max looked past his shoulder to see a flaming hunk of

metal that might have been Samuel Blackwater's ride. "Do you think he was in it?"

"We can only hope." Armed with Edward's gun, he jumped through the window, onto the grass.

He held out a hand for Max, and she landed next to him. Three men swarmed what was left of the vehicle, and Lucas urged her in the opposite direction. One of the men hollered behind them, but they'd already reached the corner and sprinted across the landscaped backyard.

From the corner of her eye, Max spotted two other men running toward them. Two gunshots sounded almost the moment she noticed them, and one of the men dropped to the ground after taking a bullet from Lucas's gun.

Seeing his buddy go down made the second guard hesitate, giving them time to get behind a small outer building that the groundskeeper likely used.

She flattened herself against the wall. "There." She nodded toward the trees roughly twenty yards away.

A chunk of siding flew off the building sheltering them before Lucas returned fire.

"Go."

Trusting him not to get himself shot again, she broke into a run. He was beside her in an instant, and they reached the woods, getting more cover between them and Blackwater's guards.

After a few minutes it was clear that no one pursued them. A strong sign that Blackwater had been in the bombed vehicle, otherwise he'd probably have every spare man hunting them down.

"Do you think he was expecting something like that?" she asked when they slowed their pace. "He looked a little panicked when I lied about a European buying the weapon from me."

"Something had him rattled. It also could have been a competitor who decided it was easier to take him out than lose more business opportunities to him." He stopped then, his gaze sliding down to where her neck stung like a bitch.

A look that was almost savage hardened his features. "I wanted to tear him apart."

She didn't have to ask to know he meant Snake. "I felt the same about Edward actually." God, when he had his gun to Lucas's head, the same sense of helplessness as the night Cara died had nearly suffocated her.

"You were great in there, you know."

Feeling a delayed sob rise in her throat, she pressed her lips together. She stared at the ground that blurred as she blinked back the tears she'd viciously struggled to hold onto in Blackwater's office.

Lucas pulled her into his arms, and his fierce hold only made it that much harder to keep a grip on the last thread holding her together.

"I don't think I've ever been so scared in my life," she choked out, swallowing hard to get past the fear that still hovered so close to the surface.

"I don't know, I think me wearing that pink sweater was pretty scary."

Since it was the last thing she expected to hear, she burst out laughing, but didn't let go of him.

He kissed her temple. "I know it's wrong, but I'm glad you were there with her."

It only took a second to realize he was talking about Cara, and she immediately squeezed her eyes shut.

"It got her through it—your strength, how brave you are. She would have needed that."

Max would have laughed at the idea of her being strong and brave if it didn't feel like her insides would shatter if she so much as breathed too deep.

Lucas cupped her cheek and guided her head back. "Open your eyes, Max."

"Can't."

His mouth closed over hers, soft and warm. With the first sweep of his lips across hers she knew this kiss was different. Too many times to count he'd left her weak in the knees or set her entire body on fire with just his mouth, but never had a kiss...strengthened her.

So used to having her senses overwhelmed by his tenderness, his frustration, his hunger, she didn't have a clue what to do with this, but take in. The heat, the determination, the quiet strength that radiated from him, the love.

She took it all in—every last breath.

His palm trembled ever so slightly against her cheek, and she knew she wasn't the only one who had barely held it together.

"Open your eyes," he whispered against her lips.

She felt a tear escape as she met his gaze, but she felt no weakness it in, no warning that she would fall apart.

"We're okay."

"We're okay," she repeated, pushing up to catch his mouth one more time. "And we'll be even better when we're far away from this place."

He grinned and released her, then dug his cell phone from his pocket and punched in a number.

When someone picked up on the other end, Lucas said, "I need a ride. Max and I are not far from Blackwater's place in Jersey. There's a good chance he might be dead, so we need to move up the timetable on retrieving the weapon." He frowned, listening a minute. "He's that close?"

Max moved a little closer, but couldn't overhear the conversation.

"We'll circle back to the main road and wait two miles west of Blackwater's. What's he driving? Thanks, Tess." He hung up and surveyed their surroundings. "Eli will meet us."

"At least we won't have to steal a car or hitchhike this time." She tucked her gun at the small of her back, then fell into step beside Lucas. "Eli is close, is that what you said?"

"Yeah."

"Did he just happen to be in the area or something?" If Lucas's team was getting ready to move on the warehouse in lower Manhattan, it seemed odd that any of them would venture too far from the area.

Lucas frowned at her. "When we weren't waiting at your cousin's for him, they used my cell signal to track us."

"That quickly? Wouldn't they have needed to figure out where you were headed almost instantly for him to be nearby so soon?"

Lucas stopped, his expression guarded. "What are you getting at, Max?"

"Just thinking out loud." She followed him through the woods as they travelled parallel to the route they'd taken away from Blackwater's.

"And implying I should question my team."

"I didn't realize you were the only one allowed to be suspicious of others. You had no problem suggesting that Glen, Wade, my Captain and probably three quarters of the people I've worked with could be on Blackwater's payroll."

"This is different, Max. Eli, Caleb and I, we put our asses on the line for each other every time we're in the field. We've bled for one another."

"So because Glen has never taken a bullet for me, I should assume the worst?"

He stopped. "That's not what I'm saying."

"That's exactly how you're acting, though. When we realized we'd been tracked to the B&B, the first thing you did was ask who I had called, and you had used the phone too."

"Joe Lassiter did not tip Blackwater off about our location."

She understood he wouldn't want to believe that someone he trusted would betray him that way, but they both needed to be realistic. "How do you know?"

"Because I do. Because he knew I was bringing you to headquarters. Why would he interfere with that?" He sounded so convinced she wanted to believe there was another explanation altogether.

He continued walking, then glanced back a few minutes later. "You're thinking awfully hard back there."

"What about the credit card you used to rent the room at Miss Maddy's? Was it the same one you used to rent the vehicle that got you to Riverbend?"

"Yeah. Tess has been trying to figure all that out, but as far as she's been able to tell, even the RCMP hit a dead-end on that front."

They lapsed into silence after that, both of them seeming to concentrate on moving as quickly as they could considering they were both hurting and sporting at least a dozen lacerations between them from the explosion.

Whoever wanted Blackwater dead had certainly made sure the blast had packed one hell of a punch.

When they reached the edge of the woods, Max could see a mid-sized car parked on the side of the road.

"That's him."

Eli had climbed out of the car by the time they reached it. His eyes narrowed a fraction when his gaze landed on her, then his attention switched to Lucas. "You guys keep having all the fun without me."

"Not really your scene. No cards, strippers or alcohol." Lucas opened the backdoor and motioned for her to slide in.

Eli grinned. "Now do you see why I prefer assignments in Europe?" He got behind the wheel as Lucas settled into the backseat with Max.

Tires spun on gravel and the car tore back onto the road like the hounds of hell were snapping at the rear bumper. Max waited, her breath lodged somewhere between her tonsils and her trachea, for him to ease up on the gas, but they continued to fly down the road.

For the next thirty seconds she was sure she preferred driving around with Snake than being a passenger with Eli at the wheel.

"Does he always drive like this?"

Lucas cocked his head. "Like what?"

The driver in question zipped around three transport trucks, completely disregarding any printed warnings for cars to keep back the specified distance. "Like he's driving a stock car."

Eli snorted, and Lucas laughed before adding, "He's more into Formula One."

"He does know he won't be able to make this car drive two hundred miles an hour, right?"

"Don't tempt him." He dug his phone out of his pocket again. "Is Caleb ready to move?"

"Just waiting on us," Eli answered. "Is she coming along?"

She waited for him to say no, but he just looked at his friend. "Where's Tess?"

"Already mobile, probably so Caleb can't insist she run her end of the show from the hotel." Eli took a corner at speeds that had to pull close to the same g-force as cars running in the Grand Prix. "What about dropping her at the hotel?"

It was on the tip of her tongue to insist on being there, but she found herself hesitating this time. "If I'm not there, it'll be easier for you to do your job, won't it?"

"Yeah, it will. But you're in this too, so it's your call."

Relief spread through her chest, and she grinned. Not because she was determined to be there, but because he trusted her enough to go along with whatever she decided.

Ignoring their audience, she pulled him down for a quick kiss. "I think you've got it covered."

The phone in Lucas's hand rang, and he answered. After a moment, he handed her the phone. "It's Glen."

"He doesn't live too far from here, does he?"

Of course Lucas knew where Glen lived. He probably knew

his food allergies and favorite brand of underwear too. "Not too far, no."

"Hey," she said into the phone. "Where are you?"

"I was tailing Burton after he got a call fifteen minutes ago and left the precinct in a damn hurry. I lost track of him though."

"I think Blackwater is dead. His car blew up. Lucas and I didn't hang around for any confirmation that he was in there, but it seems likely he was."

"Wait, you were there when it happened? Where was this? When?"

She switched the phone to her palm that didn't hurt as bad. "About twenty minutes ago at his home in Jersey."

"Son of a bitch. That must have been what Burton's call was about. What about now, where are you?"

"On my way to your place," she answered, and Lucas told Eli to make the necessary turn coming up.

"I've got to make a few calls and then I'll be there, though I'd really like to know where Burton went." Glen sighed. "If Blackwater really is dead then those witnesses are probably going to change their stories, Max."

God, she hoped so. "See you soon." She hung up and handed the phone to Lucas.

He pushed it back into her hand. "You hold on to it. I'll call you as soon as we finish at the warehouse."

Max settled back in her seat as Lucas and Eli went over some details for retrieving the case. She tried staring out the window, but everything blurred past too quickly with Eli's maniacal driving.

By the time they pulled up in front of Glen's house, her stomach was tight with worry about Lucas breaking in to the warehouse.

"Be careful. No bleeding for each other this time, alright?"

Lucas grinned. "Won't get so much as a splinter."

Eli snorted, and Max stepped onto the sidewalk. "Don't leave me hanging for too long."

"We'll be quick. And don't go anywhere else, okay? I don't want to have to bail you out of jail."

Smiling, she stepped back as the car pulled away, and turned up the driveway. The flowerbeds in front of the two-story house were barren, probably had been this year without Jillian to plant anything.

Heading around back, she noticed Glen's car. Why hadn't he said anything about being closer? He must have finished up earlier than he thought he would. The backdoor was locked, and she knocked, waiting for him to answer. She looked through the two lower windows on this side of the house but didn't see any movement inside.

Was he in the shower?

She glanced back at the car, something about it catching her attention. She walked over to it, realizing it wasn't Glen's car at all. Close but not quite...

The cross hanging from the review mirror caught her eye.

Wade's car? What the hell was it doing here? There wasn't any sign of Wade or Glen, and her partner was still probably trying to track Burton...

Max dug into her pocket for the cell phone Lucas gave her and pulled it out, dragging something else with it that hit the driveway.

Stooping to pick up Cara's lip gloss, she noticed the crack that ran along the cylinder. Ignoring it, she punched in the number Lucas had made her memorize.

A woman's friendly voice answered. "Lassiter Financial Group."

Finances? Really? "Hi. Is this Tess?"

"As long as you're not one of Eli's flings calling to confirm if he's really married."

Okay. "No, this is Max. Lucas and Eli just dropped me off

and I was wondering if you could answer a question I had."

"Shoot."

"Lucas said something about you tracking him through his cell number. Can that be done with any cell?"

"As long as it's turned on."

Wincing at a sudden pain in her injured palm, she transferred the lip gloss to her other hand. "If I gave you a number, would you be able to run it through your system?"

"Who are trying to find?"

Not exactly the *yes* Max was hoping for. "Ralph Burton."

"If I tell you, you're not going to take off are you? I've heard that's a talent of yours."

"I'll stay put, and you'll know that since you'll be able to track me on this phone."

"Good point, except you could leave the phone behind."

"True," she agreed. "But I'm not putting this phone down until I hear from Lucas."

Tess remained silent for a moment. "I've already got Burton's number in our files. Hang on a minute and I'll see what comes up."

"Sure." Okay, maybe their tracking systems really did work that fast.

Waiting for Tess, she took a closer look at her palm. At least she'd be able to do more than just wipe her bleeding hand on her pants inside Glen's.

A glint of something caught her eye, and she thought it was just light reflecting off the metal trim on the lip gloss.

"That's weird..." She frowned at the almost luminescent sheen of metal beneath the pink plastic coating, and pushed harder to break open the crack farther.

"Max?" Tess's voice cut in to her thoughts. "My screen is showing me that you and Burton are at the same location."

Max glanced at the house in front of her. What the hell was going on? Wade's car, Burton's phone and no Glen.

"Thanks for the help Tess. I need you to call me back in five minutes, okay?"

"Wait—"

Feeling only a little bit guilty for hanging up, she punched in Glen's number, willing him to answer.

He didn't.

A wave of trepidation went through her, and she withdrew her gun and returned to the back door. Assuming that if either Burton or Wade were inside they would have heard her knocking and come to arrest her by now, she used her gun to smash out the window, then reached in and unlocked the door.

She tucked the phone and lip gloss back into her pocket. The doorknob turned easily in her hand, and pushing it open, she stepped inside. Careful of the glass, she skirted the edge of the kitchen, senses attuned to any sign of movement.

Checking each room on the main level and finding nothing, she moved on to the upper floor. Her heart thumped hard in her chest and sweat slicked the back of her neck and between her breasts as she edged up the stairs.

She reached the landing and peeked around the corner. The hallway was deserted. Silently, she moved toward Glen's home office. Taking a breath, she eased the door open, and spotted someone unconscious and bleeding on the floor.

Burton?

Closing the door quietly to ensure no one snuck up on her, Max moved to her captain and knelt beside him to check his pulse. It was there, barely.

She dug into her pocket for the phone to call for an ambulance.

A creak came from the other side of the door, and she leveled her weapon at whoever was about to come through it.

"Max?" Glen stood opposite her. He immediately lowered his weapon. "If I had known you were going to be here so soon, I would have—" he stopped. "Jesus, is that Burton?"

"Yeah. Any idea what he's doing here?" Handing her phone to Glen, she sank down beside Burton once more, snagging a sweatshirt off the chair next to him. "Call an ambulance."

While Glen made the call, she set her gun aside, well out of Burton's reach, and pressed the folded-up shirt over his chest. She still didn't know how or if their Captain was connected to Blackwater, but she couldn't sit back and let him bleed out while they waited for help.

He set the phone on the corner of his desk. "Did you do a full sweep of the house?"

"Didn't finish upstairs, no." She lifted her head. "That is Wade's car out front, isn't it?" There still wasn't any sign of her ex, though. Had Burton borrowed his car for some weird reason?

Glen nodded. "I think they must have known I was tailing them. Maybe it made them nervous." He checked his weapon, then paused next to the office door. "Why isn't Lucas with you?"

"He had something else he needed to take care of."

Glen frowned. "Right after Blackwater was killed?" His expression said something didn't add up, but he didn't ask anything else before slipping into the hallway to finish securing the house.

On the floor, Burton stirred, his eyelids fluttering. He mumbled something she didn't catch.

She touched his shoulder, wanting to reassure him even when she didn't know where his loyalties lay. "You've been shot and an ambulance is on its way."

He opened his eyes, his normally sharp blue gaze seeming fuzzy and unfocused. "Careful...Max."

Not so unfocused that he couldn't recognize her, apparently.

"He might still be here."

"Who? The shooter? Was it Wade?" Despite that his name had come up, she still had a hard time wrapping her mind around the possibility. "Was he working for Blackwater?"

Burton's brows drew together like he couldn't understand the question, then he nodded and tried to move.

"Lie still. Help is coming." God, how much longer for an ambulance? How far away was the closest hospital?

Sensing movement, she lifted her head, and found only Glen in the doorway.

"Is he awake?"

"Yeah. Is the house clear?"

"Yeah. Nothing left behind but a partial footprint in the kitchen."

"Max," Burton whispered. His lids slid down and he forced them back up. He stared hard at Glen, who stood over her shoulder.

"How's he doing?" Glen crouched next to them, and if she hadn't been watching Burton closely, she would have missed the way he flinched when Glen moved closer to him.

Coincidence. The man had been shot, likely by a cop he knew. He was entitled to be a little nervous, wasn't he?

Burton moved his eyes in Glen's direction over and over, and every time she felt something in her stomach get tighter and tighter.

Already the sweatshirt was soaked through with blood. "I need something else to slow the bleeding, can you get me some towels?"

The second he left the room, Max reached for her phone. She pushed redial, telling herself it was crazy to think for even a second—

A recorded voice for Directory Assistance sounded in her ear.

Lucas stared out the passenger-side window, trying to figure out what was nagging at him so hard.

"You're wishing now you'd brought her along, aren't you?"

Yes. "No."

"So you're not worried about anything happening to her?"

"Max can handle herself."

She'd been on her own a lot longer than she'd been with him. He knew she'd be fine, had to believe that. Otherwise the oily twisting in his gut was going to get in the way of the job they still had to do. He wasn't at all used to being so protective of a woman, and one who was quite capable of looking out for herself.

Eli scoffed. "That didn't answer the question."

Lucas straightened in his seat, trying to shrug off the anxious vibe rolling under his skin.

"You gonna marry her?"

He shot Eli a disbelieving look. "What? That's a bit premature don't you think? We haven't even spent twenty-four hours together where we haven't been running from something."

"Sometimes you just know." His friend spoke with a lot of conviction for a man who swore up and down he wasn't built for long-term relationships.

Lucas fiddled with the bag of gear at his feet.

"Do you love her?"

Hard as he tried, Lucas couldn't get a read on whether or not Eli thought that was a good thing. He didn't need anyone's approval when it came to his feelings for Max, but he still wanted Eli and Caleb to like her, seeing as he planned on having her in his life.

"I think we have other things to focus on."

Eli stared at him, waiting.

"You really want to have this conversation?"

"I'm not offering to plan the wedding. It's just a question."

"No, do you take sugar in your coffee, is just a question."

His friend held up a hand. "Consider the subject dropped."

Grateful, Lucas went back to staring out the window, saying nothing for a minute then, "Yeah, I love her."

Eli grinned.

"Anything else you want to know?"

"I'm good."

They lapsed into silence once more, then, "If you *were* getting married, you'd pick me to be your best man, right?"

Lucas rolled his eyes.

"You think she'd take your name? Maxine McAllister," Eli recited, testing it out.

Something caught in Lucas's mind, something...

"Fuck."

"Take it easy, man. If you want to ask Caleb instead, that's cool."

"Turn the car around."

Eli looked him like he was crazy. "You really think proposing now is a good idea?"

"He knew my name." Lucas hit the dash, pissed at himself. "Blackwater called me by my last name and I didn't even notice." Hadn't noticed anything but the knife Snake had to Max's throat.

Eli didn't wait for him to finish his explanation before doing a U-turn that probably would have had Max digging her fingers into the seat.

If that bastard touched her...

"You might want to share the conversation going on inside your head with the rest of the class."

He released a breath, fighting the tightness clamped across his chest. "I told Max's partner my last name." He snatched up Eli's phone and put a call in to Tess.

She didn't wait for him to say anything, but started with, "If this about me helping Max—"

"Help her what?"

"Lucas?" Clearly she'd been expecting it to be Eli calling. "Max wanted me to track a number for her. Ralph Burton's. The thing is, his location matched hers. Then she told me to call her back in five minutes. That was six minutes ago and she's not picking up."

Jesus, were Glen and Burton working together?

He glanced over at the speedometer, and Eli followed his gaze.

"If I could turn this thing into the Delorean for you and fly over the people slowing me down, I would."

"I know."

Eyes focused on the road, Eli frowned. "Maybe Blackwater found out your name from another source. Maybe he caught a good close-up of you on surveillance footage from the night of the party and ran it through some facial recognition software." He shrugged. "Didn't Max's partner lose his girlfriend because of all this?"

"Yeah, she was killed in a car bomb." *Mother fucker.* "Tess, I want you to check Glen Novak's file and tell me if he's had any bomb squad training or anything else that points to a knowledge of explosives."

He watched Eli swerve around cars as he listened to Tess's fingers tapping over her laptop.

"No bomb squad training but his father spent the last twenty years working as an explosives expert."

Lucas closed his eyes, forcing back the fear that Max had already been blindsided by her partner.

"What do you want me to do, Lucas?" Tess asked.

"Be Caleb's eyes and ears, and if he can make a move on his own to retrieve the case, tell him he should take it."

"If Max is in trouble you might need backup."

"I've got Eli and he's been bitching about missing out on all the action anyway."

They were almost back to Glen's when he hung up the phone and checked the cartridge on his gun.

Chapter Fifteen

Max disconnected the call and hit redial again.

She needed to hear the voice again, needed to be sure all the second-guessing she'd been doing lately hadn't made her mishear anything.

Except deep down she knew she'd heard correctly. Glen hadn't called 9-1-1 and there was only one reason not to—he'd been the one who shot Burton.

If it had been an accident or self-defense, he wouldn't have acted as though he'd just arrived.

Jesus. Burton wasn't the one on Blackwater's payroll. It had been Glen all along.

"Who are you calling?" Glen handed her the towels, his expression unreadable, and for the first time it was like looking into the eyes of a stranger.

"I was calling Lucas, but my call was dropped," she lied.

"You sure he isn't just ignoring your call?" He crossed to the window, doing a convincing job of looking for an ambulance that wouldn't be arriving.

With his back turned, she reached down for her gun, but felt only carpeting. A quick glance confirmed that he must have taken it when he'd crouched down next to her a minute ago.

Facing her, Glen crossed his arms. "How do you know he doesn't have some kind of ulterior motive?"

"Like retrieving the same missing weapon you're looking

for?"

Glen's lips curved in a chilling smile, and his gaze landed on Burton. "He gave me away, didn't he? Because if you came here suspecting me, you wouldn't have put your gun down." He withdrew it from his jacket and laid it on the far corner of his desk.

She didn't say a word, refusing to show him how rattled she was.

He pushed away from the window. "But to answer your question, it's not the weapon I'm most interested in." He opened a drawer on his desk, unzipped a long and narrow leather case and produced a hunting knife. "It's the flash drive, I'm after. The one your friend insisted she didn't have the night I killed her."

Oh god.

She shook her head, her stomach cramping violently, protesting the reality that Cara's murderer was the man she'd worked with side by side, never suspecting a fucking thing.

The phone in her hand rang, and Glen shook his head. "Don't answer that, Max." He dragged the tip of the knife across the desk. "Put it down. Slowly."

She set it on the floor next to Burton, then stood, refusing to be in a position that physically gave Glen the edge.

"You know, I was sure you had realized it was me that night, right up until you called to tell me what happened." He cocked his head, as if remembering. "But they had roughed you up a little, probably couldn't see so well with one of your eyes swollen up so badly."

Her lungs burned from the effort it took not to lash out at him. He had two weapons within easy reach and she didn't have one. She needed to keep her head, needed to bury the fury at what he'd done to her friend.

He gave her a quick once-over. "Snake wasn't very rough with you today, was he? I'd say the bomb did more damage." Something in his eyes brightened.

"You set the explosive that killed Blackwater," she guessed, and when he nodded, her mind made the next disturbing leap. "Jillian. It wasn't some attempted hit on you gone wrong, was it? You killed her."

"Is this the part where you're all shocked at what I'm capable of?" He moved toward her. "Jillian stuck her nose where it didn't belong. Kind of like you."

She forced herself to hold her ground, instinctively knowing that some part of him wanted her to run so he could use his knife. "Then why am I still alive? You could have made a move the night we met at the diner."

"Had you gone to stay at my family's cabin when I suggested it, you would have died months ago. But you always were stubborn. Then of course when the case and flash drive didn't turn up, Blackwater became convinced you knew something, so I had to behave myself until we knew for sure."

Her gaze fell to the knife he tapped against his thigh.

"And then when I was visiting your parents a couple weeks ago, checking in on them, they mentioned a woman named Sherri. She used to date your brother, apparently, and lived in Canada. They thought maybe they should see if she'd had heard from you. Seemed like a long shot, but what the hell."

"My parents trusted you. *I* trusted you." Over and over again. They'd been friends. They'd bitched about work, laughed together. God, she'd mourned with him over Jillian's death and it had all been a lie.

"You know, your parents I understand. But you, Max? We worked side by side and you never saw or suspected anything. What kind of cop does that make you?"

Anger ripped through her. "Go to hell."

Whatever Glen saw on her face seemed to excite him. "I always sort of liked you, even when you were being a pain in my ass by pursuing Blackwater."

"Why spend all that time covering up for him only to kill him?" She wanted to hope that Tess would call Lucas when Max didn't answer her phone, but that wouldn't guarantee he'd get back here before Glen decided to use his knife.

And it only took one look in his eyes to know that he had no plan of letting her walk out of the room alive.

"I was tired of dealing with his shit, and it just so happened that other people felt the same way."

"So you were paid to screw him over? Must be some big bucks in whoring yourself out like that."

His eyes narrowed, and she braced for his response, but he seemed to catch himself at the last moment. "Since you were the first to mention the weapon, I feel like I should at least offer you some control over your fate."

The phone rang again, and this time she saw Burton stir, his fingers brushing it.

"If you tell me where the case is holding the device," Glen began, "then I promise I won't let you suffer." He got in close, dragging the knife across her abdomen. "But I have to admit that I'm secretly hoping you don't say a word."

"What's on the flash drive?"

"Names of just about everyone Blackwater has dealt with or paid off, and records of some of those transactions."

No wonder Blackwater had looked rattled. He must have suspected someone was about to retaliate for his screw up. "Including your name, right?"

He grinned again. "There are people who will pay an obscene amount of money for the flash drive *and* the case, and frankly, I'm done with being a cop."

"You sell that information and you'll make more enemies than you can out run in a lifetime. And if you don't think the buyer would use the information on that flash drive to extort everyone else, painting you with one hell of a bulls-eye at the same time, then you're clearly not the mastermind you think you are."

A flash of anger crossed his face, and he shoved her back a

step.

Max caught his wrist and twisted, wrenching his arm back as she pivoted to get behind him. He slashed back with his knife, catching her across the thigh.

She stumbled backward, hitting the desk. With her gun still out of reach, she closed her fingers around the lamp on the corner of it and whirled, smashing it against his face.

He dropped the knife, and when he doubled over, she drove her fist up under his chin, snapping his head back.

"Bitch," he snarled, lunging for her.

Max was fast, but the weight of his body knocking into hers stole her breath even before they hit the ground. Kicking out, she nailed him in the chest, but he landed a blow of his own this time.

She curled in on herself, protecting her abdomen from a second assault, but leaving her back vulnerable. Pain radiated up her spine from the kick, and she rolled away from him, but not fast enough to escape the lamp he brought down on her head.

Lucas stayed close to the wall as he moved soundlessly up the stairs. Sounds of a struggle came from the room at the far end of the hall, and it was all he could do not to sprint toward it. A struggle was better than silence. She was alive and fighting him, fighting hard.

Adrenaline and fear pounded through his veins, riding him so damn hard, he barely heard Eli start up the stairs behind him. They'd planned on each taking a floor, which turned out to be unnecessary when they heard voices coming from upstairs.

He was halfway down the hall when everything went completely silent, but he didn't slow down, didn't let his mind latch on to any possibility of what that silence might mean.

The door was ajar, and he kicked it open, immediately

spotting them. Glen stood next to the desk, one arm wrapped around Max, using her as a shield, his gun at the base of her skull.

She leaned heavily into Glen, visibly struggling to keep her gaze locked on Lucas.

Without a clear headshot, he edged farther into the room, Eli right on his heels.

"Drop them," Glen ordered, tugging Max closer to him. "I don't think I need to tell you how this goes down if you don't."

"How much time do you think shooting Max will buy him?" Lucas asked Eli.

"Five, maybe ten seconds and then you'll be so far down his throat he won't be able to breathe without choking on your gun."

Glen didn't even blink at their exchange. "Do you know what happens to cops in jail? If I had to choose between that kind of hell and death, what do you think I'd go with? Put your guns on the fucking floor or Max dies."

"Don't do this, Glen." The sound of Max's voice drove a spike through his chest, and Lucas prayed Glen was stupid enough to move another inch or so and give him the shot he was so desperate to take.

Eli took a step away from him, seeking a better shot himself.

Glen jammed his gun against Max's head hard enough to make her cry out. "Put. Them. Down."

"Don't." Max shook her head. "Take a shot."

Lucas cursed, then held out his gun, slowly bending to set it on the floor. Looking just as frustrated, Eli followed.

His friend had barely straightened when Glen shifted his aim and pulled the trigger. Eli stumbled back, hitting the wall behind him and sliding to the floor.

Son of a bitch. Lucas managed only a step, before the gun was back on Max's head.

"I know where the flash drive is."

Both men's attention snapped to Max. She sounded even more convincing than when she had lied to Blackwater.

"I'll take you to it," she vowed, "but not if you shoot him."

Uncertainty blinked across Glen's face. "And how do I know you're not lying?"

"The flash drive was in her lip gloss."

Lucas kept his expression neutral. How in the hell did she know that? And why hadn't she mentioned finding it to him before this?

"And where is it now?" Glen demanded.

Max scoffed as if the question were almost too stupid to answer. "First we get in your car and drive, then I tell you."

"Or I put another bullet in your boyfriend's partner and see if that doesn't change your mind."

"Tell him to go fuck himself, Max," was Eli's strained reply. Blood ran down Eli's arm, pooling on the floor.

Her gaze snapped to Lucas before she answered Glen. "And how would you know if I was telling the truth or just what you needed to hear?"

Glen remained silent for a moment, then nodded for Lucas to move a little closer to Eli. "Over there." He waited until Lucas was next to his friend, then inched Max forward, toward the door.

There was no way Lucas was letting him leave with Max. If Max had lied to Blackwater when she had a knife to her throat, it was doubtful she had any intention of telling Glen where to find the flash drive.

And the second Glen realized that, Max was dead.

Once they passed through the door, though, Lucas had every intention of going for the backup weapon tucked in his pants near the base of his spine. He knew he was fast, knew his aim was more accurate—even on a bad day—than Glen's, but one second was all Max's partner needed to press the trigger.

He mentally counted off the distance they travelled. One foot. Three. Five.

Glen's eyes shifted just a fraction, and Lucas suddenly knew the man wasn't leaving without putting a bullet in him. Max seemed to realize that too, and wrenched free, lunging for Lucas as Glen brought his gun up.

Her hands slammed into his chest, shoving him off balance. Lucas heard the gunshot then felt the hot spray of Max's blood on his face as the bullet pierced her neck.

Jesus, no.

She fell against him, her body sliding down his, her fingers raking his back as she dropped. He locked his arms around her, keeping her from hitting the floor.

Her head was back, her eyes locked on his—and her hand locked on the gun at his back.

He pivoted, angling his body away from Glen's and giving her a clear shot that caught her partner in the stomach.

Knocking into his desk, Glen doubled over.

Using his left arm to keep Max upright, Lucas reached behind him with his right and slipped the gun from Max's hand. One bullet would have ended it, but Lucas didn't stop pulling the trigger until he felt Max go slack against him.

"Stay with me, Max." He gently lowered her to the floor, yanking off his shirt and holding it to the wound on her neck.

So much blood, but not enough, he prayed, to indicate the bullet had severed her carotid artery.

"Here."

Max's phone slid across the floor and hit his knee. Nodding in thanks at Ralph Burton, he dialed 9-1-1, rattled off the address and mentioned two police officers and one civilian had been shot before hanging up.

Bone-deep fear that help might arrive too late made it difficult for him to breathe. "Eli?" Lucas couldn't tear his eyes away from Max's pale face. "You okay?"

A pained snort. "Maybe you missed the part where that asshole shot me."

"How bad?"

"I'm not dead." He managed to get himself into a sitting position. "Toss the phone over here so I can call Tess."

He did as Eli asked and then felt for Max's pulse. Panic sliced through him at the thready rhythm. *Fuck.* He shouldn't have left her alone here.

It seemed to take forever before Lucas heard sirens, and he clung to the hope that it wasn't too late for Max. When he heard the EMTs enter the house, he hollered so they knew to come upstairs.

"All gunshot wounds," Lucas explained to the first two EMTs through the door." She took a bullet in the neck." He nodded to Burton and Eli. "Abdomen and upper chest." He didn't waste his time pointing out Glen. "The shooter is already dead."

If the EMTs doubted his assessment of the latter, they didn't say anything and crouched to assess Max.

Two more EMTs arrived just as Max was ready to be loaded into the ambulance.

"Go with her," Eli insisted when Lucas glanced back at his friend. "This is just a scratch."

The EMT working on his friend snorted.

"I'll find you when I can." Lucas darted out the door, careful to stay out of the EMTs way when every part of him demanded he hold on to Max to keep her from slipping away from him.

Inside the ambulance she looked so vulnerable and pale. What had she been thinking shoving him out of the way like that?

The monitor tracking her pulse began to beep in warning as her pulse slowed down. Heart frozen in his chest, Lucas watched the beats grow farther and farther apart, until she flat-lined.

No!

The EMT's movements seemed to slow, as though Lucas watched the entire scene in instant replay. She still wasn't responding when they reached the hospital. The second she was wheeled inside, hospital staff swirled around her, and he was forced to the side.

A nurse gently touched his arm. "You can wait over there," she said, motioning to an area that seemed miles away from Max. She tried to move him, but he didn't budge, unable to look away from the people working on Max.

"You'll only be in the way. Let them do their job," the nurse added, sidestepping to prevent him from following her down the hall when they wheeled her away for surgery moments later.

God, he couldn't lose her.

It was the only thought that repeated in his head, over and over, until he heard it in every breath, felt in every fierce beat of his heart.

Lucas had already checked on Eli—who had also been taken into surgery—twice, talked to Tess about Caleb's success in retrieving the case, and contacted Max's family before a doctor finally let him know that she'd pulled through.

So damn grateful, he'd nearly missed the chair when he finally allowed himself to sit. All he wanted was to talk to her, to see for himself that she was fine. Max's family arrived before anyone was allowed to see her, and though he'd tried to blend into the waiting room background, having no clue what to say to them just yet, a nurse finally mentioned that he'd come in with Max.

Tempted to go wait with Eli, he couldn't bring himself to go anywhere until he got to see Max, leaving him at her family's mercy. And coming from a family of cops, there was no shortage of questions for him.

"What the hell happened?"

"Is she going to be okay?"

"Who the hell are you?"

"Were you with her when she was shot?"

And dozens more. He answered what he could, well aware of the fact it wasn't to their complete satisfaction, but with her family just as eager to see with their own eyes that she was alright, they let it slide.

Judging by more than one speculative look from her family, they were just as curious about his relationship with Max, but he wasn't having that conversation with any of them until he talked to Max.

And god, he needed to talk to her. Touch her. Kiss her.

Once her parents had been in to see her—and watching them walk down the hall while he was forced to stay put had taken the last of his restraint—Max's mother motioned for him to go in.

As eager he'd been to see her for the last few hours, he found himself hesitating on the room's threshold. Even though he knew she was fine, the relief that slid through him at seeing her there, a little more color in her cheeks, left him weak enough he needed to lean in the doorway.

He'd come so close to losing her.

Slipping into the seat next to her bed, he linked their fingers, resting his forehead on their joined hands.

He wasn't sure how long he'd been sitting that way when he felt her fingers move across the back of his hand. When he lifted his head, he found her eyes open, her expression groggy.

"Hey."

Her lips parted in a weak smile. "Hi." Her voice was no more than a whisper. "Did I dream my parents were in here earlier?"

"No. They're outside, along with your brothers."

She nodded, then winced. "My throat hurts."

"Getting shot in the neck does that to a person. You know,

most couples usually go for matching tattoos over gunshot wounds."

Instead of smiling at his joke, her brows drew together. "What happened to Glen?"

"He's dead."

She glanced at her blanket, her gaze strangely distant. "And Eli and Burton?"

"I haven't seen your captain since they took him into surgery. Tess spoke with him though. Eli is doing good. Apparently he took one look at his nurse and predicted it would be a long recovery process."

"I'm glad he's okay." Her eyes drifted shut, and she mumbled something about needing to rest.

Pressing his lips to the back of her hand, he stayed by her side until her mother returned and insisted he grab a shower and something to eat.

Lucas did both in record time and was back by her side in just over an hour, but didn't catch her awake again until he woke up from spending half the night asleep in the chair next to her.

Although she looked to be feeling better, she didn't seem as happy to see him as he expected.

"Have you been here all night?"

He nodded, trying to get a read on her and getting nowhere.

"You didn't need to do that."

Hell yeah, he did. He would have gone crazy wondering how she was doing if he hadn't been right there with her. The guarded look on her face, though, warned him she might not want to hear that.

She glanced past him to the door. "Is my family still here?"

"I saw one of your brothers a little while ago. And your mom said she'd be back first thing."

Max nodded, looking a little relieved to hear it. She fiddled with the blanket for a minute. "He was the one who killed

Cara."

"I know," he said quietly. "Burton told Tess everything he'd overheard before I got there."

"Did you find the lip gloss in my pocket?"

"Yeah, Tess has it." He'd completely forgotten about it until Eli, in between bragging about his hot night-shift nurse, had told Tess about it.

"Good."

"When did you realize it was Cara's flash drive?"

"I dropped it on the ground outside Glen's, but didn't put it all together until I was inside."

They lapsed into an awkward silence that suddenly felt way more strained than anything before this, and he couldn't figure out what he was missing that would explain why she seemed to be looking everywhere in the room but at him.

"Any idea how long they're going to keep you here?" Lucas asked, hunting for something to fill in the silence.

"Another couple of days at least." She glanced at the doorway again. "After that I'm going to stay with my parents for a few days, until I get things figured out."

Why did that sound like some kind of, it's-not-you, it's-me brush off? "Things like us?"

She refused to meet his gaze. "I know we've been through a lot together, I'm just not sure... I need some time."

"Time to what exactly?"

Something in his tone—probably the irritation he felt at how quickly their whole conversation seemed to be going in the opposite direction he'd anticipated—seemed to get her back up.

"You and I have been through a lot, under really intense circumstances. I think we both could use some time—"

"We?"

A flare of familiar determination flashed in her eyes. "Fine, *I* need some time."

He shook his head, resisting the urge to hold a hand to the

stomach that was suddenly killing him. "I thought you were tired of running, Max?"

"I'm not running from anything," she insisted, just enough edge to her words to really get him worried and move the ache in his stomach up into his chest.

She looked away from him. "It hurts to talk, so I think I just need to rest for a while, okay?"

Awhile turned out to be two days. Two days of her family putting him off, or her pretending to be asleep when he managed to get in to see her. He understood that Glen's betrayal had blindsided her, that she'd been through a lot and he was more than fine with giving her time to deal with that.

But shoving him out of the picture while she did, wasn't going to happen no matter what she thought.

"When are you gonna snap out if this slump?"

The sound of her father's voice brought Max from her trance. She frowned, letting his words sink in before she picked up her coffee mug and carried it to the kitchen sink.

She'd been asking herself the same question since her release from the hospital. Because she still didn't have an answer, she kept her back to him, wishing he'd drop the subject.

"Maxine Marie Walker, your mother and I did not raise you to tuck your tail between your legs and run. And I'm not talking about the hiding out in Canada."

"I haven't run from anything."

Just shy of six feet and built like an ox, from his big brown eyes and broad shoulders to the steady strength, Fred Walker crossed his arms. "Why the hell are you hiding out here then?"

"I'm not hiding. I'm spending time with my parents. The ones I didn't see for three months, remember?"

Her father arched a brow, clearly not believing a word she

said. Hell, she couldn't even convince herself that it was her only reason for staying either.

Sinking back into her chair, she drew circles with her finger on the table. "I'm not sure what to do."

"What's to decide? The only mistake you made was to believe that son of a bitch was looking out for you. You're still a good cop."

She shook her head. "I should have seen it, should have picked up on some vibe." She'd relied on her instincts for so long and they'd ultimately failed her. How would she be able to trust her gut after such a colossal mistake?

"You weren't the only one Glen fooled. I've been a cop for over thirty years, Maxie, and never suspected him of taking payoffs. Does that mean I should give up, quit being a cop?"

"Of course not."

He turned her around. "Don't you let Glen make you lose faith. Don't let him make you afraid to believe in yourself, afraid to believe in others."

She knew her dad was right, knew she was giving Glen one more victory over her by constantly questioning herself. Only she didn't know how to stop it.

"What about Lucas?"

"What about him?" This wasn't the first time her father had brought up him either. The way her father went on about him made her suspect they had spent entirely too much time together while she was in the hospital.

"Maybe you should give him a call."

"Playing matchmaker doesn't suit you, Dad." By now Lucas had probably gotten tired of waiting for her to figure things out, if he even wanted to hear from her after the way she'd shut him out at the hospital.

She hated that most of all, how Glen had made her question her feelings for Lucas, if she could have truly fallen for him after such a short time.

"I just want to see my little girl happy."

"I know, Dad. I just need—"

"To get back on your feet."

Max looked up at him. "Are you kicking me out?"

He dropped a quick kiss on the top of her forehead. "It's just time to get your life back."

She knew he was right, knew how determined she'd been to reclaim her life, but the thought of making another costly error in judgment terrified her. She wanted to trust herself, trust her gut, but she wasn't sure she knew how.

"I'll let your mother know you won't be staying for dinner since you'll want to get back to your apartment and all. And you can thank your sister-in-law later for watering your plants while you were gone."

It didn't escape her notice that he'd failed to mention her parents had taken care of her rent while she'd been away.

She stared after her father once he'd walked out of the room. They both knew if she insisted on staying with them, he wouldn't turn her away, but maybe he was right in giving her a push.

Parked outside her apartment building, Max had finally worked up the nerve to call Lucas, using the number for the Lassiter Group, only to have Tess tell her that he'd taken a leave of absence and she wasn't sure when he'd be back.

Unsure what she wanted to do with that information just yet, she told Tess she'd call her back later.

Grabbing the few groceries she had stopped to get on the way home, she trudged up to her apartment, no longer feeling as good about her decision to leave her parent's place.

With her arms full, she couldn't hit the light switch, and nearly set her bags by the door to do a full sweep of her apartment. A habit she'd been struggling to break, even while staying at her parents' house.

Even with her name cleared and Snake and Edward Blackwater in police custody, it took a little more effort than she expected to walk from the doorway, into her kitchen, in the dark.

Setting her bags on the table, she decided she'd get something to eat and then figure out what to do about Lucas.

Light from the fridge spilled at her feet when she opened the door to put away the carton of eggs and jug of milk. Instead of a bare fridge like she'd expected, it was loaded with food.

Okay...

Something warm bumped up against her ankle, and she stumbled back, barely resisting the instinct to go for her weapon.

A fat orange cat stared up at her. A foot away from him, she noticed a bowl on the floor that read *Cujo.*

The lamp beside the sofa clicked on. "I promise he doesn't eat much."

Her heart went from zero to sixty at the sight of Lucas in her apartment. "Leave of absence, huh?"

"Figured I could use a real holiday."

Suddenly needing something to do, she picked up the cat curling around her feet. It helped keep her from staring at Lucas, at how good he looked in the plain white T-shirt and jeans. How good he looked in her apartment, period.

"Cats do need oxygen, you know." He grinned, and she realized Cujo was trying to jump out of her arms.

She set the cat down—and wished she hadn't the second Lucas walked toward her. She'd barely wrapped her mind around being wrong to push him away and doubting if her feelings were real, and here he was.

Butterflies soared in her stomach, and with every step he took, she knew she'd been out of her mind to think she needed time to figure out anything. All it took was seeing him for the first time in days to know she was hopelessly in love with him.

God, he hadn't even touched her yet and already every cell in her body was dying for it.

Lucas slipped a hand around her nape, drawing her forward. His mouth slid over hers with a painstaking slowness that left her aching inside. If she had known it would only take one devastating kiss to remind her of how intense their connection was, she wouldn't have tried to keep him away.

Drawing back slowly, he pressed a kiss to her forehead. "So Cujo and I were thinking we might stay with you for a while."

"Just like that, huh?"

"Well, not exactly. There is the matter to settle of who gets the right side of the bed."

She wrapped her arms around his neck, thinking of the cat food dish and full fridge. "Exactly how long have you and Cujo been staying here?"

His gave her a slow, sexy grin. "Long enough to snoop through your underwear drawer."

"I think that's a serious invasion of privacy."

Lucas pressed his mouth to the sensitive spot just above her collarbone. "I like to think of it as taking stock."

"I'll bet."

He nipped the unbandaged side of her neck before gently tugging her skin between his lips. "As a matter of fact," he murmured against her, "I seem to recall seeing a sassy red lingerie set in there I'd like you to model for me real soon."

"I'll think about it." This time she brought his mouth back to hers, savoring the tenderness and hunger she felt radiating from him, letting it consume her bit by bit until she whimpered softly against his lips.

Lucas groaned. "Do you have to do that?"

She slowly sucked his bottom lip into her mouth. "Do what?"

"Sound like I'm already buried so deep inside you, you can't think of anything but how good it feels."

She smiled against his mouth. "Maybe that's what I am thinking about." And she damn well was now that he'd put the image in her head.

Without warning, he swung her into his arms and headed for the bedroom. "So how does a real vacation sound to you?"

She nuzzled his neck, grinning against his skin when he practically growled. "Got any place special in mind?"

"Well there was this little bed and breakfast across the border I heard about."

She laughed, tightening her grip as he set her on the bed and followed her down.

Heavy and warm, his body pressed her into the mattress. "Any other ground rules we need to establish?"

"Just one for now. No more borrowing my clothes."

He did a pretty convincing job of looking hurt. "But pink is so my color, girlfriend."

She laughed, but before she let him sweep her into another drugging kiss—and god he was good at that—she put her hand over his heart and suddenly struggled to meet his gaze.

"I freaked out in the hospital. I got scared and let what happened with Glen make me doubt myself and my instincts."

Cupping her cheek, he drew the pad of this thumb across her cheek. "And what are your instincts telling you now?"

"That I should hold on tight and never let go."

"Sounds like a plan to me." He teased his lips softly over hers, but each time she rose up to deepen the kiss, he held back. "Tell me you trust me, Max."

She swallowed past the sudden tightness in her throat, her emotions running high. "I trust you."

Lucas nodded, his tongue finally parting the seam of her mouth and pushing inside. He kissed her until she couldn't breathe without taking him in. "Now tell me you love me."

"Your ego needs another little boost, huh?"

He grinned. "I just want to make sure the really hot, really incredible sex we're about to have won't be based purely on adrenaline."

She laughed and trapped his face in her palms, willing his intense gaze to see deep inside her and know that what she felt for him went far beyond adrenaline, far beyond anything she'd felt before. "I love you."

His serious expression slowly gave way to a playful, heart-stopping smile. "You sure about that?"

She nodded, letting him drag her heart-first in a deep, wild kiss that claimed her body and soul. "Trust me."

About the Author

A born and raised Maritimer, Sydney Somers fell in love with writing at the age of eight. Since finishing her first book in 2002, Sydney has written over twenty-five romances—one of which will forever remain hidden under her bed.

When she's not tracking down remote controls, chasing after three very energetic children or exterminating rogue dust bunnies, Sydney can be found curled up reading or working on her next book. She loves to hear from readers and invites them to e-mail her (sydney@sydneysomers.com) or drop by her website (www.sydneysomers.com) any time.

CPSIA information can be obtained at www.ICGtesting.com
Printed in the USA
LVOW091750131211

259230LV00004B/50/P